Alexander McCall Smith is the author of over one hundred books on a wide array of subjects, including the award-winning The No. 1 Ladies' Detective Agency series. He is also the author of the Isabel Dalhousie novels and the world's longest-running serial novel, 44 Scotland Street. His books have been translated into forty-six languages. Alexander McCall Smith is Professor Emeritus of Medical Law at the University of Edinburgh and holds honorary doctorates from thirteen universities.

Praise for the 44 Scotland Street series

'Perfect escapist fiction'
The Times

'Simple, elegantly written and gently insightful'
Good Book Guide

'A joyous, charming portrait of city life and human foibles, which moves beyond its setting to deal with deep moral issues and love, desire and friendship'
Sunday Express

'Does for Edinburgh what Armistead Maupin did for San Francisco: seeks to capture the city's rhythms by focusing on a small, emblematic corner ... A light-hearted, genial soap opera'
Financial Times Magazine

D1347528

By Alexander McCall Smith

ALEXANDER McCALL SMITH

A PROMISE
OF ANKLES

A 44 Scotland Street Novel

ABACUS

First published in Great Britain in 2020 by Polygon, an imprint of Birlinn Ltd
This paperback edition published in 2021 by Abacus

1 3 5 7 9 10 8 6 4 2

Copyright © Alexander McCall Smith, 2020

Illustrations © Iain McIntosh 2020

The moral right of the author has been asserted.

A CIP catalogue record for this book
is available from the British Library.

ISBN 978-0-349-14471-9

Printed and bound in Great Britain by
Clays Ltd, Elcograf S.p.A

Papers used by Abacus are from well-managed forests
and other responsible sources.

Abacus
An imprint of
Little, Brown Book Group
Carmelite House
50 Victoria Embankment
London EC4Y 0DZ

An Hachette UK Company
www.hachette.co.uk

www.littlebrown.co.uk

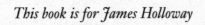

This book is for James Holloway

A PROMISE OF ANKLES

1. At the Window, with Binoculars

Standing at her kitchen window, Domenica Macdonald, cultural anthropologist, denizen of Scotland Street, citizen of Edinburgh, lowered the binoculars that for the last fifteen minutes she had trained on the street below. She had owned the binoculars for over twenty years, having been given them by her first, and late, husband. Domenica had been married to a man she had met while working in South India, a member of a prosperous family who owned a small electricity factory outside what was then called Cochin, in Kerala. Her husband, a mild and somewhat melancholic man, had been electrocuted, and Domenica had returned to Scotland to pursue an academic career. That had been a success – or 'sort of success', as Domenica described it – but she had gradually slipped out of full employment in the University of Edinburgh to the status of *independent scholar*, which enabled her to undertake various anthropological research projects in various parts of the world, while keeping her base in Edinburgh. That, of course, was at 44 Scotland

Street, a comfortable address in a sharply descending street – 'only in the topographical sense', as Domenica amusingly pointed out – towards the eastern limits of Edinburgh's Georgian New Town.

Domenica's anthropological field trips had included an eventful spell in Papua New Guinea, where she studied kinship patterns and friendship networks amongst a tribal group living along the upper reaches of the Sepik River. These people, known for their worship of local crocodiles, had become accustomed to academic interest, and alongside their important *spirit house* maintained a lodge specifically for visiting anthropologists. This lodge, known in Pidgin as *Haus bilong anthropology fella*, had hot and cold running water and copious supplies of mosquito repellent. Anthropologists could stay there for as long as they liked, as the locals enjoyed talking to them and recounting ancient legends, many of which were made up on the spot in return for cartons of Australian cigarettes.

Domenica's small monograph, *Close Friends, Distant Relatives: Patterns of Contact Amongst the Crocodile People of the Sepik River*, had been well received, being shortlisted, but eventually not being awarded, the *Prix Claude Lévi-Strauss*, one of the more sought-after awards in the world of cultural anthropology. That was enough, though, to ensure that her next project, *Marriage Negotiations and the Role of the Astrologer in Madhya Pradesh*, was given adequate funding by the Royal Society of Edinburgh, the British Academy, and the Carnegie Trust. That led to an article, rather than a book, but it was still widely quoted in the footnotes of other anthropological papers, the measure by which, in an age of quantification, the success of a scholarly paper tends to be measured.

Thereafter, there had been only one overseas project of any significance. That had involved a period living with a community of contemporary pirates on the Malacca Straits. These pirates lived at the mouth of a river, in houses surrounded by thick mangrove. They spoke an obscure dialect, but Domenica had been able to communicate with them reasonably effectively in a variant of the Pidgin she had acquired in Melanesia. She concentrated on the home life of the pirates, taking a particular interest in their domestic economy. For their part, the pirates' wives had given her a generous welcome, and had been only too happy to discuss with her their housekeeping issues. Domenica had been taught how to cook the dishes local to that part of the country, and over the months that she spent there she had developed a taste for the coconut curries dominating pirate cuisine.

At the end of her stay, of course, she had made a discovery that somewhat overshadowed the entire project. That had come about one morning when, out of curiosity, she had slipped a small boat of a mooring and discreetly followed the pirates as they set off for work in their larger vessels. She had followed them round the headland that marked the end of the river mouth, and then, straining her small outboard engine to keep up, she had trailed them into another river system a few miles up the coast. There all was revealed: the pirates, it transpired, were employed in a pirate CD and DVD factory, and it was to this plant that they travelled each morning and from which they returned early every evening.

That discovery had been slightly disappointing to Domenica, but it did not compromise any of the data she had assembled on domestic economy issues and formed no more than a footnote in the paper she later published on the subject. When she left the Malacca Straits to return to Scotland she was given an emotional send-off by the pirates' wives, whom she had taught how to make shortbread and clootie puddings. She was still in touch with them years later, sending them a copy of the *Scotsman* calendar each December and a gift subscription to *The Scots Magazine*, which they assured her they so enjoyed reading.

On her fiftieth birthday, Domenica decided that there would be no more research trips in the field, or, rather, that the field could be visited, provided that it was local. Her scholarly time was now largely spent on freelance editing for a number of anthropological journals, occasional lectures, and work on a project that she had long nurtured – a study of the networks and customs of Watsonians, the graduates of George Watson's College, who played an important part in Edinburgh life and whose influence extended into the furthest reaches of the capital city. This research was different from that which she conducted on the Crocodile People of New Guinea, but it had risks of its own. It was also a project that would require far more time to be completed – Domenica was thinking of years, rather than months – as access was an issue and the layers of association and meaning in Watsonian affairs required a great deal of semiotic analysis.

But there she was – standing at her window overlooking Scotland Street, lowering her Carl Zeiss binoculars and turning to her husband, Angus Lordie, who was seated at the other end of the kitchen, his dog and familiar, Cyril, at his feet. Angus, a portrait painter, was wearing his studio clothes – a paint-spattered jacket that Domenica wished he would throw away, a shirt of faded tartan material, and a pair of trousers that was slightly too large for him and that was kept from falling down by an improvised belt – a tie threaded through its loops. This tie was that of Glenalmond College, a school tucked away in Perthshire, where Angus had been all those years ago a moderately unhappy boarder and member of the school pipe band. Whenever he heard *Mist-Covered Mountains*, that most haunting of pipe tunes, he saw Glenalmond under soft veils of rain. He saw his friend playing the pipes beside him in the ranks of the band; and they smiled at one another, because that friendship had been such a profound one, and we must keep alive the happiness we experience before the world closes in on us.

2. *Épater la Bourgeoisie*

Domenica said to Angus, 'Nothing yet. They're certainly taking their time.'

Angus laughed. 'Patience is required of the curtain-twitcher. It's like fishing, I think. You have to be patient.'

Domenica defended herself: no anthropologist could ever

be a curtain-twitcher. 'I am *not* that at all,' she said. 'For a start, we have no curtains – on this particular window, at least. Curtain-twitchers operate behind lace curtains, and their motives ...'

Angus waited. 'Yes? Their motives? Curiosity?'

'*Idle* curiosity,' Domenica corrected him. 'I am not indulging idle curiosity here. It's important we should know who's going to move into that flat. It could be anybody. They might be turning it into a party flat, with hen parties coming up from places like Manchester to spend the weekend here. Imagine that. You'd soon take an interest if that happened.'

'That's not what we heard,' said Angus. 'I told you: I bumped into the agent in the Wally Dug and he said that it was likely to be students. He said that they could charge students more rent than they could charge ordinary people ...'

'Ordinary people,' interjected Domenica. 'By that ...'

'By that I mean *respectable* people,' said Angus. 'Students are, by definition, not respectable.'

They both laughed.

'Nobody talks about respectable people any longer,' said Angus. 'Perhaps that's because it has become unfashionable to be respectable.'

'Respectable people disapprove of things,' mused Domenica. 'And Edinburgh used to be very disapproving. Now it's only moderately so. Do you remember that councillor? The one who hated the Traverse Theatre because it represented a threat to public decency.'

Angus smiled. 'That was a long time ago. Nobody can be shocked these days.' He thought about the effect of that. 'Of course, that's a matter of great regret if you're a cutting-edge artist. How can one épater la bourgeoisie if the bourgeoisie declines to be shocked? That rather takes the wind out of the sails of the artist.'

Domenica agreed, and wondered what the definition of a cutting-edge artist might be.

'One who can't paint,' said Angus. 'Nor draw. Nor sculpt. The real cutting-edge types are distinguished by their inability to do any of these things. And now, to make things worse, they're finding it increasingly difficult to épater the bourgeoisie.'

'How sad for them,' mused Domenica. 'I suppose the bourgeoisie is unshockable now. It has seen everything there is to be seen.'

'And has no energy left to express disapproval, even if it felt it,' remarked Angus. 'Except when the Turner Prize is announced each year, and there's a ritual huff and puff in the press about the mind-numbing banality of what's served up.'

At the mention of the Turner Prize, Cyril stirred in his sleep, and uttered a barely audible, somnolent growl. He had been trained to lift his leg at the mention of the Turner Prize, one of the few terms that Cyril recognised, along with *walk*, *biscuits*, *sit*, and *bad dog*. Domenica had disapproved. 'You can be very childish, at times, Angus,' she said, adding, 'like many men.' But Angus did not mind, and enjoyed demonstrating Cyril's trick to people he bumped into in the street. Childish it may have been, but we were, after all, *homo ludens*, and if we couldn't have a bit of fun at the expense of an artistic establishment that took itself so seriously, then what could we do? If anybody needed to be épated, it was that cultural establishment with its shibboleths, obsessions, and deadening, *Pravda*-like conformity.

He looked down at Cyril, still fast asleep at his feet, occupying the subfusc rug that was his undisputed territory. Then he transferred his gaze to the blue Spode teacup on the table in front of him. This teacup was as powerful a trigger of memory as the madeleine cake had been to Proust. In this case, the memory evoked was not one of a room, like that in the house at Combray, but of an unfortunate incident that had occurred several years previously and that had involved their neighbour, Antonia Collie. Antonia had experienced an episode of Stendhal Syndrome in the Uffizi Gallery in Florence and since then had become closely involved with an Italian socialite nun and aphorist, Sister Maria-Fiore dei Fiori di Montagna. Relations between Antonia and Domenica had long been prickly, owing to a long-running dispute as to the ownership of a room that Antonia believed had been wrongly incorporated into Domenica's flat despite its belonging, in Antonia's eyes, to her own flat. In spite of this argument – every bit as significant, in the mind of both parties, as the dispute between Peru and Ecuador as to the ownership of a contested section of the Amazon Basin – the two women had continued to recognise the normal incidents of good-neighbourliness, including a willingness to lend each other things needed at short notice. One such loan had involved a blue Spode teacup that, in Domenica's view, Antonia omitted to return. That had led to Domenica and Angus secretly letting themselves into Antonia's flat to repossess the cup. It was some time later that Domenica discovered that she had two blue Spode cups in her flat, which meant that they had, in fact, wrongfully taken one that Antonia possessed legitimately. It was because of this background that Angus always felt uneasy when drinking his coffee out of the blue Spode cup. And it was a guilty unease that he felt, although of course it was now far too late to remedy the situation. If they took the cup back, then it would be noticed by Antonia, who might suspect them of involvement. Doing nothing, although strictly speaking the wrong thing to do, was in this case exactly the right thing.

His thoughts were interrupted by a cry from Domenica. 'There they are,' she alerted him, lifting the binoculars to her eyes. 'They're coming out.'

Angus rose to his feet and joined Domenica at the window. 'He looks like a student,' he said.

Domenica squinted into the binoculars. 'He looks very . . . very respectable. Neat hair. Not at all scruffy.'

'Appearances can be deceptive,' Angus warned her.

Domenica lowered the binoculars. 'I shall go out while they're standing there,' she said. 'In that way I shall be able to strike up an acquaintance and get the measure of our new neighbour.'

Angus had taken the glasses from her and was conducting his own assessment of the young man on the street down below. 'Red trousers,' he said. 'That tells us a lot.'

Domenica burst out laughing. 'Is it all in the genes (jeans)?'

Angus looked at her. He gave a shrug. 'I d(i)na ken.'

That was a highly sophisticated response, although the difficulty of rendering parenthesis in speech meant that the joke fell quite flat.

3. Student Neighbours

Outside in the street the letting agent was finishing off his conversation with the young man whom Domenica had spotted from her window. The viewing of the flat had been entirely satisfactory from the point of view of both parties. The agent had proposed a rent that was fifteen per cent above the going rate for such a property, and this had been accepted without demur. From the point of the lessee, the agent's flexibility as to date of entry and willingness to countenance a sub-let during the Festival – subject, of course, to a rent increase during that period of thirty per cent – made the entire deal an attractive one.

'We'd like to move in tomorrow,' said the young man. 'I know that's not much notice, but we're all sleeping on friends' couches and you know how that is.'

The agent thought for a moment. When had he last slept on somebody's couch? A long time ago, and he had been woken rudely when somebody came into the room and sat on him. As luck would have it, though, the person who sat on him was very attractive, and that made all the difference ... It was at this point that Domenica appeared from the door at the foot of the No. 44 common stair. She smiled at the agent and offered her hand to the young man. 'I take it,' she said, 'that you're our new neighbour in the ground-floor flat. I thought I'd come and say welcome to Scotland Street.'

The young man nodded his head and smiled. 'I'm Torquil,' he said. 'And I am. Or will be tomorrow.'

The agent looked at his watch. He had business to attend to, and so, after hurriedly agreeing on the collection of the keys, he left Domenica and the young man standing at the front door.

Domenica looked at Torquil. He was a tall young man, with a neat haircut and a broad, friendly smile. His features were immediately appealing; in fact, she thought, this was a remarkably good-looking young man.

'I take it you're a student,' she said.

Torquil inclined his head. 'Classics.'

Domenica's eyes widened. 'I didn't know anybody still studied classics,' she said. 'Well, I suppose some must, but it's a bit unusual, isn't it?'

Torquil fixed his warm smile on his new neighbour. 'Maybe. But there are more of us than you might imagine.'

'My husband will be pleased to hear that,' Domenica said. Angus was in favour of classics, and enjoyed quoting snippets of Horace and Virgil. She gestured towards the windows of the ground-floor flat. 'I imagine you'll be sharing.'

'Yes,' said Torquil. 'There are going to be five of us.'

Domenica made a quick mental calculation. She knew the flat in question, and as far as she could remember there were only three bedrooms. Of course, there was a living room at the back that could be used as a bedroom, but even then, somebody would have to share.

'I hope it's not going to be too crowded,' she said. 'These

flats are not as big as some in Drummond Place or further up the hill.'

Torquil grinned as he replied. 'We're not fussy,' he said.

'The other boys?' she asked. 'They're students too?'

'Two of them are boys,' said Torquil. 'Two of them apart from me, of course. Three boys and two girls.'

Domenica continued with her calculation. If they kept the living room as it was, as a common room, then they would have three bedrooms at their disposal. If the girls shared a room, that would mean that one other room would have to be shared by two boys, and one would then have a bedroom to himself. Or it could be that one of the girls was in a relationship with one of the boys – possibly Torquil – and that would mean that the two of them could share, the other could have a room to herself, and the two remaining boys could share the third bedroom.

Domenica put the sleeping arrangements out of her mind and asked what the others were studying. 'Well,' said Torquil, 'there's Rose, for starters. She's in her third year of architecture. She comes from Kelso. Then there's Dave, who used to go out with Rose but doesn't any more. They're still good friends, though, and I think Rose might want Dave back, except I don't think that's going to happen. Because Dave . . . well, it's just not going to happen.' He looked bemused.

How could he be so sure, Domenica asked herself. Had Dave said, *I'm not going back to Rose – and that's final?* Or was it because Dave was enamoured of somebody else – and Rose was unaware of this? Could there be something between Dave and Torquil? If there was, then Torquil could be reasonably certain that Rose's chances were slight, but why would Dave have been involved with Rose in the first place if his inclinations had been otherwise?

'Dave is studying environmental science,' he continued. 'Third year – we're all third year, actually. Dave is a good friend of Alistair – they were at school together in Stirling. Alistair is doing mathematics, which he doesn't like very much but which he's going to have to stick with because you can't change just like that in your third year. Anyway, I think Alistair is too thick to be doing mathematics. You shouldn't do mathematics if you're thick. You should do something like estate management or sports science. Sports science is a really good course for thick people – it's made for them, really.'

Domenica raised an eyebrow. She was not sure whether he was being playful. 'I'm not sure everybody would agree,' she said.

Torquil did not argue. He moved on to Phoebe. 'She's a bit odd,' he said. 'We all love her – don't get me wrong – but she's definitely not your average person. She comes from Findhorn and some people say that they're all weird up there. I don't think that's necessarily true. But I think that Phoebe definitely has weird parents. She admits it. She says, "My parents are seriously weird." That's what she herself says.'

So that's that, thought Domenica. 'I mustn't keep you,' she said. 'We're two floors above you, but I'm sure we'll be seeing a lot of one another. It's a very pleasant street.'

Was it? She thought, on balance, it was. But the problem with a pleasant street was that it could rapidly become less pleasant if difficult or noisy neighbours moved in. Students were, on the whole, difficult neighbours, but she would give

Torquil and his friends the benefit of the doubt and welcome them. *Build a silver bridge and it will be friends who will cross on it*. That was probably true, even if it had about it the ring of a Sister Maria-Fiore dei Fiori di Montagna aphorism.

She looked at Torquil again. He really was very striking, an Adonis in every respect, and she found herself wondering: *who does he share a room with?* It was not an appropriate thought – at least, not one for *her* to think – but she was certainly pleased that the new neighbours would be interesting. Life would be dull, Domenica reminded herself, if we all ended up living next to people who were just like ourselves.

4. *That Dreadful Woman*

The following day was a Saturday. In the Pollock flat in Scotland Street, one floor below Angus and Domenica, Stuart's mother, Nicola, was making breakfast for her son and two grandsons. She had spent the night in the flat rather than return to her own flat round the corner in Northumberland Street; she would usually do this if babysitting in the evening for Stuart, as she had done the previous night. Stuart was reluctant to ask his mother to babysit in the evening, as she gave up most of her days to look after Bertie and Ulysses, but on this occasion he had arranged to have dinner with his new friend, Katie. That was something that Nicola was keen to encourage; in the earlier days of Stuart's marriage to Irene, Nicola had done her best to keep good relations with her daughter-in-law before eventually realising that it was just impossible. After reaching that conclusion, she had simply kept out of Irene's way, not doing anything to provoke a matrimonial split, but being immensely relieved when the fault lines in the marriage eventually made themselves clear. And when Irene announced that she was leaving Edinburgh to pursue studies for a PhD in Aberdeen, Nicola found it impossible to conceal her glee.

'I can't say I'm exactly devastated,' she said to Stuart. 'Much as I admire Irene ...'

Stuart had looked at her balefully. 'You don't admire her, Mother. You may as well be honest.'

Nicola hesitated, but then she said, 'No, you're right. I can't stand her. I've never been able to. Sorry about that, darling, but she really is the most dreadful cow.'

It was not the language of a tactful mother-in-law, but at least it was direct, and Stuart knew that his mother was at heart completely devoted to him. Like so many mothers, all she had ever wanted in this life was that her son should be happy. That was her *raison d'être*, he had decided, and it was a humbling thought – that another should devote herself so wholeheartedly and unconditionally to your interests. Mothers loved; mothers plotted; mothers turned a blind eye to the most egregious defects in their sons. Daughters were different, and were often judged more severely by their mothers, but when it came to sons, mothers could forgive anything.

And yet this maternal objective of Nicola's was clearly

incompatible with Irene and all her works. Something had to give, and that, it transpired, was Irene. Up until her announcement that she was going to Aberdeen, she had seemed invincible, a stubborn fact of life, as immutable and solid as the Hoover Dam or the Great Wall of China. Well, stone and cement will last, while our human arrangements may prove less firm of foundation. Irene, whose shadow he thought of as a long one, was suddenly no longer there – except for the occasional weekend – and he was like a prisoner suddenly released from durance vile. It was heady, it was exhilarating, even if he was still in the foothills of freedom.

'I'm sorry it's come to this,' he said to his mother. 'I tried to make it work – I really did.'

'Of course you did, darling. You tried and tried. I saw it. I would never have had the patience you showed. I would have poisoned her long ago … Sorry, darling, I don't really mean that. What I should say is that I would have been *tempted* to poison her.' She smiled as she remembered something. 'Speaking of which, I read something terribly amusing the other day. It was about the way in which the CIA made plans to dispose of various leaders they considered to be hostile. You'll remember the exploding cigars they tried to get Castro to smoke?'

Stuart had read about those.

'They had various committees to plot that sort of thing,' Nicola continued. 'And they gave these committees code names. One of them was set up to plan the poisoning of the then Prime Minister of Iraq – that was back in the early sixties. They called it the Health Alteration Committee.'

'That's a bit scary,' said Stuart.

'Indeed,' said Nicola. 'But there we are. I really am sorry you've had to put up with that dreadful woman ... sorry, your wife ... for so long. But now, at long last, freedom!'

'To an extent,' said Stuart.

'She hasn't changed her mind, has she?' asked Nicola anxiously.

'No, but she always said that she'll come back for weekends from time to time – to see the boys.'

'As she should,' said Nicola. 'As long as she doesn't stay too long.'

'She's coming back today,' said Stuart flatly. 'She sent me a message. She said: *Back today. Get boys ready.*'

'That was all?'

Stuart nodded. 'That was all.'

'Oh well,' said Nicola. 'It takes a very low mind to talk in telegraphese. However, be that as it may, I shall make myself scarce. I can come back tomorrow – if she's gone by then.'

Stuart explained that Irene had announced she would catch a three o'clock train back to Aberdeen the following day – Sunday. Nicola did a rapid calculation. That meant that she would only be in Edinburgh for twenty-six hours or so – and there was a limit to the psychological damage one could do in twenty-six-hours.

That Saturday, as it happened, Bertie had with him his friend, Ranald Braveheart Macpherson. Ranald had been brought over to the flat after school on Friday by arrangement between Nicola and Ranald's mother. Ranald's father had been subject to a significant Community Payback Order, imposed on him by Edinburgh Sheriff Court after pleading guilty to an offence relating to company accounts. It was not an offence of dishonesty as much as one of negligence, and the sheriff had thought that community service would be a fitting punishment. With this he had imposed a period of two hundred hours of Scottish country dancing, and it was this sentence that Ranald's father tackled each Friday evening when a variety of country dance enthusiasts descended on the Macpherson house in Albert Terrace and clocked up the necessary hours in the doing of 'Gay Gordons', 'The Dashing White Sergeant', and 'Dukes of Perth'. Ranald found these evenings tedious, and so was relieved when Nicola had suggested to his mother that there should be a Scotland Street sleepover.

Now Bertie and Ranald were in Bertie's room, poring over a previously clandestine copy of Baden-Powell's *Scouting for Boys*, when Bertie suddenly looked at the clock on the wall and said, 'My mummy's coming soon, Ranald – we'd better look out.'

Ranald looked disappointed. His hours with Bertie were the highlight of his life. They were the firmest of friends; they were blood-brothers, the bond having been sealed by the stabbing of two palms with a pin; they were comrades-in-arms in all the battles that went with being seven. 'My dad says your mummy is a real minger,' said Ranald. 'I'd never say that, Bertie – it's my dad. But I think lots of people agree with him, you know.'

Bertie bit his lip. 'I can't help it,' he said, struggling to keep his voice even. 'You can't help your mummy, Ranald.'

'Maybe she isn't your real mother,' offered Ranald, helpfully. 'Maybe there was a mistake at the hospital and they gave her the wrong baby. Maybe you really belong up in Morningside or somewhere, rather than down here in Scotland Street.'

'Maybe,' said Bertie. Morningside, or even Glasgow, he thought, allowing himself a vision of freedom enshrined, distilled, apotheosised.

5. *The Speaking of Italian, etc.*

Irene cast her eye about the kitchen in the Pollock flat on Scotland Street. Stuart and Nicola had tidied it before her arrival, but even so it was clear that she was ready to find fault.

'I see you've moved the breadbin,' she observed. 'Whose idea was that?'

Stuart, who was far from relaxed, gave a nervous start. 'Whose idea? My ma's, I think. But ... ' He realised, too late, that this was not a wise answer. 'Or me,' he added lamely. 'It might have been my idea. Who knows?'

'Your mother's?' crowed Irene. 'I didn't expect her to come in here and start moving the breadbin. Not that I don't appreciate her help with the boys, but still ... '

Stuart felt the back of his neck getting warm. It always did that when he was under stress; it had done that yesterday in a meeting at the office when the chairman of the finance company he now worked for questioned a report he had written.

There was nothing wrong with the report – Stuart knew that – but there was everything wrong with the chairman's grasp of the figures in it.

'It doesn't matter,' he blurted out to Irene. 'It doesn't matter whether the breadbin is on that table or this one. What difference does it make?'

Irene pretended to be placatory. 'Oh, it makes no difference, Stuart. Don't be so sensitive. It's just that there's an obvious place for the breadbin – the place it *used* to occupy – and then there's a place that's not so intuitive. That's all I'm saying.'

He should have let the matter drop – he knew that – but there was something that made him persist. This was a symbolic rather than a real battle. What was at stake here was the principle of autonomy. Nicola did not have to accept Irene's way of doing things; she had the right to move the breadbin around if she so wished.

'I don't think,' he began, 'that you should come down from Aberdeen and start going on about the breadbin the moment you set foot in the house.'

Irene glared at him. 'May I remind you, Stuart: this is still my house. I may be located in Aberdeen at present, but I still live here, you know.'

'A funny sort of living,' Stuart muttered.

Irene would not let that pass. 'Oh yes? And what do you mean by that, Stuart?'

'I mean that you now live in Aberdeen. You went there. I didn't say to you *Go and live in Aberdeen*, did I? You went to Aberdeen because you wanted to be with that shrink. It was your decision. And that implied loss of control over any breadbin in Edinburgh.'

'Don't be so ridiculous,' snapped Irene. 'And don't call Hugo a *shrink*. That's a very demeaning word.'

'Well, that's what he is, isn't he?'

Irene sighed. 'Listen, Stuart, I haven't come down to Edinburgh to argue with you about matters in respect of which I am quite clearly right. I've come down to Edinburgh to see Bertie and Ulysses.'

Stuart made an effort to control himself. 'All right. Ulysses is sleeping at the moment . . . '

'Good,' said Irene. 'I'm pleased that at least something is being properly handled. His afternoon sleep is very important.'

Stuart ignored the implication that there was much else that was not being properly handled. He would let that pass because he knew, from experience, that arguments with Irene could go on for ever, were inevitably bitter, and were never won by anybody but Irene herself.

'And Bertie is with Ranald Braveheart Macpherson. They're in his room – reading, I think.'

'Reading what?' asked Irene.

Stuart shrugged. 'I don't know. They go in there and play with trains and read. They like reading to one another – or Bertie does the reading because Ranald can't exactly read yet.'

Irene was silent for a moment, and then said, 'I thought you'd know what Bertie was reading. It could be something unsuitable, you know.'

'Unsuitable? Of course it won't be. It's probably that scouting book he's so fond of.'

No sooner had he uttered these words than he realised that this was going to lead to trouble.

'Scouting book?' asked Irene. 'You're not letting him read that dreadful book I confiscated, are you? That Baden-Powell book?'

Stuart was defiant. 'There's nothing wrong with it. That's the sort of thing that boys like to read.'

The effect of this was immediate. 'Excuse me, Stuart, there is no such thing as what boys like to do. That sort of talk is no longer acceptable. It's as simple as that – no longer acceptable.'

Stuart took a deep breath. 'But that, I'm afraid, is just the way it is, Irene. You may not like it, but there are certain differences between boys and girls. They often have different interests.'

Irene closed her eyes. 'I can't believe I'm hearing this,' she said. 'Not today, not after all the conversations that this country has had over gender.'

'Conversations?' said Stuart. 'I thought a conversation implied the free exchange of ideas.'

'I shall ignore that,' said Irene icily. She moved towards the door. 'I shall go and see Bertie. We can talk some other time, Stuart.'

She left the kitchen and walked across the hall to the door that led into Bertie's room. 'Knock, knock,' she said. 'Guess who's here, Bertie.'

The door opened and Bertie appeared. He stood still for a moment, and then rushed to embrace his mother.

'*Bertissimo*,' Irene whispered. '*Bertissimo mio.*' Then she added, 'Have you been practising your Italian, darling?'

Bertie disengaged. 'A bit. Not actually speaking it, Mummy, but thinking it – a bit.'

'That's good,' said Irene.

'Granny says that French is more use than Italian,' said Bertie.

Irene ruffled his hair. 'Does she now? I wonder why Nonna would say something like that.'

'She says it's because Italian is a one-country language. She says that they speak French in other places too. She also says that Spanish is a good language to learn as there are lots of countries that speak it. Did you know that they speak Spanish in South America, Mummy? Did you know that?'

Irene said that she had heard this to be the case. 'But it's not just a question of how many people speak a language, Bertie,' she said. 'It's what the language represents. You and I know – don't we, Bertie? – that the Italian language is the language of the Renaissance. The language of Petrarch and Dante, of Michelangelo and da Vinci – not that your granny has probably heard of them, but still.'

Irene went into Bertie's room. She smiled at Ranald and asked him when he was going home.

'But can't Ranald stay?' asked Bertie.

'We all get back to our own houses, Bertie,' said Irene. 'Ranald's house is over in Morningside or Church Hill or somewhere like that, Bertie. We mustn't monopolise him.'

'When are you going to go back to Aberdeen?' asked Bertie. 'I'm just asking, Mummy. You can stay as long as you like, of course, but I just wanted to know.'

6. You Tattie-bogle

That night, while Irene conducted a lengthy telephone conversation with a friend from the Carl Gustav Jung Drop-in Centre, Stuart put Bertie to bed. The ritual was always the same: with the main lights out and the room lit only by the glow of a small night-light, Stuart would ask Bertie about his day, listen to the reports of activities down amongst the children, as he thought of it, and then he would tell his son a story. That story did not have to be a new one: stories that had been repeated many times were still appreciated, even more so, perhaps, than those that were new. Like so many children, Bertie was, at heart, a traditionalist – in the broadest sense of the word: he did not want things to change. Which is perhaps not such a surprising position: the child, for whom all things are new, might be forgiven for not wanting to abandon that which is only recently experienced and, for the most part, found good – because anything better has not yet been experienced.

A few days earlier, Bertie had asked about kelpies. His interest had been piqued by a newspaper photograph he had seen of the great metal kelpie statues near Falkirk – towering horses' heads that had become so popular. 'Were there really any kelpies?' asked Bertie. And then answered himself with a further question, 'They're mythical, aren't they?'

Stuart had been relieved. Kelpies were typical water spirits, and there were few water spirits that were consistently benign. From what he remembered of the Scottish folklore on the subject, kelpies were particularly unpleasant. If you unwittingly climbed on a kelpie's back, you would be stuck there, unable to get off, and would in short order be taken into the water and drowned. Thereafter the kelpie would eat you. This, after all, was folklore, and folklore is generally not for the faint-hearted. In that respect, the kelpie barely differed from the sirens whose charms lured sailors onto the rocks. With sirens, one must avert one's gaze to have any hope; but there was only one way in which the kelpie could be mastered, and that was by seizing their bridles. It was for this reason that the Clan MacGregor was said to possess a potent bridle, passed down from generation to generation, exclusively for use on troublesome kelpies.

Stuart was happy to allay his son's concerns. 'Kelpies definitely do not exist,' he said. 'Nor do many of those other creatures people talk about, Bertie. There's no need to worry.'

From his drowsy pillow, Bertie muttered, 'And tattie-bogles, Daddy? What about tattie-bogles?'

Stuart smiled. He knew all about Scottish scarecrows. 'Oh, they exist, Bertie. But they're just tattie-bogles – nothing more. They can't chase you or do any of the things in stories. You won't find any tattie-bogles walking about.'

He remembered a poem he had learned as a child. Now it came back to him, dredged from the recesses of memory. It was by Willie Soutar, a bed-ridden Scottish poet who had had such a short life – a little longer than Robert Fergusson's, but still curtailed. Now he recited it to Bertie:

The tattie-bogle wags his airms:
Caw! Caw! Caw!
He hasna onie banes or thairms:
Caw! Caw! Caw!

We corbies wha hae taken tent,
And wamphl'd round, and glower'd asklent,
Noo gang hame lauchin owre the bent:
Caw! Caw! Caw!

(The tattie-bogle wags his arms: Caw! Caw! Caw! / He hasn't any bones or insides: Caw! Caw! Caw! / We crows have taken heed of this and flown around, and looked sideways at him, and now go home in fits of laughter over the moor: Caw! Caw! Caw!)

Bertie listened quietly, and then, his voice increasingly drowsy, he asked his father to recite the poem again. Stuart did so, and by the time he finished, he realised that the little boy was asleep. He gazed at him for a few minutes, fascinated by his son's face in repose. There was such vulnerability, as there was in the face of any sleeper, although in the case of a child that vulnerability can surely break any heart. *Could surely melt ilka heirt* ...

He thought of Willie Soutar's poem. His English teacher at school – one of those inspiring teachers who can arouse a love of poetry in even the most sceptical of young people – had told them about Soutar, reading to them Douglas Young's touching tribute to the young poet. *Twenty year beddit*, ran that poem, *and nou the mort-claith* ... Twenty years confined to bed, and now the shroud ... *Was his life warth livan? Ay, siccar it was. He was eident, he was blye in Scotland's cause . . .*

He returned to the kitchen, where Irene was finishing her telephone call.

'We need to bring that up with the committee,' she was saying. 'They have to face reality.'

Stuart stared at her. It was typical of Irene that she should be more concerned with the affairs of the Carl Gustav Jung Drop-in Centre than with her own small son, that little boy with all his anxieties about kelpies and his thoughts of tattie-bogles. But there was no point in going into that now. There was no point in talking to Irene about anything, really, because she simply did not hear what you said to her. Everything was filtered through a belief system that excluded any opinions – or evidence – that she did not want to hear.

Irene tucked her telephone back into a pocket and looked expectantly at Stuart. 'Well?' she said.

'Well, what?' Stuart countered.

'What are you up to, Stuart?'

Stuart gave a gesture that embraced the flat about them. 'Running this place,' he said. 'Getting Bertie to school in the morning. Taking Ulysses for his inoculations. Earning the money to pay for all this.' He wanted to add, 'Using up my life in keeping our heads above water,' but he did not. Irene was quick to detect self-pity and Stuart did not want to give her any ammunition.

'Are you happy, Stuart?'

He thought for a moment before he answered. He could say that while he was not sure that he was as happy as he

27

might be, he was certainly happier than he used to be. 'Enough,' he said. 'I'm happy enough, I suppose.'

Irene looked at him quizzically. 'I suppose one gets accustomed to failure,' she said.

He said nothing.

'Ambition is not for everyone,' Irene continued. 'There are those who want to get ahead, and those who are content with staying where they are.'

Stuart held her gaze. 'I suppose you're putting me in the second category. Division two.'

'If that's where you see yourself,' said Irene. She paused, as if waiting for a *mea culpa* to emerge. 'Surely you know in your heart of hearts that it doesn't matter what you do or don't do. Nobody much is going to notice it.'

Stuart bit his lip. She was a tattie-bogle – that's what she was. A real tattie-bogle.

Now she lowered her voice. 'I'd be most interested to hear if you're seeing somebody, Stuart,' she said.

He looked at her. Why would she want to know that? Their marriage was over and he regarded himself as perfectly free to see somebody if he wanted to; and the same was true of Irene.

He affected surprise. Surely she could not know about his romance: it was far too recent, too discreet, to have registered with anybody whom Irene might know.

'I might be,' he said. 'But I feel that we don't need to inform one another of this sort of thing. There are no requirements, I would have thought, of full disclosure . . .'

Irene drew in her breath. 'I take it that means yes,' she said.

'I didn't say that,' protested Stuart.

Irene spoke as if *ex cathedra*. 'Often what you don't say is more important than what you say.' She paused. 'Who is she?'

Stuart did not reply, and Irene moved on.

'I've made up your bed on the sofa,' she said.

He closed his eyes. She was the visitor; she should sleep there. She was the one who had left, and he saw no reason why she should now feel she could return and put him out of his bed.

The injustice of it, he thought, the sheer injustice.

'Tattie-bogle,' he whispered under his breath.

'What?' said Irene.

7. *More Than Anything Else in the World*

On Monday morning Matthew planned to arrive at his gallery in Dundas Street earlier than usual. It was the day on which he would be hanging the paintings in his new exhibition, and he was single-handed; Pat, his part-time assistant, had an interview for another part-time job and would not be able to get into work until after lunch. The task of hanging was difficult enough with two people doing it – with one, it became even more demanding. And yet Matthew was looking forward to it: as he drove into town from Nine Mile Burn, he reflected on how fortunate he was to be doing a job that he loved so much, in an incomparably beautiful city, in a country that, for all its faults, was an interesting and *kind* place to live. Scotland was a kind place because people still worried about one another and believed in the good of community, and in a rough – and reassuring – equality too. Only read Robert Burns to understand what that is about.

And there was the weather to be considered, too, in any counting of blessings. Scotland's weather would not accord with anybody's idea of an ideal climate, but it was better than many other possibilities. Many places were simply too hot: you could live on the plains of India, in the red heart of Australia, or the coast of the Persian Gulf, but in the height of summer such places were barely habitable. Many other regions were too cold, as was true of large swathes of northern Canada. There, in winter, the mislaying of a glove would quickly lead to the loss of fingers from frostbite, and people who stumbled off their path and into the snow might be frozen where they stood. Scotland was never too hot, but neither was it too cold. It might be blustery, but it would be blustery *and* fresh. It might be wet, but it would be wet only intermittently, and between the veils of rain there would be shafts of dreamy sunlight, rainbows, patches of soft-blue sky.

And there all these things were, laid out before him, as he made his way along the final stretch of road descending to the city's boundary. Off to his left were the Pentlands, the hills that stood between the coastal plains and the rolling, feminine interior. Down on those plains, a few wisps of *haar*, of sea-mist, now lifting, blanketed the cluster of rooftops, the occasional church spire, of the Midlothian towns, of Carrington, of Roslin, of Dalkeith. And then beyond all that were the cold blue fields of the North Sea across which lay Denmark, and the places beyond Denmark. He saw the conical absurdity of Berwick Law, a geological *scherzo*, and the Bass Rock, guano-white even at this distance, and he spotted a dot on the blue that was a ship ploughing its course northwards to Dundee or Aberdeen.

He thought of the two artists whose work he would show in his new exhibition. One of them painted Homeric subjects, placing figures from Greek myth in a landscape made up of bits of Greece and bits of Scotland. The Cyclops, with that hesitation of those whose vision is less than 20/20, stood astride a path in a landscape that could be right here, where he was driving, although the sky in the painting would be Aegean. Circe worked her magic in another painting, where men became pigs, delving greedily in the half-worked earth. The other artist was a watercolourist who painted architectural studies with a palette of earthen colours – sienna, umber, gold – and with a view of the world that was of light and shadow and an underlying order.

His mind wandered to the house he had just left behind him – to his triplets, Rognvald, Fergus and Tobermory. He had left them that morning seated at the small table that was their domain, their breakfast before them – and on the floor, too, as they were messy eaters, even by the standards of small children. There had been the smell of burnt toast in the air, as one of the boys had stood on a chair and been able to interfere with the toaster settings, producing slices of smouldering black and provoking an exasperated scolding from Elspeth. Matthew thought: each morning I leave all that behind me: the noise, the rough and tumble, the chaos that lurks beneath the surface of any household of children, and yet Elspeth, who stays behind with it and for whom it is her whole day, still actually loves me. He knew that. She loved him, because suddenly she had said just that in the bathroom that morning as he shaved with his new triple-action floating-head electric razor, the achievement of some unsung Dutch designer of shaving technology. She had touched his arm, as if to remind him of something he had promised to do, and had said, 'I love you so much, Matthew – I really do.' And then, above the buzz of his shaver, she had said, 'And your boys love you too, you know. Tobermory said as much last night. He said, *I love Daddy more than anything else in the world*. Which is not bad for three, don't you think?'

He had not thought too much about it then, because when he had finished shaving he had to get dressed and make the private muesli he made for himself to keep sugar out of the equation. He had not thought about it because when you have mundane things to do you do not contemplate your good fortune. Now he did, though: I am so fortunate, he thought. I could die right now, and still be considered lucky for what I have had so far.

He slowed down. He was now on the edge of the city and approaching a roundabout. It would be easy to describe a circle at that roundabout and return in the direction from which he had just come. He could drive right back to Nine Mile Burn – he would be there within fifteen minutes – and say to Elspeth that he had decided to stay at home that day to be with her, to help her with the boys, perhaps to take them all off for a picnic on the beach at Gullane (pr. *Gillin*) or on an expedition to explore Tantallon Castle. He could do that, and Elspeth, who loved spontaneity, would readily agree and would quickly prepare sandwiches and boiled eggs wrapped in tinfoil with salt and pepper in little twists of newsprint. And they would go off together and forget about Edinburgh and the claims of the gallery.

But you didn't do that – you just didn't. You went into work and you did what you had to do, although at times in the working day you might pause and think about what was said to you in the bathroom, and bathe in it, as one bathes in the warmth of a profession of love, or even just friendship.

8. *A Bit of Forever*

By ten o'clock, Matthew had hung six pictures, two of which he had subsequently taken down and substituted with others. By ten-thirty he had swapped a further two and moved one to a new position. He was pleased: the effect was good, and he seemed to be achieving what he set out to achieve, which was to give each painting the room to be itself without fighting with its neighbour.

He looked at his watch and saw that it was time to cross the road for his morning coffee. He put on his jacket and hung up, on the glass front door, the sign given to him by a German friend: *Ich bin bald wieder zurück*. Then he made his way across the road towards Big Lou's coffee bar.

He only remembered as he descended the steps to Big Lou's basement premises that fifty-one per cent of Big Lou's, as the café was widely known, now belonged to him and Elspeth. This had come about as a result of a rescue operation mounted by Matthew: Big Lou, in need of money to send her adopted son, Finlay, to ballet school in Glasgow, had been on the point of accepting an offer for her coffee bar from a developer; Matthew had stepped in, offering to buy half of the business for Elspeth. She and Big Lou would then expand the coffee bar and run it as a partnership. They would employ another au pair to help with the boys and thus make Elspeth available to work in the coffee bar for at least half the day. That would give her time out of the house, away from the incessant demands of the triplets, without the constraints of a full-time job. 'When you have more than one small child on your hands,' a friend had advised, 'you need a retreat if you are to maintain your sanity.'

That had proved to be true: there had been times when Elspeth had been at the end of her tether and had only survived thanks to the help she received from Matthew, from James, their young male au pair – nephew of the Duke of Johannesburg – and from a bottle of Tio Pepe bone-dry sherry kept in the fridge and self-administered judiciously, and responsibly, when the mayhem got too overwhelming. James, the au pair, had exceeded all expectations. He was an exceptional cook, with a particular talent for turning what Matthew called *nursery food* – fish fingers, baked beans etc. – into concoctions that the triplets found irresistible. The cajoling and persuasion that had been a feature of the boys' dinner time before James's arrival quickly became a thing of the past: now plates were licked clean and demands made for more even as the food appeared on the table.

And the same culinary skills were in evidence when James cooked for Elspeth and Matthew, which he did four nights a week. His preference was for Italian cuisine – for rich Tuscan bean stews with floating chunks of bread that he himself had made; for antipasto plates decorated with marinated artichoke hearts and dried tomatoes that he prepared in the baking oven of Elspeth's Aga; for delicate sauces that accompanied home-made tagliatelle. These dishes he would announce as he served them at the table, explaining their origin and the circumstances in which he had learned to make them. Once a week, he took a bus into town to visit Valvona & Crolla and stock up with the provisions that he used in these dishes, although he had also found local sources of which he made full use – a farmer who sold him chickens; a woman in the nearby village who cultivated chanterelles in her shed; an angler who had a source (not investigated too closely) of trout and occasionally of langoustines.

But James, of course, being an au pair, would not last for ever. Elspeth had hardly dared ask him about his plans, but she knew that he was intending at some point to go to university, and that she would lose him. He was now just a few weeks short of his twentieth birthday, and she realised that sooner or later she would have to discuss with him the climbing trip that he planned to take to Switzerland with Pat, Matthew's assistant in the gallery. Elspeth had her misgivings about that relationship: Pat was four years older than James and although there was nothing inherently wrong in that age gap, she still felt that James was, in some vague way, vulnerable and that Pat should be careful.

Matthew did not share that concern. 'What's four years?' he asked. 'And anyway, if it were the other way around – if she were twenty, or whatever, and he was twenty-four, would anybody bat an eyelid? They wouldn't, would they?'

Elspeth looked wistful. 'I know, I know. But still. James is just so ... so special. I suppose that's what I want to say. He's special.'

Matthew was puzzled. 'What do you mean? So, he can cook. And he's good with the boys. And he ...'

'And look at how kind he's been to his uncle,' Elspeth added. 'After the Duke crashed his flying boat up in Argyll, look at how James went to the hospital every single day and then took him to physiotherapy for weeks. He never complained.'

'Yes, he's great,' said Matthew. 'But we must face the fact that James won't be with us all that much longer. We'll have to get somebody else.'

Elspeth looked thoughtful. 'I've had an idea, Matthew.'

'You've thought of somebody?'

She shook her head. 'No, but it's occurred to me that we could somehow hold on to James.'

Matthew frowned. 'He's not going to want to be an au pair for the rest of his life.'

'No, I know that. Obviously not. But he's spoken about going to university in Edinburgh, hasn't he? He's never said anything about going away.'

Matthew agreed: James had indicated on more than one occasion that he wanted to study in Edinburgh.

'Well, why don't we give him a part-time job? That's what

Pat had all the way through her student days. He could do the same. We could employ him.'

'At the gallery?' asked Matthew. Pat had worked for him in the gallery, and still did.

'I wasn't thinking of that,' said Elspeth. 'He could do some work there, I suppose, but I was thinking of Big Lou's. He could do shifts at Big Lou's once we get going there. Then he could do the odd weekend for us, perhaps. The triplets would love to have him about the place, Tobermory in particular: he loves him to bits. You can see that.'

Matthew smiled. 'We can't keep him for ever,' he said. 'Boys like that grow up.'

'We can at least keep him for a bit of forever,' said Elspeth.

9. Mr Fifty-One Per Cent

'We need to have a chat,' Matthew said to Big Lou as he entered the coffee bar. Looking around, he saw that there were a few customers who had been served with coffee and, in one case, a bacon roll. In the air there hung the smell of freshly cooked bacon, that enticing smell that is, for the newly converted vegetarian, the most painful temptation, a distilled evocation of a life now rejected. Matthew had often thought that were the manufacturers of aftershave lotions and men's fragrances to do their market research properly, the scents they would offer their customers would not be the usual cedarwood or sandalwood, but fried bacon, the smell of a new shirt fresh out of its cellophane wrapper, or freshly ground coffee. These were the scents that men liked, but that somehow did not appeal to the advertising agents. *Porc pour l'homme* had a ring about it, but not quite the ring desired by the marketeers, and so there was no range of men's products that catered to that side of men's sensibilities.

Big Lou gave him a cheerful nod. 'And the usual, Matthew?'

She knew that she did not have to ask, but she did so anyway. It was a Monday, and on a Monday Matthew always had a skinny latte (medium) and a small bottle of Pellegrino sparkling water on the side. On Wednesday and Friday, that would be broadened to include a bacon roll with a dab of English mustard. These bacon rolls were, as Matthew described them, *off the record*, as he did not report them to Elspeth. Her policy was to restrict bacon to a once-a-week treat – for health reasons – and she would not have approved. Matthew felt guilty about this, but only slightly. In terms of matrimonial deceptions, this was at the most innocent end of the scale, and even then he was planning to confess his secret bacon rolls to her when he got round to it, which for some reason had not yet happened.

Matthew sat down on one of the stools at the bar. Behind the stainless-steel counter, Big Lou operated the large Italian coffee machine: steam hissed and clouded; water within boiled and gurgled; from a concealed spout came a stream of dark brown coffee. Into this, heated milk was poured, the surface being topped off with a creamy twirl of foam depicting a thistle-head.

'You wanted to talk?' Big Lou said as she passed the cup to Matthew. 'It's about this place, I take it?'

Matthew nodded. 'You and I need to have a meeting with Elspeth. We need to agree a business plan.'

Big Lou pursed her lips. 'My accountant keeps talking about making a business plan. I tell him I'm here to make coffee, not business plans. Coffee and bacon rolls – which are proving gey popular, by the way.'

'I'm sure they are,' said Matthew. 'But we do need to have some idea where this place is going.'

'It's not going anywhere,' said Big Lou quickly. 'I haven't noticed any movement.'

Matthew laughed dutifully. 'Of course not. But you know what I meant – it's a question of knowing where the business is going in a general sense. That's why we need a business plan.'

Big Lou shrugged. 'If you say so, Matthew.'

'And Elspeth and I already have some ideas,' Matthew continued. 'Would you like to hear them?'

'Aye,' said Big Lou. 'I'm happy to hear them.'

Matthew gave her an intense look. He was fond of Big Lou – as everyone was – and he had been quick to help her when he heard that a developer was circling round. But he wondered now whether his offer had been too quick, and whether running a business with Big Lou would be more difficult than he imagined. Elspeth had a good relationship with Big Lou, but she did not know her all that well and of course they had never worked together. It was working with somebody, with all the compromises and adjustments that involved, that could be a real test of a relationship.

'Of course, I'm happy to hear your own ideas, Lou,' he said. 'We're going to be partners, after all – I didn't get involved to . . . ' He struggled to find the right form of words. He wanted to reassure Big Lou, but he did not want to condescend to her. 'I didn't get involved to tell you what to do.'

He heard Big Lou take a deep breath. This was not a good sign. People took deep breaths for a reason.

'Tell me what to do?' said Big Lou. '*You* tell *me* what to do, Matthew?'

Matthew was flustered. 'That's exactly what I don't intend to do, Lou. That's why I brought the subject up, you see.'

Big Lou reached for her cloth and began polishing the counter surface energetically. Matthew decided that was another bad sign. 'I didn't mean to offend you, Lou,' he offered.

The polishing increased in vigour.

'You couldn't tell me what to do,' she muttered.

Matthew took a sip of his coffee. He was not fond of conflict, and the idea of arguing with Big Lou over anything was anathema to him. And yet it was important, he felt, to make the terms of their business relationship clear. If he did not, then he would merely be putting off an inevitable row to some point in the future. No business, he thought, could leave the issue of ultimate control unsettled. At some juncture, sooner or later, somebody would have to know where real power lay.

'Listen, Lou,' Matthew began. 'We need to be aware of where each of us stands.'

Big Lou put down her cloth. 'Aye, Matthew,' she said. 'I'm standing behind this counter, running this place, and you're sitting on the stool on the other side. That's where we are, I think.'

Matthew sighed. 'You're not making this easy for me, Lou.'

'Easy to do what?' she challenged.

'Easy to work out what we do.'

Big Lou frowned. 'But what's there to do?' She gestured to the tables, only one of which was unoccupied. 'See them over there? They're the customers, and they're not complaining, are they?'

Matthew glanced over his shoulder. He was uncomfortable about having this discussion in the open, in the middle of the coffee bar. But he had started it and it would only be more difficult in the future if he put it off.

'You see,' he began, 'the arrangement we reached, you'll remember, was that I acquired just over half of the business – and all its assets, including this bit of the building – when I paid you that money. Remember? It was three hundred thousand. Three hundred and fifty thousand, to be precise.'

'I know how much it was,' said Big Lou. 'I put it in the bank.'

'Yes,' said Matthew. 'You put it in the bank and so I became the controlling shareholder in the little company we set up. Remember that? *Big Lou Limited?*'

'That's me and you,' she said. 'Aye, I mind that well. And I'm happy to be in business with you, Matthew. And I'm grateful to you for coming up with the money and joining me.'

'I was happy to help, Lou, but . . . '

Big Lou did not let him finish. 'And I look forward,' she said, 'to working with Elspeth – when she has the time.

There's no hurry, as far as I'm concerned – you know that, I think.'

10. Tribal Markings

While Matthew and Big Lou engaged in these preliminary exchanges at the counter, at the back of the café, seated at a table directly in front of the window giving onto the shared green, were two men in their mid-forties. They were smartly dressed in grey, pin-stripe suits, one suit being slightly darker than the other, although both disclosed an attention to cut. The tie that each wore revealed, to any experienced spotter of such plumage, the wearer's institutional affiliations. Ties, for men, can be a tribal marking, as clear in their statement as any system of facial tattooing to be found in Polynesia. A tie can demonstrate the wearer's preferred sport, his education, and, in the case of politicians, his party membership and position on the left-right spectrum. A deep red tie indicates uncompromising attachment to socialism, while a tie of a lighter red is a sure sign of the left-centrist; a tie shading into pink may be making a different statement altogether. A navy blue tie is an indication of bone-deep conservatism, while one that is sky-blue will proclaim a more liberal disposition, yet still be a tie of the right. Green ties are worn by Greens – and are almost always recycled. There is a small but thriving industry that takes red, blue and yellow ties discarded by other politicians and dyes them before selling them to Greens. In Big Lou's that morning, one tie, sported by the taller of the two, a man with a fine aquiline nose and a general air of distinction, even if faded, bore the motif of the Bank of Scotland; the other proclaimed, in bold silver and maroon stripes, membership of the Watsonian Rugby Club.

To the casual observer, these two would seem to be typical Edinburgh businessmen, one obviously employed by the Bank of Scotland, the other possibly a member of one of the law firms that had migrated from Charlotte Square to the financial quarter behind the old Caledonian Hotel. Such an observer, had he or she bothered to speculate, might suggest that their meeting would be the prequel to a larger meeting to take place at one of the banks or investment firms – an opportunity to discuss strategy or explore a position before the dynamics changed and people from London joined in the discussion.

Such an assessment would, of course, be wrong, as the look of concern on the face of one of these men, leading to a frown on the face of the other, was nothing to do with the vagaries of business affairs but had everything to do with the continuing difficulties of a voluntary association that was against its will being drawn into territory in which it would prefer to remain uninvolved.

The man wearing the Bank of Scotland tie was, in fact, a senior figure in Scottish Widows, a life assurance and pension company set up in 1815 to look after the female dependents of men who had lost their lives in the Napoleonic wars. He was a successful middle-level manager in a solid company, but that was by no means all that he was. In addition to his business role, he was the Chairman of the Association of Scottish Nudists, and his companion at the table, a partner in a firm of commercial property managers, was the Secretary of the Association. When they had both recently assumed office, neither had been aware of the looming crisis that now threatened to divide the Association. It was this crisis that had disturbed the sleep of the Chairman for the last two nights and had prompted him to telephone the Secretary with the suggestion that they meet for coffee and a chat at Big Lou's. Big Lou's was, in fact, convenient for both of them that day as they were both to attend an earlier meeting at the headquarters of the Association, which was only a few blocks west of Big Lou's in Moray Place – an elegant Georgian circus looking in upon a sedate urban garden. The garden, with its shady canopy of trees and its well-kept paths, was a favourite haunt of members of the Association, and was the site of the well-attended annual Scottish Nudist Country Dance Weekend, an event coinciding with the main Edinburgh Festival each year and drawing its audience from all over the world.

The Chairman looked up at the ceiling, as if for guidance from some hidden oracle. 'It's very difficult to know what to do,' he remarked.

The Secretary nodded his agreement. 'I feel as if we're destined to lurch from crisis to crisis,' he said. 'There was that entryism debacle a few years back – remember that? And I thought we'd got over that whole wretched business.'

'Just when you thought it safe to get back into the water ...' mused the Chairman. It was a metaphorical observation, although even as he made it, the Chairman was reminded of the particular hazard that swimming now presented to Scottish nudists with the proliferation of jellyfish species along the West Coast of Scotland.

The entryism episode had been a bruising experience for Scottish nudists: a group of Glaswegian nudists, smouldering with resentment over Edinburgh's domination of the committee, had plotted to take over the Association and all its assets. These attempts had required a quick response from the Edinburgh membership, and this defence had eventually succeeded. But it left bad feeling that had not been entirely dispelled and had, in fact, been fanned by the choosing at the last election of a committee made up exclusively of members from Edinburgh and its environs.

'What about us?' one of the Glasgow troublemakers had complained. 'Do we count for nothing over here? What about Paisley? They have one of the most active memberships in the country and they don't have a single voice on the council. Not one.'

The crisis had been weathered, and the committee was now hoping for a period of stability. But nobody on the committee had anticipated the consequences of appointing a new editor and editorial board to the Association's bi-monthly magazine, *The Scottish Naturist*. This new editor, who had impressed the sub-committee set up to make the appointment, had seemed plausible enough. He had given an address in South Queensferry, and it had been assumed that this was where he came from. But that proved not to be the case. The editor, it transpired, was only staying for a few months with his sister-in-law in South Queensferry while his house was being renovated; his real address, disclosed nowhere on the application form, was in Pollokshields. And everybody knew that Pollokshields was in Glasgow.

11. Muckle Birkies

'Oh jings!' said the Chairman of the Association of Scottish Nudists. 'We should have been more careful. There are plenty of ways of telling where somebody is from – if you look out for the tell-tale signs.'

The Secretary shook his head sadly. 'You're right. We haven't been vigilant enough.' But then he thought: just how did one tell whether somebody claiming to be from South Queensferry was really from Pollokshields?

The Chairman answered the unspoken question. 'The verbal cues are the really important ones. We should have noticed that he spoke rather quickly. Remember? He ran his words together with scant regard for the natural break between words.' He sighed. 'I sometimes wonder how people in Glasgow manage to *breathe*. All the words come tumbling out without any pause for breath. It's extraordinary.'

The Secretary knew what the Chairman meant. 'It's as if they can't wait to get things out,' he said. 'It's as if speed adds force to what they say.'

'Perhaps that's intentional,' mused the Chairman. 'If you

speak so quickly that nobody can understand what you've said, you've probably scored an initial victory. The person to whom you're speaking is left in doubt.'

'And then there's the inflection,' added the Secretary. 'There's an underlying challenge in most Glaswegian sentences. Each statement implies: *contradict me if you dare*. The tone goes up at the end, and you're left there.'

'These are subtle matters,' said the Chairman. 'We haven't even considered the patois. Do you remember when we offered him a glass of sherry at the end of the interview ...'

'It being past twelve o'clock,' interjected the Secretary, primly.

'Yes, and remember what he said?'

The Secretary frowned. He had not paid particular attention to the interview, such was his relief that somebody had actually applied for the post of editor of the magazine. 'What was that?' he asked.

The Chairman grimaced. It was not easy for an Edinburgh financier to use the demotic, irrespective of its origin. 'He said ... and I quote, of course, *ipse dixit*, as we say, *I wouldnae mind a wee swally*.'

The Secretary gasped. 'Oh no! And I didn't notice!'

'Well, that's what he said. A *wee swally*, no less. I thought that he was being ironic, in the same way in which you and I take leave of one another with *see yous*. We would never pluralise the second person singular, because we know, of course, that the same form includes both singular and plural. But we do use it ironically.'

'Like those people who say *au reservoir?*'

The Chairman nodded. 'Exactly. And so I just smiled and

said *Oloroso?*' He paused. 'And you know what that led to? He looked at me and said, *Where's that?*'

'No!' exclaimed the Secretary. 'What a hoot!'

The Chairman nodded. 'Of course, one can't count on any degree of knowledge about anything these days. You would imagine, would you not, that a senior official in the Department of Culture and the Arts could be expected to know who Giotto was? You'd think that, I believe. And yet I met one a few years ago who thought Giotto was a sort of cheese. Yes! He asked whether you could get Giotto at Valvona & Crolla – he really did.'

'Astonishing,' exclaimed the Secretary. 'Giotto, of all *French* painters!'

'Hah!' said the Chairman. '*Très drôle.*'

Their mirth seemed to cheer them up – and there was more to come.

'That same chap,' said the Secretary, 'might have thought *pointillism* was a skin disease.'

The Chairman doubled up, laughing so much that a seam on his waistcoat split. 'Characterised by extensive spots,' he said.

There was more laughter. Up at the counter, Big Lou interrupted her conversation with Matthew to observe, 'Those twa over there,' she muttered. 'See them, Matthew? Those twa lang-nebbit chiels who run roond with their bahookies on show – something's making them cheer-ful the day.'

But the chat at the two men's table had already reached its comic apogee. Now came a descent into concern and anxiety.

'You see,' said the Chairman, 'he didn't indicate at all what

48

his editorial line would be – other than to say *no change*. Do you remember that? Because I thought: any new editor who says *no change* gets my support. I have *always* supported those who say *no change* – and I am *always* disappointed when they are swept away.'

'I can see why you believed him,' said the Secretary. 'You mustn't reproach yourself. South Queensferry, after all, is completely acceptable. Nobody would imagine that Glasgow was lurking in the background.'

'It's not Glasgow,' said the Chairman. 'I like Glasgow – in its place …'

'Which is forty miles west of here.'

The Chairman smiled, but the time for laughter was over. 'I like their cheerfulness and their good humour. I don't always see the point of their jokes, but that might just be me …'

'*Au contraire*,' said the Secretary. 'It's me as well.'

The Chairman smiled. He and the Secretary were, he thought, almost always on the same page. It was very reassuring. 'Well, there you are,' he said. 'But the real point is this: Glasgow should keep its nose out of other people's business. The Association has always been based in Edinburgh and run by Edinburgh people. And did anything go wrong? It did not. And the magazine has always been neutral on political issues – we've always made a point of welcoming everyone, no matter what their political views may be. We're all Jock Tamson's bairns, after all, aren't we? Once the clothing's off, we're all the same underneath.'

'Well, to a degree,' said the Secretary. 'Some of us have perhaps allowed ourselves to go to seed a bit. But we're never ashamed of the human body, whatever its contours might be.'

'That's a very good metaphor,' remarked the Chairman. *'Take ownership of your contours!* I think that would be a very good slogan.' He paused. 'But to write that provocative editorial and then to fill the magazine with pictures of a South Ayrshire naturist pilgrimage to Bannockburn where everybody – and I mean everybody – had Saltires painted all over them ... Well! There was no mistaking the political message there.'

The Secretary sighed. 'I take a broad view of the national question. I respect both camps, and I really don't think that our magazine should identify with one side or the other.'

'My views entirely,' said the Chairman. 'But what do we do?'

'We could ask him to show editorial balance,' said the Secretary. 'Are there any big Unionist naturist events coming up?'

The Chairman looked at the ceiling. 'I have heard of something,' he said. 'But I don't think we should discuss it just yet.' He made a sign to the Secretary – a strange movement of the fingers across the lips.

The Secretary recognised this immediately. This was the New Club sign for *omertà*.

'Lips sealed,' he said, and made the sign back to the Chairman.

From behind the counter, Big Lou whispered to Matthew, 'Look at them, Matthew. Twa muckle birkies.' She shook her head. 'Mair coffee, Matthew?'

12. Down Among the Men

'Please feel free to go out, Stuart,' Irene said over her shoulder, as she browsed through the contents of the food cupboard. She did not wait for a response before continuing, in a slightly sarcastic tone, 'Now what have we here? *Smoked oysters. Product of China.* Well, that's a thought, isn't it? Chinese oysters.'

She turned to face Stuart, who was sitting at the kitchen table, a copy of the *Scotsman* crossword in front of him. He was trying to ignore Irene, but her presence made it very difficult for him to concentrate on the crossword. '*An air force man looks jaunty,*' he muttered, more for his own benefit than for Irene's.

Irene smiled. 'Pretty obvious.' She paused. 'Is that the children's crossword or the adults'?'

The slight was intended. Irene had always been better at crosswords than Stuart, and she took considerable delight in coming up with solutions that were, in retrospect, glaringly obvious but which had for some reason not occurred to Stuart.

'Well, then?' goaded Irene. '*An air force man looks jaunty.*'

She waited. Stuart tried to ignore her. He would move on to the next clue, he thought, rather than give Irene the satisfaction of solving this one. Long experience had taught him that if you moved the conversation on, you could wrong-foot her. Sometimes.

'I've got it,' he muttered, and then, '*An old woman at first is followed by part of a backward analyst: tasty in January!*' Haggis, he thought. Hag, followed by the first part of Sigmund, backwards. That would show Irene.

'You solved that first one?' asked Irene. 'The jaunty aviator?'

Stuart hesitated. He was truthful by nature, but Irene was a force that disturbed all known patterns of type and character. He felt justifiably irritated. She had the right to visit the boys, but she had no right to go through the kitchen cupboard, make comments on tins of smoked oysters – implicit at this stage, but doubtless with more to come; nor had she the right to interfere with his doing of the *Scotsman* crossword. You never told people the answers to a puzzle they were doing. You just did not. It was the equivalent of telling somebody about the ending of a book or a play: it was a *spoiler*. Irene loved spoilers, as long, of course, as they originated with her.

'Yes, I've moved on,' said Stuart.

'So?' Irene persisted. 'What was it?'

Stuart bit his lip. Sometimes Irene made him feel as if he were Bertie's age, or even less. He had put up with that in the past, swallowing his pride as a grown man must on being treated as a small boy, but now that he was free at last – and that was the word he used: *free* – that small, so emotive word, heady in its potency – now that he was free he did not have to put up with this.

He looked up at Irene. He was seated – she was standing. This, he thought, was how the world must seem to Bertie, with all these adults a few feet above one's own head. This was the view from down among the children.

Down among – that phrase could be used in so many different contexts where there was an upper and a lower level. *Down among the children; down among the desperate; down among the* ... He stopped, remembering a paper that Irene had once delivered to a meeting of her Progressive Book Group. This was a book group that was based in the New Town and met once a month in places such as North West Circus Place and Howe Street to excoriate those who, for one reason or another, were not considered progressive, or at least were not progressive enough. The group consisted entirely of women, as far as Stuart could ascertain; he had once enquired of Irene whether there were any male members, only to be told that none had been deemed suitable. Stuart had very tentatively proposed himself, but this suggestion had been met with silence, and was not aired again.

It was for delivery at this book group that Irene had written her paper *Down Among the Men*. Stuart had discovered this on the family computer, and had printed it out to read it in a more leisurely way. For reasons of security, he had read it while sitting on one of the benches in Drummond Place Garden, where the chances of being discovered by Irene or any of her allies were low.

The main premise of *Down Among the Men* was that all male writers worked under the influence of a subconscious archetype to which Irene had given the name *The Inner Hemingway*.

'Scratch any male writer,' Irene had written, 'and you will find a Hemingway not far below the surface. This *Inner*

Hemingway is a *Weltanschauung* that sees the world as a *tabula rasa* upon which the dominant male must mark his territory – just as a wolf does. But there are other wolves around – we must never forget that – and they will be required to be subdued by the projection of strength. It is this projection of strength that informs every male endeavour, whether it be the subduing of Gaia (Earth, femininity) through big civil engineering projects, the annexation of the Crimea, or the creation of a fictional universe. It is all the same. Every man is a Hemingway. Every man is a Norman Mailer. Do not be fooled by those writers who claim to have a different vision: *men are never different*. Go down among the men and see for yourselves.'

Stuart had waded through this, feeling increasingly angry and despondent in roughly equal measure. It was just so unfair. There were Hemingways – of course there were – but there were also plenty of sensitive, sympathetic men who did not see the world in these terms. How unjust to describe half of humanity, or whatever percentage men were, with this dreadful stereotype. It was every bit as bad as those misogynistic comments that slipped from the lips of unreconstructed men from time to time and resulted in their rapid suspension or dismissal from their university chair.

He sighed, and laid *Down Among the Men* to one side. He closed his eyes. He did not think he could take this for much longer.

A voice spoke – a gentle, Italian voice.

'Oh, Mr Pollock, here you are,' said the voice. 'I turn a corner in the garden, and what do I see? I see you, seated like one of Poussin's shepherds on a convenient bank.'

He opened his eyes and saw Sister Maria-Fiore dei Fiori di Montagna standing before him, clad in her nun's habit of Marian blue, like one of those visions that appears from time to time to surprised bystanders in places like rural Fatima, or credulous Knock, or, perhaps, even Drummond Place Garden.

13. Looking for Mother

Stuart had been pleased to see Sister Maria-Fiore dei Fiori di Montagna. There were some people whom he normally did not wish to see in Drummond Place Garden, particularly those members of the Garden Committee who policed access. This was a much-contested point: the founding charter of the Garden stipulated that it was for the exclusive use of the proprietors of Drummond Place flats and houses. That was clear enough, but then there had arisen a number of difficult issues over whether those whose windows overlooked Drummond Place, but whose doors were on a different street, were eligible to use the Garden. That had, by immemorial custom, been interpreted in favour of access, and it meant that there were some whose address was Dundonald Street or Nelson Street who were allowed to parade around the Garden with all the assuredness of those who had an actual Drummond Place address. There was, of course, always a certain qualification to their entitlement – a whiff of the narrow shave – but nobody openly called into question their rights. In addition, there were certain properties in nearby streets that had been given a right of access under some ancient letter of comfort, and whose position was therefore more parlous. Stuart was one of these. They had inherited a key when they bought the flat, and that key had originally been accompanied by a letter from the committee saying that the owners of flats in 44 Scotland Street could enjoy the gardens in perpetuity. But did that mean that any owner of a flat in 44 Scotland Street could enjoy that right until his or her demise, or did it extend to their heirs? That was the issue, and on several occasions it had been brought up in a confrontational way by a member of the committee.

'May I ask what you're reading?' said Sister Maria-Fiore dei Fiori di Montagna.

Stuart folded the piece of paper and tucked it into his pocket. The nun was notoriously nosy, and even had the document in question been an uncontroversial one, he would have resisted any effort on her part to discover the contents.

'It's just a report,' he said, and then, deliberately changing the subject, he observed how neat and tidy the gardens were looking. 'Midsummer produces such luxuriant growth – it's very easy for the gardens to look a little bit jungly.'

'Ah,' said the nun. 'Like the background of a Rousseau painting? Very green. Very large leaves. Very dense.'

Stuart smiled. 'I wouldn't go so far as that, perhaps. But certainly, nature looks a little less ordered in summer than at other times.'

'So, what sort of report?' asked Sister Maria-Fiore dei Fiori di Montagna.

Stuart shrugged. 'About the state of the world, I suppose.'

The nun sat down next to him on the bench. 'Could I see it? I am most interested in the state of the world. Indeed, I spend long hours considering that very issue.'

Stuart pretended not to hear. He was aware, though, of the nun looking at him intently.

'Sometimes we are inclined not to hear what we do not wish to hear,' she said, after a while. 'There is always that temptation, you know. If we do not like something, we act as if we are ignorant of it – but we are not ignorant, Stuart. We are far from ignorant. That to which we close our ears bypasses our hearing and goes into our heart, where it may fester away for a long time. So, by denying it to begin with, we lend to it great power in the long run.'

Stuart pursed his lips. What had he done to deserve this relentless persecution by women? There was Irene, there was Sister Maria-Fiore dei Fiori di Montagna, there were others – he was sure of it. But then he thought: am I becoming paranoid? And with that, he decided not to resist the nun's inquisitiveness.

Reaching into his pocket, he extracted the report. 'My wife has written this,' he said. 'It's for her progressive book club.'

He passed the nun *Down Among the Men* and the nun began to read it. When she finished, she folded it again, taking care to observe the same creases that he had used, and then handed it back to him. Then she crossed herself.

'That is very culture-specific,' she said calmly. 'Not all men are like that.'

Stuart expressed relief. 'I'm not,' he said. 'Nor is Angus Lordie. Nor anybody, really.'

'Of course they aren't,' said Sister Maria-Fiore dei Fiori di Montagna. 'And you will see that she is only quoting northern, mostly Protestant writers, although Mr Mailer was Jewish, I believe.'

'That's true,' said Stuart.

'And where are the Italian writers in all that?' asked Sister Maria-Fiore dei Fiori di Montagna. 'Where is Ariosto? Manzoni? Calvino? Eco? Where are they?'

Stuart frowned. Irene made a great deal of her interest in Italian culture, and so the absence of Italian writers was surprising. 'They're not mentioned because they don't fit the argument.'

'Exactly,' said Sister Maria-Fiore dei Fiori di Montagna. 'Italy is not a male-dominated society. It would not fit the mould.'

'And yet,' said Stuart. 'And yet it has the Catholic Church. Surely that is more or less entirely dominated by males? Where are the female cardinals? Where are the women in the higher echelons of the Vatican – or even in the lower echelons?'

The nun sighed. 'They are there,' she said. 'But only in an idealised state. There may be no real women in those places, but they are there in the cult of the Virgin. The feminine principle infuses Latin Christianity, Mr Pollock, because of the absent father in Mediterranean culture. That is why pre-Christian religions in those parts had powerful female goddesses who simply became the Virgin Mary later on. And because the father was not present, men looked for a female figure to replace their mother when she was no longer there. And they created the Virgin Mary as the expression of all that longing for a feminine presence in their lives – these sad, lonely men expressed their longing for the feminine by creating a figure whom they could venerate. That explains the Marian cult, you see.'

She smiled sweetly. 'Whereas in Scotland, men did not feel the same need to have a mother-substitute. Nor any statues, nor superstitions. Scots looked for love in Reason, and in sympathy.'

Stuart smiled. 'You're sounding more and more like a Protestant,' he said.

'I understand that,' said the nun. 'I have been moving gently towards Protestantism, although not going as far as your Free Kirk, I'm afraid.'

Stuart laughed. 'What are they looking for?'

'They're looking for mother too,' said Sister Maria-Fiore dei Fiori di Montagna. 'If you listen to those Gaelic psalms of theirs, the keynote – the authentic note – is this: *Where are we? Where are we going? Why is there so much rain?*'

14. The Merits of an Open Mind

Stuart had found the encounter in Drummond Place Garden with Sister Maria-Fiore dei Fiori di Montagna strangely comforting, and now, in the combat zone that was the kitchen of his flat in Scotland Street, he thought back to the socialite nun's words. It was so easy for women to make men feel desperate – and there were many women who seemed to enjoy doing just that. Stuart was fair-minded enough to realise that men's current discomfort was but as nothing when compared with the humiliation and oppression of women by men over the ages, but he still felt that the ending of one wrong was no excuse for the encouragement of another. He felt that he, personally, had never been party – at least not consciously – to the subjugation of women, and he felt, then, that he did not deserve the treatment that he had had from Irene during the entire currency of their marriage. Nor did he think it helpful for people to belittle men, as this involved something that he had never seen as justified: collective guilt.

Yet Irene and her co-zealots seemed to be everywhere, and their influence extended even into the remotest of corners. Bertie's situation was an example of that: Stuart had recently become aware of what Bertie had to put up with at the hands of Olive, the girl in his class at school who most closely approximated to Irene in her seemingly relentless agenda of persecution.

It was Stuart's mother, Nicola, who had reported on a conversation she had had with Bertie on the 23 bus back from Morningside.

'Bertie was a bit upset this afternoon,' she told Stuart. 'I was travelling back with him and Ulysses on the top floor of the bus, which he normally likes. Today, though, he was a bit *piano*, and so I asked him if everything was all right at school.'

'They normally give you a monosyllabic answer to that,' Stuart observed. 'They say *fine*, and leave it at that.'

'Not today,' said Nicola. 'He said, "It's that Olive, Granny. I hate her like poison."'

'There's never been any love lost between them,' said Stuart. 'Olive has been hounding Bertie for years. She insists that he promised to marry her when they're twenty. I even came across a letter she had written to him about it.'

'No!' exploded Nicola. 'The little minx!'

Stuart explained how he had found the skilfully forged letter tucked away behind Bertie's bookcase. 'She had obtained a genuine solicitor's letterhead,' he said. 'She had cut out the top part that gave the name of the firm. It was Morton Fraser, I think, and then she had typed underneath it – or had typed for her, as I don't think she can write yet – a whole spiel about breach of promise and how, if he failed to discharge his responsibilities, an action would be raised against him in the Court of Session, with damages, and interest on damages.' He paused. 'Heaven knows where she got it from, but it all looked very official.'

Nicola groaned. 'Poor wee boy. She knows how to turn the knife, that young lady.'

'Oh, she does that all right. But what's the latest?'

'Apparently Olive and her sidekick . . .'

'Pansy.'

'Yes, Olive and Pansy have been telling Bertie that they think he's really a girl – psychologically, that is – and that he should get counselling about this.'

Stuart frowned. 'Where on earth does that come from?'

Nicola smiled. 'Well, whatever the source, they've put

the wind up him. They told him they've been observing him and that any time he feels he wants to talk about it, they're ready.'

Stuart shook his head in despair.

'He was very upset,' said Nicola. 'It all came out as we made our way along George IV Bridge and down the Mound. He said that he likes being a boy and he sees nothing wrong with it, although he did say that he did not think that Tofu was a very good role model.'

'There's something to be said for that,' said Stuart. 'So, what did you say?'

'Well, I listened,' said Nicola. 'It's a difficult issue. Children pick things up and don't understand, as you know. All this discussion about gender filters down eventually, and they can get a bit confused.'

'But Olive doesn't exactly help.'

'No. So I told him that it was very clear that he was a boy, and that Ulysses was a boy as well. Then I gently tried to find out exactly what Olive had said. And then it all came out.'

Stuart listened.

'Apparently, Olive said that the acid test of whether a boy was a boy was whether he could whistle. She said that if you couldn't whistle, you were more or less certainly a girl.'

Stuart gasped. 'She said that?'

'Yes. And, as you know, Bertie can't whistle – he's too young, anyway.'

Stuart looked away. He was unable to whistle – or at least, to whistle convincingly. He had always envied people who could put two fingers in their mouth and emit a loud whistling sound – sufficient to hail a taxi in a noisy street, for example. But he was not one of them – and of course being unable to whistle, he had not taught Bertie.

'What can we do?' he asked.

'I've been thinking about that,' said Nicola. 'I suppose we can have a word with the school. This is a form of bullying, after all, and they have a very strong policy on that.'

'We could,' said Stuart. 'I'm sure they'd be supportive.'

'And we can give him a boost,' Nicola went on. 'We can build him up. Make him confident as to who he is.'

Stuart nodded. 'Of course.'

Nicola hesitated. 'There is another possibility.'

'Oh yes?'

'Boarding school,' said Nicola. 'We could take him away for a while and send him to a boys' boarding school. That would get him away from the baneful influence of Olive and Pansy.'

Stuart shook his head. 'I'm not a great believer in boarding schools,' he said. 'It seems so unnatural to take a child away from the home and send them off like that.'

'I know what you mean,' said Nicola. 'But there are plenty of children who do very well at boarding school. There are plenty of children who seem to benefit.'

Stuart was unconvinced. 'And anyway, they're terribly expensive.'

'I'll pay,' said Nicola. 'I have the means, as you probably know. I can pay.'

'But where?' asked Stuart. 'Most of these places are co-ed now. Fettes, Strathallan, Dollar. Are there any boys' schools left?'

'There's a boys' boarding school right here in Edinburgh,'

said Nicola. 'Merchiston. It's academically very strong and they have plenty of rugby and so on.'

'Mmm,' said Stuart.

'All I ask is that you keep an open mind,' said Nicola. 'I know that open-mindedness is very unfashionable these days. But it has its merits, you know.'

15. A Lover in Aberdeen

Stuart had been dreading spending the evening in Scotland Street with Irene, and when she announced that she did not object to his going out, he immediately retreated to the bathroom – the one place in the flat where he felt secure from Irene's prying eyes – and telephoned his new friend, Katie.

'Look,' he said, his voice lowered, 'I know that I said I was likely to be tied up this weekend, but ...'

'Why are you whispering?' she asked. 'Are you in a library?'

'No, I'm in Scotland Street. I'm in my flat ... It's just that Irene is down from Aberdeen and I don't want her to hear me.' He waited. He had told her about Irene, but he was not sure that he had explained the situation adequately. Stuart was loyal by nature, and it went against the grain of his character to disparage somebody to whom he was still married and who was, after all, the mother of his children. It was possible, he thought, that Katie simply did not grasp the full extent of

Irene's contrariness. It was possible, too, that she would think that his explanation of their estrangement was no different from the unexceptional *my wife doesn't understand me* plea of so many wandering husbands.

There was silence at the other end of the line. Then Katie said, 'I'm uncomfortable with this, Stuart. I've never been involved in anything like this before. I don't like the idea.'

'Of what? Of seeing me?'

'Of having to communicate in whispers. Of deceiving somebody.'

Stuart sighed. His fears were proving well founded. 'I'm not deceiving anybody,' he pleaded. 'The situation really is as I've explained it. Irene left me to go to Aberdeen because she has ...' He hesitated. It was still hard for him to say this, but he felt that he had to. 'Because she has a lover there. She has a lover in Aberdeen.'

There, he had said it. *She has a lover in Aberdeen.* It was such an *explosive* thing to say. A lover in *Aberdeen*. Having a lover *simpliciter* was unremarkable enough; to have a lover in Glasgow or London was a little bit more exotic, but to have a lover in *Aberdeen* was in a different league altogether. It was a bit like confessing to having a lover in the Arctic Circle.

'Well, I suppose ...'

'She's the one who left,' he interjected. 'It wasn't my fault, and I don't see why I should feel guilty about it.'

'No, I suppose not.'

'And she was never all that keen on marriage,' Stuart continued. 'Especially marriage to me.'

Katie made a sympathetic noise.

'So that's why I don't think I'm deceiving anybody,'

Stuart concluded, his tone now that of one who has been unfairly accused.

There was a brief silence, then Katie said, 'I'm sorry, Stuart. I shouldn't have said what I said.'

He breathed a sigh of relief, and just at that moment there was a knocking on the door.

'Stuart,' shouted Irene, 'what are you doing in there?'

Katie overheard. 'Is that her?' she asked.

'Yes,' whispered Stuart. 'She's knocking on the door.' He was glad that Katie had heard Irene shouting. Now she might be able to understand what he had put up with. He moved the phone a bit closer to the keyhole, so as better to pick up Irene's voice.

'Stuart?' repeated Irene. 'Are you talking to somebody?'

'What did she say?' asked Katie.

Stuart cupped his hand over the receiver. 'I'm dictating a memo,' he called out to Irene.

'What about?' asked Irene, knocking again as she spoke.

'Something private,' said Stuart.

'Have you gone mad?' asked Irene.

Stuart now addressed Katie. 'Listen,' he said. 'Can I see you in about half an hour?'

Katie replied immediately. 'Yes. Where?'

Stuart thought of the first place that came to mind. 'The Wally Dug Bar. Northumberland Street. On the corner.'

'I know it,' said Katie.

'I have to go,' said Stuart.

Outside the bathroom, there was an ominous silence. Plucking up his courage, Stuart unlocked the door and began to open it. As he did so, his eye caught a drawing that Bertie had done and that he himself had stuck on one of the door panels. It was a portrait, in the stick-man style of a child's drawing, and it portrayed Stuart in a kilt, wielding what looked like a claymore. Underneath was written, in faltering lettering, MY DAD IN HIS KOLT, and beneath that the signature, BERTIE.

He stared at the drawing, his emotions welling up within him. That was him: MY DAD – seen from the perspective of a little boy who was barely seven, who wanted from the world no more than that which any seven-year-old boy wants – a Swiss Army penknife, a dog, friendship and adventure, and a mother and a father. That was all. And yet even if he could provide some of these things for Bertie, he could not provide them all, no matter how hard he tried.

He saw that Irene was no longer waiting outside the bathroom, and so he was able to look again at the drawing. Why had Bertie chosen to portray him with a large sword in his hand? He thought he knew: Bertie had recently expressed an interest in William Wallace, of whom he had read in a book that Nicola had found for him: *A Boy's Book of Scotland and Scottish Things*, published by Messrs Nelson, at their printing works in Edinburgh in 1956. Nicola had obtained it from her friend Mary Davidson, who collected books for the Christian Aid sale and who had spotted this as being ideal for somebody of Bertie's age. Bertie had been thrilled because the editors of *A Boy's Book of Scotland and Scottish Things* had a vision of Scotland that was misty, romantic and totally at odds with the contemporary official version of the country. Scotland, in their view, was all about plotting, revenge, acts of astonishing bravery, explorers, inventors, the Forth

Railway Bridge, and oatmeal porridge. People such as Olive and Pansy were written out of this conception of the country, as were the English, who were only marginally portrayed in their role as members of Edward's army, ruthless Redcoats at Culloden, and frightened occupants of Northumbrian farms cowering in the face of entirely justified Scottish raids to retrieve stolen cattle from English stock-thieves.

And here, thought Stuart, am I, imagined in that vanished world that never was anyway, pictured by that little boy with his wavering pencil, pictured with love, with pride, and with an intensity that shone through with as much force as that which drove Michelangelo, Titian or Rembrandt van Rijn to put pigment to canvas, board, or plaster.

Oh, my darling Bertie, Stuart thought. I love you so much, so much. And I'm going to do everything – everything – I possibly can to make your life better, to allow you to be a boy, which is not something you need be ashamed of or apologise for. I promise you that, Bertie; I promise you.

And with that he went into the kitchen, where Irene was waiting for him.

16. At the Wally Dug

Irene said to Stuart, 'So, Stuart: dinner à deux, I imagine, with your young friend?'

Stuart ignored the taunt. 'There's a quiche in the fridge for you,' he said. 'It's chopped ham and sun-dried tomato. And there's a salad too – it's already dressed.'

Irene sniffed. 'You shouldn't put dressing on a salad until you're ready to eat it. It kills it dead after half an hour.'

'Well, there you are,' said Stuart. 'That's what's available.'

He turned to leave the kitchen.

'I take it that you're finding something you didn't see in me,' said Irene. 'Men being men.'

Stuart caught his breath. He gave Irene what he hoped was a withering glance, and made his way out of the flat. He felt his heart beating within him; that would be adrenalin, he thought, the fight or flight hormone produced by such situations of stress. Well, he had opted for flight, which was ultimately better, he decided. Bertie might see him as William Wallace, but that was not really him. He wanted only harmony and freedom from constant criticism and sniping. He wanted normality.

He went out onto Scotland Street and started the five-minute walk to the Wally Dug. Although it was summer, and the city was filling with visitors, in that quiet part of the New Town there were few people about: a man taking a dog for a walk; a young couple strolling hand in hand, completely absorbed in the miracle that was one another; a woman loading an estate car with bunches of cut flowers and plants in small terracotta pots.

It was quiet, too, at the Wally Dug, with only four or five people in the bar, none of whom he recognised. There was a point in life, he thought, where you might expect to go into a bar and recognise nobody; and then a further point, still a distant one for Stuart, but one that he could nonetheless at least envisage, where one would go into a bar and realise that one is the oldest person there.

Stuart ordered a half pint of Campbell's and sat down at one of the tables in the back. He looked at his watch. He was early, but only by ten minutes. Even if Katie were to be five or ten minutes late, this meant that within twenty minutes, at the most, he would be seeing her. The thought excited him, and he felt his heart beat more noticeably. Our revealing hearts, he thought: they give everything away. He had read somewhere that the idea of a broken heart was not an impossible one; that the heart, pre-eminently amongst organs, reacted to the emotions. So perhaps the heart was indeed where feelings of love were located. You *did* give people your heart; your heart *was* snatched away from you by one for whom you fell.

And the heart, with its chambers, may have room for more than one love; in Stuart's heart, there was a chamber for his sons, for Bertie and Ulysses, and one for his mother, and one for somebody like Katie.

He looked at his watch again. Time would drag because of his anticipation; he knew that. But then he saw the door swing open and Katie came in. He rose to his feet automatic-ally, and spilled his glass of beer across the table. She saw it happen; saw him reach forward, too late to prevent disaster.

'Oh, look,' he said. 'Just look. Stupid me ...'

She laughed. 'I'm always doing that.'

'Spilling things?' He mopped at the pool of beer with his handkerchief, now soaked.

'Yes, and breaking things too.'

A woman behind the bar came round with a cloth and tidied up.

'I feel very stupid,' said Stuart.

She laughed. 'Don't worry. It happens. Sit at that table there. This will dry.'

They moved, and Stuart ordered Katie a drink. She wanted orange juice. 'I like wine,' she said, 'but not always. Sometimes.'

He said that he thought it a good idea not to drink wine all the time. And then he laughed. 'That sounds so odd. *Don't drink wine all the time.*'

'Two or three times a week,' she said. 'That won't harm you.'

He looked at her, his eyes falling to the linen blouse she was wearing. He loved linen, particularly green linen, which this was.

'Linen,' he muttered.

She had intercepted his gaze. 'My blouse? You like it, then?'

'Love it.' And then he asked, 'Have you been working on the PhD?'

Katie was doing a PhD on twentieth-century Scottish poetry. She spent a lot of time, she had told him, in the National Library.

'No,' she said. 'I've been ...' She looked embarrassed. 'I've been indulging myself. I know I should be working on the thesis, but ... well, every so often, I want to do my own writing. And I do. Today has been one of those days.'

'Poetry?' asked Stuart. 'You told me you write poetry – and you gave me that poem once. Remember?'

She nodded. 'Yes. I've got a ridiculous plan.'

'Tell me.'

'You won't laugh?'

'Of course not.'

She took a sip of her orange juice. 'I'm writing sonnets. I want to write a series of sonnets about friendship and love. That's my plan.'

Stuart smiled. 'But that's wonderful.'

She seemed pleased. 'Do you think so?'

'Yes.'

She gave him a searching look. 'Do you know Shakespeare's sonnets?'

He replied that he knew one or two lines – nothing more. '*When in disgrace with fortune and men's eyes* . . . et cetera?'

'That's one of them. There are rather a lot. Not all of them are as memorable as that.'

'And yours?' asked Stuart.

'They'll be in strict sonnet form. Or fairly strict.'

He looked at her. He was in love. It hit him as a wave hits you when wading in the sea – or that is what it felt like. It made him feel elated. It was love, as forceful and as powerful as a wave. He wanted to say to her: *Look, I'm in love with you – head over heels, utterly, completely, insanely.* But instead he said, 'Would you read one to me? One of your sonnets?'

She blushed. 'Do you really want me to?'

'Of course.' He reached out and took her hand. He could not believe he was holding it. She did not resist. She returned the pressure of his fingers, and that meant only one thing: they were lovers. He had a lover. And suddenly it felt as if a great burden was lifted from him: a burden of guilt and regret. He had done his best with his marriage: it was not his fault. He had gone through life tiptoeing round Irene's sensitivities, apologising for being who he was, and now it was over. There would be no more apologies. He was free.

17. *Love, Like Electricity*

Stuart said to Katie, 'You said you'd read me one of your poems.'

'Yes, I did.'

He stroked her hand. 'So? Will you?'

She looked about her. 'Here? In the pub?'

'Nobody's paying any attention to us.' He gestured to the other people, none of whom seemed aware of their presence. 'See?'

She reached into a bag she had brought with her. 'As it happens ...'

He grinned encouragingly. 'Go on.'

Katie took out a single sheet of paper. Stuart craned his neck to look at it, but she kept it to herself. 'Remember, they're sonnets.'

'You said that.'

'So that means fourteen lines,' she explained, 'with twelve lines rhyming on an *abab* scheme, and the last two lines rhyming *aa*.' She paused. 'Pentameters. More or less.'

Stuart nodded. He tried to remember what he knew

about metre, but it had been forgotten. He had done Higher English, but that was a long time ago.

'I've imagined this first poem as something that might have been written by James VI,' Katie said. 'He was a very interesting figure, you know. Rather sad. He had a pretty stern tutor and very little joy in his life. His mother, after all, had her head chopped off. And then, along comes his cousin from France, Esmé Stuart, and James, as a boy, falls in love with him. For the first time there is light in his life – until Esmé is sent back to France. So I imagined James writing this. It may sound a bit old-fashioned as a result.'

Stuart listened.

> *Cousin, you came into my life too late*
> *To be the one to teach me how to see*
> *How strange it is to be a slave of Fate,*
> *Even though men should subjects be to me.*
> *But what you taught me – that I'll always hold*
> *More precious than the gifts of high estate,*
> *Those are base metal, while your words are gold*
> *Displayed in letters large at Heaven's gate;*
> *A gentle look, a secret touch, a smile,*
> *Given free and by outsider's hand unbidden,*
> *Will count for more than any trick or wile*
> *Or words in which a heart of ice is hidden.*
> *Now you are gone, you have put out the light*
> *That bathed my days in sun, that banished night.*

When she had finished, Stuart was silent. He looked at her and she looked back, unblinking.

She said, 'The departure of Esmé Stuart brought his world to an end.'

He said, 'Yes, it would, wouldn't it?'

'I have another one,' she said. 'Another sonnet. Nothing to do with James. This is about the end of a love affair. One person has gone and the other reflects on the parting.'

He waited, and she began to read:

> *When I felt lonely I would go around*
> *Lost in a crowd of those I did not know,*
> *Hoping to hear the once familiar sound*
> *The voice of one who claimed to love me so;*
> *But listened in vain, just as I listen still,*
> *For you to utter, to evoke my name,*
> *Knowing the ear's a trickster and often will*
> *Contrive to make other people sound the same;*
> *You needed do no more than write to me,*
> *You needed do no more than make a call;*
> *Writing costs nothing, email's almost free,*
> *My sorrow, though, I think counts not at all.*
> *An injured heart does not engender love,*
> *No sheltering tree will want a single dove.*

He reached for her hand again. 'Is that you speaking?' he asked. 'Did that happen to you?'

She did not answer immediately, but then she said, 'Hasn't that happened to everybody? Hasn't everybody loved somebody and not been loved back? Unreciprocated love?'

He thought about it. When he was sixteen he had fallen in love with a girl who was a year older than he was. His feeling for her had hit him like a jolt of electricity, as he had suddenly discovered the possibility of thinking about another person for a sustained period of time *with pleasure*. This was the real essence of love – that simply thinking about another, conjuring up the image of the object of your love, could fill you with such an extraordinary sense of excitement. It was like cradling a rare thing in your hands and staring at it in wonderment – the wonder being that this thing actually existed, that it *was*. How strange, how strange … and he had felt all that for that girl who had not even noticed him because he was a year younger than she was, and at that age such an age difference can be fatal.

He answered Katie. 'Yes, it probably has. It happened to me.'

He had not intended to say that, but he had, and now she asked, gently enough, but with an enquiring look, 'Your wife?'

He shook his head. It had been quite different with Irene. He had always imagined that he had loved Irene – after all, he had married her – but now he was not at all sure. He had done his best to love her, because Stuart was duteous and it is expected of husbands and wives that they should at least try to love one another, but there had never been that … that … He searched his mind for the right word, and ended up with *electricity*. It was a somewhat hackneyed metaphor, but everybody knew what it meant in the context. There had not been that electricity that went with love; it simply was not there. Perhaps it was affection – perhaps that was what there had been, at least on his part. He was not at all sure, now, that Irene had ever even *liked* him. She had been so critical, so censorious, that he had wondered whether her first and greater loyalty was to some social or political project, some greater cause in which there was no place for the unbeliever, the outsider.

He looked at Katie. 'Your poem,' he said. 'What were the last two lines of that second poem?'

She looked down at the piece of paper from which she had read the two sonnets.

'An injured heart does not engender love,' she read. 'No sheltering tree will want a single dove.'

'What does that mean?' he asked. 'I like the sound of it, but what does it actually mean?'

She folded the paper. 'It means that it's no good trying to get sympathy from the other person – the person who's indifferent to you. He, or she, will never love you because you're sad – just as a tree wants two doves that are happy rather than one that's sad.'

He looked down at the floor. Yes. That was quite true. He had not thought of it before, but it was one of those observations that had always been there and that one suddenly stumbled across and knew to be true.

Something occurred to him – a doubt. 'There's something you should know, though,' he said. 'It's this: those two little boys of mine – Bertie and his brother – I love them so much. They are more important than anything else. They're my life, I suppose. They're everything to me.'

She reached out to take his hand. 'Of course, I understand that. Of course I do.'

18. An Offer from Paris

That same afternoon, Pat had arrived at Matthew's gallery two hours later than usual. She had warned Matthew that she might be delayed at an interview she was attending for another part-time job, but had implied that she would be in for work no more than half an hour after he would normally expect her. As it turned out, it was not until almost four o'clock that Matthew saw a taxi draw up outside the gallery entrance and Pat step out. That in itself was unusual: Pat never travelled by taxi, as she made a point of walking everywhere or using the 23 bus, which conveniently made its way from the south side of the city, where Pat lived, all the way down Dundas Street, a route that took her almost to the gallery door.

'A taxi?' said Matthew as Pat came through the front door.

She looked at her watch. 'It's still, technically, three-something,' she said. 'It's not quite four.'

Matthew smiled. 'You told me. Don't worry. I knew you were going to be late.'

'But not this late,' said Pat. 'I'm really, really sorry.'

Matthew reassured her that it was not the end of the world. 'It hasn't exactly been busy,' he said. 'We almost sold a painting, and then the person changed her mind. It was that woman who lives round the corner. She came in with her husband and I could see that he didn't like it.' Matthew paused. 'Imagine being married to somebody who doesn't *understand*.'

'Doesn't understand what?'

Matthew shrugged. 'Oh, the things that you yourself understand. Music. Art. Literature.'

'A Philistine, in other words?'

'Yes,' said Matthew. 'How does the nursery rhyme go? *Jack Sprat could eat no fat, his wife could eat no lean . . .* '

'Yes, that's how it goes. But it doesn't really say much about them, does it? Or not as far as I remember.'

Matthew shook his head. He had been reading nursery rhymes to the triplets, from a book that Elspeth had had as a child, *Nursery Rhymes for Good Children*, and they were fresh in his mind. The boys, for some reason, liked Little Jack Horner – he who had sat in the corner, gorging himself on carbohydrates – and Georgie Porgie, a most unsavoury character, Matthew thought, who would be in deep trouble were he to behave like that today.

'The Sprats were actually quite happy,' he said. 'I think the message – if there is one – was that people could be happily married even if they had rather different tastes.' He paused. 'A rare example of harmony in a nursery rhyme.'

Pat sat down at her desk. 'They're full of misfortune, aren't they? Jack and Jill and their abortive trip up the hill. Humpty Dumpty too – I remember feeling so sorry for him, falling off his wall like that.' She laughed. 'He was such a nice character, Humpty Dumpty.'

Matthew considered this. He was not sure that he agreed with Pat. 'Actually, I find him a bit sinister. There's something odd about Humpty Dumpty – and I don't just mean his shape. I think there was a hint of ... well, I'm afraid to say a hint of something ...' He shrugged. 'I can't put my finger on it, but I think it's there. A psychosexual issue, I suppose.'

Pat laughed. 'Come on, Matthew. It's a nursery rhyme.'

'But innocent little stories are full of hidden meaning,' said Matthew. 'Don't be fooled. You can deconstruct anything. You should know that. You have a degree in art history – and that leaves nothing undeconstructed.'

Pat looked at her watch again. 'I'm really sorry about being so late, but that interview I told you about ...'

Matthew waited.

'That interview ... Well, it turned out to be rather different from what I had imagined.'

'The job was different, or the interview?'

'The job,' she replied. 'It was completely different. It's for a full-time post.'

Matthew said nothing. He knew that there would come a time when Pat would go after a full-time job somewhere – it was inevitable. But he had become used to having her as his part-time assistant, being there for when he needed a few hours away from the gallery, or for when he went down for a day or two to the London Art Fair or to some other trade gathering. Pat was good at her job – she was tactful with the clients, being not too pushy nor too diffident in her sales techniques, and she knew about art. She had a good eye, too, and there had been more than one occasion when she had spotted a warning sign in a painting that Matthew was contemplating buying at auction – some infelicity of style that suggested the auctioneer's attribution might be too optimistic or simply misinformed.

Eventually, Matthew said, 'You mustn't hesitate.'

She seemed surprised. 'To take this job?'

'To take *a* job. I know that I don't have a permanent claim on your time. I know that.'

She looked away. 'But you've been so good to me. All the way through. When I was a student in my first year. Right since then.'

Matthew made a self-deprecatory gesture. 'You were good at the job. Now ... well, you have to have a career. I'm not going to stand in your way.'

'It's in Paris.'

Matthew was not prepared for this. 'Paris? Your actual Paris?'

'Yes, your actual Paris. I can hardly believe it myself, but one of the people interviewing me for the part-time job, which was here in Edinburgh, said at the end that he could offer me something far better. I wasn't sure what he meant – I didn't have a clue, in fact – and then he said, "How would you like to work in Paris?" I couldn't believe it.'

Matthew shook his head. 'You can't refuse anybody who says, "How would you like to work in Paris?" You just can't.'

'I didn't,' said Pat.

Matthew thought: I should have been prepared for this, but I'm not. I'm going to get emotional. Struggling to keep his voice even, he said, 'That's wonderful, Pat.' And then he added, lamely, 'Paris.'

'It turned out that he – this guy who was interviewing me – is on the board of the Gargantuan Institute.'

Matthew drew in his breath. 'The Gargantuan? The people who . . .'

Pat nodded. 'Yes, them. Mr Gargantuan has six researchers working for him in Paris. They want to appoint a seventh who will handle British painting in general, but particularly Scottish art. They've been dealing in the Colourists recently and they felt they didn't have the necessary expertise. Not to have the final say, of course, but somebody who would know where to go for an opinion.'

'You can certainly do that,' said Matthew.

Pat turned to look at him. 'You aren't cross with me, are you? Leaving, and everything . . .'

He was quick to reply. 'Of course not. Of course I'm not cross.'

Then he thought: *This could change everything*. What if Pat took James with her? If you were going off to Paris, what would stop you from taking your younger boyfriend with you?

19. Scotsmen Don't Cry (Well, Not Much)

Pat offered to work her notice.

'I don't want to leave you in the lurch,' she said. 'You've been so good to me, Matthew.'

Matthew said nothing. Like all truly good people, he was

unaware of his goodness. He was not a moral philosopher with a theory as to why we should act in one way rather than another; he simply acted in the way he did in order to avoid pain in others. That, of course, might be called a moral theory, but it did not answer the more difficult question as to why it was *wrong*, rather than merely uncomfortable, to inflict pain on others.

Now Pat was staring at him. Had he looked at her more closely, he might have noticed that she was close to tears; but he was not looking at her at all. He was staring out of the window, engaged in a private emotional battle of his own. Matthew, at heart, did not want the world to change. He liked things to remain the same: for people to continue to do what they had always done; for the world about him to look more or less the way it had always looked – or at least the way it had looked to him over the past few years; for newspapers and clothing and what came out of the radio to be recognisable and not too surprising; for continuity to be the prevailing note in human affairs. That was not to say that he was insensitive to that which was wrong in the world about us – he was well enough aware of that, and had a stronger dislike of injustice and suffering than many others who wore their hearts more conspicuously on their sleeves; it was just that he wished such things would go away without disturbing everything else. The radical, the icono-clast, knew in his stomach that this would not happen, that only by upheaval would the wrongs of the world be rooted out, and would mock Matthew's naïvety in these matters. And yet Matthew, when it came to the minor decisions of his personal world, probably acted more kindly than many of those who loudly professed a reformist role. The loudly good are often not the best of people; the intuitively good, to whom it may not occur ever to discuss what they do, let alone why they do it, may be morally unsung, but are heroes nonetheless.

And now, consistent with that disposition, he said to Pat, 'You don't have to do that. You don't have to work your notice because . . .' He turned to her and smiled. 'Because I have no idea what your notice should be. How do you work that out with a part-time job like yours?'

She started to protest, but he cut her short. 'No, you don't have to worry, Pat. You can go whenever you like. This afternoon, if you like. I'll give you . . .' He hesitated before deciding. The gallery barely made a profit, but that was not the point. Matthew had funds behind him, and he had always been generous with these. It was that generosity that had led him to invest heavily in Big Lou's business, and now it manifested itself again. 'I'll give you three months' pay. As a sort of thank-you present.' He rapidly changed that. 'No, I shouldn't call it a present – it's not. It's something you're entitled to.'

Pat shook her head vigorously. 'I can't accept that, Matthew. That's really kind, but . . . but you don't have to.'

He brushed her objections aside. 'Please, let's not argue.' He paused. 'And I really don't mind if you finish right now. Today. It's not that I want to get rid of you – I don't. I just don't want to hold you up.'

'Oh, Matthew . . .'

'No, I'm serious. When did they want you to start at the Gargantuan?'

Pat looked embarrassed. 'They did mention next week ... I told them, though, that I had this job and ...'

'No, that's fine by me. Really.' He smiled. 'Imagine, Pat – just imagine. Working in the Gargantuan ... in Paris. Mixing with people who really know what they're talking about.'

Pat laughed. 'But I've been working with somebody like that for years now. You.'

Matthew blushed. 'Not me. No, you don't mean me.'

'I do,' said Pat. 'Maybe at the beginning you didn't, but then nobody knows what they're doing when they first do it, do they? The important thing in the art world is to have an eye. And you, Matthew, have that.'

He blushed more deeply, and shook his head. 'I don't – not really.'

Pat opened the top drawer of her desk and gazed at the contents. 'I don't want to leave a mess. I should sort this out.'

Matthew said that he would do that. 'And it isn't a mess, anyway. You've always been tidy.' He paused. 'Where will you live in Paris?'

'I have a friend,' Pat answered. 'She and I were at school together. She was half French and she went to university there. She works for UNESCO. She arranges exhibitions. Her Italian flatmate is going back to Rome.'

'Convenient.'

'Yes. It's a fabulous flat. It belonged to her grandmother, who died. She left it to Angie – that's my friend – and her sister. The sister lives in Lyon. She's older than Angie and she's married to a surgeon. He's Congolese. Angie wants to buy them out of the flat if she can. She's looking into ways of doing that.'

Matthew nodded. 'It's simpler that way. Having two people owning the same place never works ... '

'Except sometimes.'

He laughed. 'I suppose so. People can share. It shouldn't be that hard.' He looked at his watch. 'I was thinking of closing. I should help with bath-time back at home.'

Pat smiled at the thought of bathing three boys as active as the triplets were. 'That'll be splashy,' she said.

'It always is.'

And then Matthew took out his handkerchief and blew his nose. And Pat knew that he was actually crying, and she rose to her feet, crossed the room, and put her arm around him.

'Matthew, I don't have to take this job. I don't have to go to Paris.'

He shook his head. 'Don't talk nonsense. Of course you do. It's just that ... It's just that I'm thinking of how much I've liked having you ... in my life, I suppose. Yes, I have. I've liked having you in my life.'

She comforted him. 'I've liked having you in mine.'

'It's odd,' he said. 'It's odd, isn't it? We hardly ever say that sort of thing to people. We hardly ever tell them that.'

'Well, we should,' she said.

'Of course, we should. But we don't because we're ... ' He struggled to think of how he might put it.

'Because we're Scottish? Is that it?'

He nodded, mutely. His tears were flowing freely now.

'And Scottish men have to be tough, don't they?' Pat continued. 'They have to pretend not to have feelings. They have the whole football-culture, macho, hard-man rubbishy *face* to put on, while inside they're wanting to be something else altogether.'

Matthew nodded again.

'We have to rewrite our myths,' muttered Pat.

20. Rhododendrons and Missionaries

Matthew drove up towards the house at Nine Mile Burn, manoeuvring round the rhododendrons clustered by the drive. These exuberant shrubs had rampaged since he and Elspeth had purchased the house, as if they were deliberately planning to test the resolve of the new owners. The Duke of Johannesburg, from whom they had purchased the property, had warned them that this might happen. 'I have a cousin over in Argyll,' he said, 'who had a frightful lot of rhododendrons. They were all over his place, and actually eventually covered the house.'

Matthew shook his head. 'They need little encouragement. My aunt had rhododendrons at the edge of her lawn in Currie and she . . .'

The Duke interrupted him. 'Yes, yes. Currie. A great place for rhododendrons, but they really like the west. It's wetter there, you see. Rhododendrons like a spot of rain. They like that. Anyway, this poor cousin of mine, Basil Campbell-Campbell – they not only lost sight of the house, but they lost sight of Basil too. He was somewhere in there, they thought, but nobody knew where and eventually they lost interest. Somebody said he might have gone to Argentina – Basil had a boyfriend over there. A gaucho, apparently. He had spoken of meeting up with him. But nobody was sure.'

Matthew had laughed, thinking the Duke could hardly be serious. Nobody could be lost in a cluster of rhododendrons – it was inherently unlikely. And as for Basil Campbell-Campbell and his gaucho ...

'They're frightful things, rhododendrons,' the Duke continued. 'In retrospect it was not the best idea to bring them back to Scotland. They were fine in the Himalayas, but not in the Highlands. The problem was those plant collectors. We had a lot of them in Scotland, you know. Forrest, and people like that. Extraordinary people. He was pursued by homicidal lamas, you know. Up in the mountains, when he was collecting plants. These lamas took exception to his presence. Very awkward. One doesn't think of the danger of being pursued by Buddhists keen to eviscerate one, but there we are. They were different times. And I suppose we *were* on their turf, so to speak. They didn't take kindly to missionaries. And who can blame them – sometimes?'

'Oh,' said Matthew, 'I'm not ... '

The Duke interrupted him once again. 'I was stopped by a couple of missionaries in Morningside the other day, you know. In broad daylight, outside that rather nice hardware store that sells all that useful stuff. You know the place? Anyway, these two young men came up to me and asked me whether I was interested in reading some book or other. Written by some chap who saw an angel. They all did in those days, you know. There were plenty of angels flying around, we're led to believe.'

Matthew laughed.

'Oh, you can laugh, Matthew,' went on the Duke. 'But I'll tell you something about angels: a very high proportion of the population actually believes in them. They think they have a guardian angel, would you believe. A sort of government angel allocated to them. So, don't take angels lightly, Matthew.'

'If you say so.'

'Well, these two young men thrust this book into my hands and urged me to read it. They were very polite. Cleanshaven, too, which is a change these days.' The Duke lowered his voice. 'I found out something interesting, Matthew. These young missionaries are actually rather nice people. They're well behaved and courteous and cause no trouble. A nice change. But ... ' He lowered his voice still further. 'They wear the most peculiar sacred underwear, though. Not many people know that. They call them temple garments, apparently, and they're garments that you sort of slide into and which cover the torso too and the top of the arms. Must get a bit warm in the summer.' The Duke's voice was now not much more than a whisper. 'Apparently the purpose is to remind one of higher things. So I read, Matthew.'

'Well,' said Matthew. 'I suppose ... '

'It's very odd being proselytised, Matthew, don't you think? The basic assumption of the missionary is that what you – the other person – believes is somehow inferior.'

'I suppose that ... '

'Whereas the people approached may have a perfectly

reasonable set of beliefs – or at least their beliefs may be no more ridiculous than those of the people trying to convert them.'

Matthew drew in his breath. 'I don't think you should be too hard on missionaries. They set up hospitals and schools. They had the best interests of others at heart, don't you think?'

The Duke seemed to lose interest. 'You'll need to watch those rhododendrons, Matthew. It's very difficult to get rid of them once they establish themselves.'

But Matthew was thinking of Cousin Basil. 'Did he really disappear? Under a whole lot of rhododendrons?' It seemed improbable to him, but one never knew with the Duke. After all, who would have believed that the Duke would have been secretly building a microlight flying boat with his vaguely sinister Gaelic-speaking driver, Pàdruig? If you had told anybody about that, they would have thought it was one of those exaggerated stories that people in the Highlands loved to tell – most of them embellished, at best, or completely apocryphal at worst.

'Did he disappear?' echoed the Duke. 'Yes, I think he did. I thought he might turn up at a family funeral or wedding – you know, the sort of occasion that draws people out of other woodwork, but he never did.'

'And what do you think? Do you think he really could be in Argentina?'

The Duke looked thoughtful. 'I think he may be. He was a great admirer of Cunninghame Graham, you know. He felt drawn towards the continent. And then ... well, a couple of years ago somebody said they were at a polo match out there and they saw Cousin Basil. His boyfriend was playing, and he was watching from a vintage MG parked at the edge of the field. They said he was wearing Campbell trews.'

'How very strange,' said Matthew.

'Scotland is a strange country,' said the Duke. 'You know, we try to convince people that we're a rational place, but I'm afraid ...'

'You're afraid we're not?'

The Duke shrugged. 'I'm not sure that we even convince ourselves. The world is a strange place, Matthew. There are very rational, logical societies – one thinks of Sweden, for instance ...'

'And Germany, of course.'

'Yes, Germany, but Germany has a broad streak of Romanticism, and of course is prone to the occasional bout of fanaticism. And then you have the rather more – how shall I put it? – *passionate* societies, such as any society that speaks Spanish. And then you have the odd nations. But I can tell you one thing – we're not half as peculiar as the English, bless them.'

21. Men Don't Send Birthday Cards

Having negotiated the final loops of the crumbling drive, Matthew drew up at his front door. Getting out of the car, he became aware of three pairs of eyes watching him from a window on the first floor of the house. He waved, and his wave was quickly returned with excited gestures from the three boys, Rognvald, Fergus and Tobermory. They were joined by Elspeth, who hovered into sight behind them, and blew a kiss down to Matthew.

By the time Matthew had opened the front door, with its peeling green paint, the triplets had tumbled downstairs and were clamouring to welcome him. They hugged his legs, one of them – Tobermory, he suspected – giving him a small bite on his calf: an affectionate bite, but not something one would encourage in a two-year-old.

'Tobes,' Matthew scolded, 'you mustn't bite Daddy. Has Daddy ever bitten you?'

Tobermory, blushing, deflected the criticism with earnest denial. 'It was Rognvald,' he said. 'Rognvald bit you, Daddy.'

Rognvald responded by hitting Tobermory, who then pushed him backwards, causing his brother to knock over Fergus, who generally liked to keep out of trouble. This led to all three boys bursting into tears.

Elspeth appeared. 'Domestic bliss,' she said, trying to separate the boys from one another. She scolded the boys fondly, but with all the tired firmness of a mother of three. 'There will be no ice cream tomorrow if you carry on like this,' she said.

The effect was instantaneous, and calm was restored. Down below, amongst children, ice cream and chocolate are the bargaining chips supreme, as powerful as money and military force are amongst adults.

James appeared from the door that led from the hall to

the kitchen. 'Shall I take them up?' he asked. He looked at his watch. 'It's that time of day, I think.'

Elspeth answered with relief. 'Thank you, James. They all need a bath.'

'Tobermory smells,' said Rognvald.

This was met with outraged denial.

'Everybody smells,' said James. 'There's nothing wrong in having a smell.'

Matthew grinned. 'That's what comes of having a relativist au pair,' he said to Elspeth.

The triplets were corralled by James and led upstairs while Matthew and Elspeth made their way into the kitchen. As they entered, Matthew sniffed at the air appreciatively. 'Talking of smells,' he said, 'what's that in the oven?'

'Rack of lamb,' said Elspeth. 'Your favourite.'

Matthew rubbed his hands together. 'Brilliant.' He noticed a pie dish. 'And that?'

'Apple pie,' said Elspeth. 'What else?'

'And mashed carrots done in cream with lots of black pepper on top?' asked Matthew.

Elspeth smiled. 'Yes. Everything you like, you see.'

Matthew shook his head. 'You're wonderful, you know – you really are. Here I am, this completely average guy, and I get you, of all people. I get the absolute twenty-two carat, *Good Housekeeping* Institute Badge of Excellence, University of Edinburgh First-Class Honours best. The best.'

Elspeth was looking at him quizzically. 'Of course, I chose the meal specially for you.'

Matthew nodded. 'So it would seem. You chose everything I love.'

Elspeth hesitated. 'Because it is a special day, after all.'

Matthew had picked up an unopened envelope from the kitchen table and had been about to open it. Now he stopped. 'Today?'

'Yes. It's a rather special day in . . . '

He waited.

'In the calendar of our lives,' she continued. 'A special day for us.' A further pause ensued before she continued, 'That is, for you and me, in view of the fact that today is . . . '

Matthew closed his eyes. 'Oh, my God, oh . . . ' He opened them. 'Our anniversary. I . . . I should have . . . ' His voice was strangled, and he left the sentence unfinished.

'I thought you'd forgotten,' said Elspeth. 'When you didn't say anything this morning, I assumed you'd forgotten.'

'Oh, my darling,' said Matthew. 'I feel so bad. I really . . . I really hadn't thought of what day it was. I didn't look at my diary, you see, and then this morning I had a lot on my mind.' There had been Pat's resignation. That was an excuse – of a sort – although it had come later on in the day and he should have remembered their anniversary in the morning.

Elspeth made a gesture that said, *don't worry about it*. Then she smiled at him. 'I might at least get a kiss.'

Matthew rushed forward. 'A kiss for every year,' he said. 'So . . . ' He stopped. How many years was it? He had forgotten.

Elspeth was looking at him tenderly. 'Men,' she said. 'You're hopeless at these things – all of you.'

'We try,' said Matthew.

'I know you do. But it's always women who send the

birthday cards. To everyone – not just family. Have you ever had a birthday card from one of your male friends? From Angus Lordie? From that chap with the hair gel?'

'Bruce?'

'Yes. I doubt if he sends birthday cards.'

'To himself, perhaps,' said Matthew. 'Bruce is a narcissist, as everyone knows.' He paused. Birthday cards were a ruthlessly commercial business and you would imagine that amongst all the specialist cards – *to uncle*, *to nephew*, *to a best friend* and so on – the sentiment-purveyors of the birthday card industry would have tumbled to the need to offer cards for narcissists. *You know something?* The message might read. *You're truly terrific.*

But then he thought: I should not be uncharitable about Bruce, who was really no more than a casual acquaintance. He had Elspeth and the boys; Bruce had nobody. Mind you, did a narcissist want anybody other than himself? Perhaps not.

Now he answered Elspeth's question. 'You're right. I never get birthday cards from male friends. It's not what men do.'

'So sad,' said Elspeth. 'Women are always giving their friends presents and sending cards. Women understand these things.'

'Am I forgiven?' asked Matthew.

'Of course you are. Of course.'

He thanked her. 'You're so sweet,' he said. 'Some women are so judgemental of their men.'

'Let's not talk about other people,' said Elspeth. 'The important thing is that I have you and you have me.'

'And we have our little boys.'

Elspeth nodded. 'And we have the boys. And this house. And ...'

'The rhododendrons.'

Elspeth laughed. 'Yes, those too. We have everything. And I think it's important to remind oneself of one's good fortune.'

From upstairs, through the ceiling, they heard bumps and crashes. 'The boys,' said Elspeth. 'James is a wonder, you know. He handles them like ... like a lion tamer handles a lion.'

'With a chair?' asked Matthew.

'Did lion tamers really use chairs – or was that just something you saw in cartoons?'

Matthew did not answer her question. He nodded in the direction of upstairs. 'Is James having dinner with us?'

Elspeth replied that he was. 'I couldn't very well exclude him. He does live with us, after all. I hope you don't mind.'

'Of course not,' said Matthew. 'But perhaps you and I can go outside now – just for a few minutes. It's so lovely and warm. We could have a glass of champagne together. Just us. To celebrate so many years ...'

How many was it? He would remember later on, he thought.

They went outside. The sun was sinking over the hills to the west, out towards distant Lanark and the early reaches of the Clyde. Matthew shivered; it was not as warm as he had imagined, in spite of the sunlight.

The hills were blue – soft and blue. He said, 'Thank you for everything, Elspeth.'

She raised her glass to his. 'Remember Jamaica? That hotel?'

He smiled. That was where they had spent their honeymoon.

'How could I forget that hotel?' he said.

Elspeth laughed, and as she laughed, she asked herself: how many people laugh when they remember their honeymoon? Not many, she thought.

22. A Very Strange Hotel

The hotel had been recommended to them by Matthew's father. 'There's a place in Jamaica,' he said. 'I've never been there, but Uncle Charlie was there back in the late nineteen fifties, just before independence. He knew it quite well, because he used to go up there from Kingston.'

Uncle Charlie was Matthew's father's godfather. Matthew was too young to have met him, but he was a figure so central to family history that he felt he knew him. He had been a well-known yachtsman on the Clyde in his early years, having been born in Rhu, and with yachting in his blood. He had graduated in economics from the University of Glasgow and then gone to Oxford, to Balliol, a nursery for talented Scots destined for the higher reaches of the civil service. He had opted to go into banking, though, choosing posts where he would be near the water and where he could sail. Being sent to Jamaica had suited him very well, and he had

97

forgone promotions in order to stay there, ending up being responsible for a whole string of banks across the Caribbean. He stayed in Jamaica for six years after independence, having married a Jamaican – an 'unacknowledged sprig of the plant-ocracy', as Charlie had referred to her. He had then come back to Scotland, to spend his retirement sailing on the Clyde. His wife, though, had sickened in Scotland, which was too cold for her. 'She never got warm,' said Matthew's father. 'Poor Matilda. She just shivered and shivered and eventually she went home. They had grown apart. She disliked the water and could get seasick simply looking at it. She died of eating unripe ackee. They love ackee over in Jamaica but you have to be careful. It's like that poisonous fish the Japanese love to eat. You have to make sure you don't eat the wrong bits.'

Matthew had heard the story of Aunt Matilda and the unripe ackee as a young boy and had refused for years to eat any fruit with seeds. Uncle Charlie's demise, too, had put him off sailing; he had fallen overboard while sailing up Loch Fyne in a gale. He had been wearing a safety line, but it was too long, and failed to keep him on board. His going overboard was noticed by his crew only ten minutes after it occurred, and by then it was too late and he had been dragged through the water at the end of the line for too long.

'Uncle Charlie loved that part of the island,' Matthew's father said. 'He was a great fan of a hotel not far from Ochos Rios. He went up at weekends, from Kingston. He had lots of friends, and they used to go up there with him. It was quite a sociable set, I believe.

'The hotel that he liked had a bar that was famous for

its rum cocktails. They served rum with tonic water and Angostura bitters. Uncle Charlie drank there with some pretty exotic customers. Noël Coward was a regular. He had a villa called Firefly not far away, and would drop in on a Friday evening. They had a piano, but Uncle Charlie said that Coward never touched the piano in the Green Island. He didn't like its tone, apparently, calling it "that *soi-disant* piano". And Ian Fleming was seen there too. It was quite the place.' He paused. 'The original owners sold it, I believe, but it's still there. And I wondered whether you and Elspeth would care to spend your honeymoon there – I'll pay, of course.'

Matthew had accepted. There had been a time when he would have declined, but he had stopped doing that when he had realised that his father got such pleasure from buying him things. There was such a thing as gracious acceptance, Matthew thought. So he said, 'That's really generous, Dad,' and arrangements were made.

They flew from Edinburgh to London, and then from there to Kingston. On the flight, as their plane soared over the clouds and the cabin filled with light, Matthew took Elspeth's hand in his and pressed it. 'Excited?' he asked.

She smiled. He loved her smile. He loved it, and his heart soared. He could not believe his good fortune that he had found somebody as perfect as she was – a person completely without fault. But then, he thought, was that love speaking? Was love, as the Latin phrase would have it of anger, a *furor brevis* – a brief madness? And if one could fall in love suddenly – in just the same way as one catches a cold – then could one fall out of love equally quickly and equally unpredictably? He thought of a poem he had once picked up by chance: it was Betjeman, at whom his English teacher had sniffed, and he was talking about a couple in a restaurant; *Eingang*, they were in love again, and *Ausgang* they were out. Something like that, he thought. He knew, of course, what his English teacher had meant. He had talked of sentimentalism, and warned against it. 'It cheapens real emotion,' he had said. 'Real attachment. Real loss. Real love.' But then he had said – and Matthew remembered his precise words – 'The problem is that Betjeman was *popular*. It's a great sin to be popular.'

Matthew had put up his hand. 'But Scott was popular. Burns too. They were great writers, but they were popular.'

The English teacher had gazed out of the window and stroked his chin. Matthew had noticed that he often seemed to cut himself when shaving in the morning. He treated the nicks with an old-fashioned remedy, a styptic pencil, which left a line of white where applied to the skin. Could the Edinburgh Academical Association not pass the hat round to buy the English Department an electric razor? They could leave it in the staff common room for general use. Matthew smiled at the memory. This was exactly what the same English teacher had meant when he talked to them about *intertextuality*, about how one piece of writing lives on in another; how one thought prompts another, until a tapestry of association and cross-reference results. That talk, of course, had been above the heads of most of the people in the class, and Matthew, closing his eyes briefly in that pressurised cabin above the Atlantic, could see them now. Tommy Maclean, who thought only about rugby, and who almost played for Scotland, but not quite; Bill Sullivan, who thought about the Red Hot Chili Peppers most of the time, and who spent hours cultivating what he described as a 'cool way of walking'; Eleanor Mactavish, who spoke a lot about moisturiser and shampoo and who probably thought about them too – she had split ends, poor girl; and Bob Anderson, who thought about nothing at all, as far as anybody could ascertain. None of them would think about intertextuality on a plane, with a freshly poured gin and tonic in hand, and on the way to a honeymoon in Jamaica.

He turned to Elspeth, who smiled at him.

'What were you thinking about?' she asked.

'Too complicated,' said Matthew.

Elspeth gave him a reproachful look. He could not work out whether it was playful or serious. 'I'm married to you now,' she said. 'I'm entitled to know.'

Matthew hesitated. Was that true? Was that what marriage involved?

23. Not Your Average Hotel

Their honeymoon hotel occupied a commanding position on a hill. The view to the front was of the coast, a short walk away through a thick growth of sea grape, coconut palm and Cuba bark trees. To the rear, the ground fell away sharply until it rose again in another hill, densely covered with the ubiquitous, dark green shrubs of the island. The hotel had been built as a private house in the early years of the twentieth century by an artist called Wilma Paterson. She was famous in Jamaica for painting only one scene – the view from the front veranda – to which she returned in canvas after canvas. 'I shall get it right one day,' she said. 'The sky keeps changing. It's most vexing.'

Wilma Paterson was American, the daughter of a professor of human anatomy at Harvard. She married Macfarlane Paterson, a wealthy dipsomaniac originally from Portland, Maine, and left him after five weeks. It was widely believed that he only became aware of her departure two years after she had gone; they had lived in separate wings of a large colonial-style house in Concord, and during the brief marriage they rarely saw one another, and when they did he was almost always drunk.

The more-than-generous divorce settlement set Wilma up first in Key West and then in Jamaica. While the house was being built, she stayed in Kingston, in a house she rented from the French consul general. The consul general had a son called Hubert, who was a fascist. He was twenty-five, five years younger than Wilma, but she found him irresistible. She paid no attention to his political views – 'I always thought he was joking,' she said – and took great pleasure in showing him off to her girlfriends. 'Isn't Hubert unspeakably handsome?' she used to ask them, and they all agreed. 'Handsome and dangerous,' said one, but Wilma paid no attention to the warning, as is often the case with friends.

Hubert moved in with her, and after a year of cohabitation

Wilma became pregnant, giving birth in 1920 to a daughter, Marie Josèphe Rose Tascher de la Pagerie, named after Napoleon's first wife, who had been born in Martinique, where Hubert himself had been born. In 1930 Wilma was widowed when Hubert, who had organised a picnic for a small group of French fascists, fell off the edge of a cliff. Three of the fascists, seeing him lying on a rock halfway down the cliff face, attempted to rescue him, but failed to do so. There had been heavy rainfall the day before and the ground was unstable. A large slab of cliff face tumbled into the sea below, taking with it all three rescuers and Hubert. Only two fascists returned from the picnic.

Wilma decided that she had never really liked Hubert, nor his friends, about whom she felt there was always a reek of sulphur. She took to being a widow, and devoted her energies to painting and entertaining. Marie Josèphe was sent to a convent school in Kingston, from which she was expelled at the age of seventeen for spitting at a nun. She married a coffee planter called Haldane McIntosh, and gave birth to a daughter, Barbie, in 1950.

On Wilma's death, Marie Josèphe inherited the house and in 1955 turned it into a hotel, naming it after her grandmother, Wilma. She was a natural hotelier, and as that part of the island became increasingly popular with a racy, artistic set, the hotel became the favourite haunt of the high-living and the socially ambitious. Hemingway stayed there shortly after it opened and was said to have worked in one of its rooms on *Islands in the Stream*, a novel that he had begun many years before and never published. Noël Coward and Ian Fleming lived nearby, and were to be seen with their glittering visitors in the bar and sometimes in the dining room, where the speciality of the house was lobster thermidor. Local legend had it that it was in this bar that a friend had asked Fleming whether he had been to the doctor that day. 'Doctor? No,' replied Fleming, and then said, 'However, that gives me an idea . . . ' Like most stories about such places, this was almost certainly apocryphal.

Marie Josèphe handed the hotel over to her daughter Barbie, who in due course passed it on to her own daughter, Clottie, who was the result of an ill-judged affair she had with a diving instructor called Captain. Barbie did not enjoy managing the hotel, and after training Clottie to run it, she left the island to live on Antigua with an ill-mannered tax accountant. Clottie's main interest was tennis, and since the hotel had its own tennis court, she was happy to stay there, spending a lot of time on arranging specialist tennis holidays. She renamed the bar the Centre Court, but the locals ignored this name and continued to refer to it as Wilma's Bar.

Clottie had a woman friend called Tippy, who was German. She invited Tippy to run the hotel with her, and Tippy agreed. They lived in a small cottage behind the main house, outside which a round sign, of the sort that normally prevents parking, or walking dogs, or some other such activity, showed a picture of a man, with a red line crossing him out.

'Did you see that sign?' Elspeth asked Matthew after she had completed her exploratory walk around the hotel grounds.

'Yes,' said Matthew. 'And I'm not sure how to interpret it.'

Elspeth looked at him. 'I think that . . . '

She did not get to finish. They were in their room at the

time of this conversation, and there was a sudden, rather peremptory knock on the door. Elspeth opened it, to find herself faced with Clottie.

'Dinner,' Clottie said, 'has been served for the last twenty minutes.'

Elspeth glanced at her watch. 'All right,' she said. 'We were just going to have a bath and then we'll come along.'

Clottie glared at her. 'I would appreciate it if you showered,' she said. 'That uses far less water – particularly if you don't linger.' She looked past Elspeth, to where Matthew was sitting on the bed. 'And if you could possibly tell *him* about that – about the need to conserve water – I'd appreciate it.'

Elspeth gave a momentary start. '*Him?* Matthew?'

Clottie nodded. Her lip curled. 'Indeed,' she said. 'And seven-thirty for dinner, by the way, doesn't mean eight. It certainly doesn't mean nine either. It means seven-thirty.'

Elspeth opened her mouth to say something, but Clottie had turned on her heel and was halfway down the corridor.

'Well!' she said, turning to Matthew.

Matthew smiled. 'There you are,' he said.

24. *Kamikaze Mosquitoes*

Their first night in the hotel was far from comfortable. Their sleeplessness might have been put down to the effects of time differences on their circadian rhythms, but a more immediate cause suggested itself in the presence in the room of flights of mosquitoes. Wave after wave of these tiny warplanes launched themselves against the target presented by the recumbent forms of Matthew and Elspeth, diving in to attack, kamikaze-fashion, ignoring the desperate swats of their victims. There was a mosquito net, but this provided inadequate protection as it was too small for the double bed.

'Those women have given us a single-size net,' muttered Matthew, as he tried in vain to tuck the edge of the net under the mattress. 'This is just too small. It won't stay where it should.'

'What about repellent?' asked Elspeth. 'Is there any in the bathroom?'

Matthew went to check, but there was none. On the way back, he donned trousers and socks in order to minimise the area of exposed skin that would be susceptible to mosquito bites.

The next morning, after the mosquitoes, sensing the onset of dawn, had retreated to base, Matthew made his way to the reception desk to raise the issue of a larger mosquito net. Clottie answered the bell when he pressed it.

'Breakfast is not until eight,' she snapped.

Matthew struggled to be civil. 'This is not about breakfast,' he said. 'I've come to talk to you about mosquito nets.'

'You've got one,' said Clottie. 'I put it up myself. You shouldn't have any trouble from mosquitoes.'

'Well, we did,' said Matthew.

Clottie pursed her lips. 'You shouldn't mistake the sound

of mosquitoes for actual bites,' she said. 'Mosquitoes are always buzzing about. But if you have a net, you're safe.'

Matthew showed her his bare forearm. There were several angry red spots discernible on it. 'What are these?' he challenged.

Clottie glanced at his arm with distaste. 'You seem to have some sort of skin condition,' she said. 'There's a pharmacy in town. You could pick up something there. Some sort of lotion.'

Matthew gasped. 'I do *not* have a skin condition,' he exclaimed. 'These are mosquito bites. And there are more. I could show you plenty more.'

Clottie shuddered involuntarily. 'But you have a net,' she said. "You should have used your net.' She paused before fixing Matthew with a disapproving stare. 'It's not our fault if guests fail to use the things we try to provide for them.'

Matthew took a deep breath. He was naturally mild in his manner, and he generally avoided confrontation. But this was pressing him to his limits. It was not unreasonable, surely, to raise – as politely as he had done – an issue of this nature. He was not blaming the management for the presence of mosquitoes – that was a matter of geography and, he imagined, elevation, and nobody, not even these sour and unwelcoming women, could be reproached for their height above sea level. But they *could* be held responsible, he thought, for providing a single-bed-sized mosquito net for a room that clearly had a double bed.

'We used the net,' Matthew said. 'But there's a problem with it, I'm afraid. That net is for a single bed, you see, and as a result it doesn't tuck in properly. It comes untucked if there's any movement in the bed, and then the mosquitoes get in.' He paused for dramatic effect, the staccato phrases each an item in a solemn indictment. 'And then they bite you. Badly. On the arm. And elsewhere.'

He would leave that to her imagination. She had seen his arm; she could only speculate.

Clottie's eyes widened. 'Movement in the bed, you say? What exactly are you doing in that bed?'

Matthew gasped. Then, through clenched teeth, he answered, 'Trying to sleep.'

'Hah!' said Clottie. 'So you say. The point is, you have a net and you haven't used it properly. We can't go round changing our net arrangements if one set of guests fails to use them properly, can we? There are other guests in this hotel, you know.'

'I'm surprised,' said Matthew quickly. 'I'm surprised you have any guests at all.'

Stalemate had been reached, and they disengaged. Matthew returned to the room to tell Elspeth of his failed attempt to deal with the mosquito-net issue. She sighed. 'We'll have to get some repellent in the village,' she said. 'I saw a pharmacy down there. We can try them.'

'Or one of those coil thingies you light,' suggested Matthew. 'They smoke the mosquitoes out.'

'Yes.' She looked at Matthew. 'Dear Matthew,' she said, 'you look as if you have a skin disease on your arm. Poor you.'

And then later that day, to pile Pelion upon Ossa, there had been the incident of the snake in the swimming pool.

That had occurred when the two of them had gone down to the hotel's pool, which was deserted at the time; in fact, they had not seen anybody else swimming in it, even if there were towels laid out on loungers at the poolside. Elspeth had been about to dive in when she stopped herself and pointed to a long, thin object in the water below her.

'Is that a snake, Matthew?'

Matthew looked. 'Yes, it's a snake all right. I'd better go and get somebody.'

The snake was swimming along the rim of the pool, moving through the water in elegant, untroubled serpentine sashays. Matthew took another quick look at it, and then he and Elspeth made their way up to reception. There they found Tippy.

'*Ja?*' asked Tippy, and then added, '*Und so?*'

'So you claim there's a snake in the pool,' said Tippy after Matthew had explained the situation.

'I'm not *claiming* there's a snake,' he retorted. 'There *is* a snake. A big one.'

'I doubt it,' said Tippy. 'You're from Scotland, aren't you? You don't see snakes there.'

'Excuse me,' protested Matthew. 'There are plenty of snakes in Scotland.' Well, not plenty perhaps, he thought, but at least there were adders on some of the hills, not that he had seen them.

'Wait here,' said Tippy, and disappeared.

Ten minutes later she returned. 'There was no snake,' she said.

Matthew and Elspeth did not argue, but made their way back to the pool. There was no snake, but there were large puddles of water around the edge of the pool, and a long-handled net had been left dripping at the poolside.

Matthew sighed. 'I'm so sorry, my darling,' he said. 'This might not have been the wisest choice.'

'But you are,' said Elspeth, kissing him. 'You're the wisest choice *I* ever made.'

25. *Roger's Porcini Soup*

Now, sitting outside their house at Nine Mile Burn, looking out towards the blue folds of the Lammermuir Hills in the distance, they finished their anniversary glass of champagne together with a gentle touching of empty glasses. Returning to the kitchen, they found that James had finished putting the boys to bed and was peering into a pot that Elspeth had left warming on the side of the range.

'Sorry,' he said. 'I can't resist finding out what's for dinner – and I think I know what this is.'

It was the first course – the one that Elspeth had not mentioned to Matthew when he had guessed the rack of lamb and the apple pie.

'Roger's Porcini Soup,' she said. 'From . . . '

'From one of Mary Contini's books,' supplied James. 'Yes, I know the recipe.'

'Roger is Roger Collins,' Elspeth explained to Matthew.

'He and Judith McClure are friends of Domenica and Angus, I think. He writes books on medieval Spain and the papacy, but he's also a famous cook.'

James sniffed at the soup. 'I love porcini to bits,' he said. 'They're the only mushroom I'd go out of my way for.'

'What about chanterelles?' said Matthew. 'Porcini are delicious, but so are chanterelles.'

They sat down at the table.

'It's very kind of you to invite me,' said James. 'I mean, I know it's your anniversary dinner and everything, and I could very easily have gone into town. Or even into Peebles.'

'Nonsense,' said Matthew. 'You live here. You're the au pair. And we wanted you, anyway.'

'Matthew's right,' said Elspeth. 'You come with the house, so to speak.'

They laughed. Elspeth served the soup.

'The boys went straight to sleep,' said James. 'I read to them, as per usual, but I could see them struggling to keep their eyes open. They've had a very physical day. They spent hours on the flying fox I rigged up for them. And then we went on a bear hunt in the rhododendrons. For ages.'

'The hunting instinct,' said Elspeth, a note of regret in her voice.

'I'm afraid that's the way boys are,' Matthew said. 'We can try to put them in touch with their feminine side, but nature, when all is said and done, tends to reassert itself.'

James looked doubtful. 'I think you can do a lot to make people grow up non-violent. I was never allowed to play with toy guns, for example. And I don't like guns as a result.'

'You never played Cowboys and Indians?' asked Matthew.

James looked blank. 'Cowboys and Indians?'

'You see,' said Elspeth, who had returned to the table with the soup tureen. 'That's completely gone. At least here. I don't know if boys still play it in Arizona or New Mexico, or places like that.'

'Perhaps they have a modernised version,' suggested Matthew. 'A modernised version where the cowboys lose.'

Elspeth smiled. 'Called Retribution?'

'I remember playing Chase the Dentist when I was small,' observed James, sniffing again at his soup. 'Gorgeous. What a soup!'

'I know that game,' said Elspeth. 'Its rules are very simple, I think. One person is the dentist and the rest all run after him.'

'And what about British Bulldog?' asked Matthew.

'A Unionist game,' said James.

Matthew grinned. 'Possibly.' He paused, as he remembered another game of his childhood. 'Of course, there's Bonnie Prince Charlie. One person goes off and hides – preferably in the heather – and then everybody looks for him. It's quite simple. When you find him you shout *Jacobite!* and then it's somebody else's turn. I played that. We were living in Moray Place in those days. We played it in the Moray Place Gardens.'

'Before the nudists took over?' asked Elspeth.

James looked puzzled. 'Nudists? What nudists?'

'The Association of Scottish Nudists has its headquarters down there,' explained Matthew. 'You often see them in the Moray Place Gardens.'

'How odd,' said James. He looked thoughtful. 'Why do people take off their clothes?'

'It's to do with being natural,' said Matthew. 'It's a whole philosophy. They call themselves naturists. It's to do with feeling at one with nature and the elements.'

'That's why Scottish nudists have such a thin time,' said Elspeth. 'It must be great being a naturist in the South of France or Greece, or somewhere like that. It's another matter here in Scotland.'

'Not for me,' said James, with a slight shiver.

'Well, British Bulldog is safer,' said Elspeth with a smile.

'My uncle taught me to play that,' said James.

Elspeth glanced at him. 'Your uncle the ...'

'Yes, the Duke,' said James. 'Yes. He showed me and my friends how to play it. I distinctly remember. It was on the lawn at Single Malt House.'

Matthew reached out to pour the wine. 'I haven't seen your uncle recently. There was that business with the flying boat. I hope he's all right.'

'He got over that,' said James. 'He was hirpling for a while, but he was all right.'

'Good,' said Elspeth. 'The whole thing was ridiculous. It could have ended far worse.'

They finished their soup. Then, while Elspeth was taking the rack of lamb out of the oven, Matthew said to James, 'There's something I wanted to talk to you about, James.'

James looked at him expectantly.

'It's the future,' said Matthew.

'It's all right,' said James. 'I won't stay for ever.'

'No,' said Matthew. 'We don't want to get rid of you. Anything but. In fact, we were rather hoping that you would stay for another year – maybe even two. You're in no hurry to go to uni, you said.'

'No. Not really. I want to go eventually, but I want a bit of a break from education.'

Matthew agreed. 'I can understand that. I think you can get far more out of university if you go a bit later.' He fiddled with his fork. 'I was wondering whether you might be able to help me in a new business I have a stake in.'

James waited.

'There's a coffee bar run by a woman called Big Lou. She's great. I'm now her business partner and I want to get somebody in to help her expand what she offers. She does bacon rolls at present, but that's about it. You're so good in the kitchen ...'

James interrupted him. 'Yes,' he said. 'Yes. Count me in.'

'It would be part-time,' said Matthew. 'You'd still do some looking after the boys. But we'd get you an assistant here, so to speak. We thought if we got an au pair girl from somewhere like Denmark, she could help Elspeth while you're working at Big Lou's. You'd divide your time.'

'Let's get her tomorrow,' said James.

Matthew sat back in his chair. He was glad the conversation had gone so well. 'I take it that's a yes.'

'I already said yes,' said James. 'In so many words. So take it as an underlining of the first yes.'

'Good,' said Matthew.

Then James said, 'Actually, there was something I wanted to talk to you about. It's my uncle. Something odd is going on.'

Mathew listened, and James told him. When the young man had finished, Elspeth, who had begun to carve the rack of lamb, put down her knife. 'But that's seriously worrying, James,' she said. 'What are you going to do?'

James shrugged. 'I'm only nineteen,' he said. 'And when you're nineteen, you sometimes run out of ideas.'

26. The Kelpie Cult

'Neanderthal man,' said Domenica. '*Homo neanderthalensis.*'

She was sitting in her kitchen in Scotland Street, paging through a recently delivered copy of *Evolutionary Anthropology*, one of the half dozen journals to which she subscribed. *Evolutionary Anthropology* tended to drop through the letter box ten days or so before *The Literary Review*, which she shared with Angus, and not long after the *Australian Journal of Anthropology*, on the advisory board of which she sat. That was not a particularly onerous role, one that she had been offered by a previous editor of the journal, with whom she had done fieldwork in New Guinea some time earlier. Their work on the Crocodile People of the Sepik River had been published by the Australian National University in Canberra as a small monograph, *Crocodile Cosmology*, and had been widely discussed. The cosmology in question, based on the notion that the people of the Sepik valley were the descendants of a young woman dragged into the river by a crocodile, was found to have its counterparts in creation myths of many other cultures, prompting the conclusion in the final chapter – indeed, in the final sentence of the book – that human notions of where we came from have the same deep structures whichever culture one chooses to examine. In Scotland, as Domenica pointed out, there are, of course, no crocodiles, and so Scottish mythical beasts are somewhat different in form, even if their tricks and devices are much the same. Kelpies, for example, are horse-like, but nonetheless sea-going, and nasty to boot. The Kelpie Cult still had its followers, she pointed out, who have raised two large Kelpie idols by the side of the road between Edinburgh and Stirling. The mysteries practised there at full moon were never reported in the Scottish press, but were rumoured to be both regular and colourful.

On the other side of the table, her husband, Angus, was prising flecks of paint from under his nails with the pick-end of a nail file. He made a habit of scrubbing his hands thoroughly at the end of each day in the studio, but inevitably traces of paint remained.

'If they ever fish me out of the canal,' he observed, 'they will have no difficulty in identifying me from the paint under my nails.'

'What a morbid thought,' said Domenica.

Angus shrugged. 'Well, we are mortal, aren't we? As a man in a pub once said to me, *à propos* of nothing, *Nobody gets out of this life alive.* I remember thinking: what a profound observation, and how true.'

'Immortality is a very brief experience,' said Domenica. 'We're immortal until what age? Eight? Nine? When does it occur to us that *we* might actually die?'

'It's a slow process,' said Angus. 'You start with no conception at all of your end, and then gradually it dawns on you that the rules of mortality brook no exception. But then you think that it's going to be so far away that it hardly needs to be thought about. Then you turn forty, and it becomes a bit more vivid. And so on, thereafter, until you realise that it's more or less tomorrow.'

Domenica sighed. '*Carpe diem*. Gather ye rosebuds,' she said, and added 'Et cetera, et cetera.'

'Actually,' said Angus, 'I tend to think of one of Shakespeare's sonnets when this sort of thing crops up. Sonnet Seventy-Three.'

'Refresh my memory,' Domenica said.

'It's the one where he reflects on growing old. He wonders whether his lover will still feel anything for him and decides, somewhat optimistically, if you ask me, that he will, in spite of his physical decline.'

Domenica put down her copy of *Evolutionary Anthropology*. 'And?'

'I used to know the whole thing off by heart,' Angus said. 'No longer, I'm afraid. But it's one of the most beautiful of the sonnets – at least I think it is. It starts off: *That time of year thou mayst in me behold / When yellow leaves, or none or few, do hang / Upon those boughs which shake against the cold / Bare ruin'd choirs where late the sweet birds sang . . .*'

Domenica closed her eyes, as if in rapture. '*Bare ruined choirs where late the sweet birds sang . . .* How could that line ever be bettered – by anything?'

'It couldn't,' said Angus.

'It's sad, isn't it? The whole tenor is sad.'

Angus put down his nail file. 'Yes,' he said. 'All those earlier sonnets are terribly sad, in a sense. You can see the way things are going to end. Poet falls for a much younger man. Writes wonderful poems addressed to him. Younger man inevitably finds something else to entertain himself with. Poet reflects on the nature of love and mortality.' He paused. 'But why did you say *Neanderthal man*? Something in ...' He squinted to read the title of the journal. 'Something in *Evolutionary Anthropology*?'

Domenica picked up the journal again. 'Yes. A paper by somebody I know, as it happens – a palaeoanthropologist from Berlin. We met at a conference in Vienna. We visited Freud's house in the same small group. Very disappointing, because all the furniture went to London.'

'One of those Professor Dr Drs the Germans go in for?'

'Yes. Just Professor Dr, in this case, although I once came across a Professor Dr Dr Dr.' Domenica paused. 'And his wife was Frau Professor Dr Dr Dr. Of course, if she had her own doctorate she would be Dr Frau Professor Dr Dr Dr. It becomes complicated. But then German professors are *inherently* complicated. Look at Hegel. Even Hegel didn't understand Hegelianism.' She paused for a moment, remembering something. 'Kierkegaard said something terribly funny about Hegel, you know. He said, "If he'd only said after he had written his books, 'It's all a joke,' Hegel would have been a great man."'

Angus smiled. The joke was the one thing that German professors often did not see. 'Have there been any anthropological studies of German professors?' he asked.

'Not to my knowledge,' Domenica replied. 'Academics like to study everybody else. They don't like to look too closely in the mirror.' Even as she said this, it occurred to her that it would be a rather enjoyable project – with fieldwork possibilities in agreeable places like Heidelberg and Göttingen. Perhaps, after she had completed her long-awaited study of Watsonians – if she ever got round to starting that – she would move on to an anthropological study of the German professorial class. She heard the mood music: *Carmina Burana*, of course, the *Gaudeamus*, naturally, and Brahms's *Academic Overture*.

Angus interrupted her reverie. 'Neanderthal man?'

'Yes,' said Domenica. 'It's another rehabilitation of the Neanderthals. You remember how we used to regard them as very primitive? Low forehead types?'

'Well, they did have low foreheads.'

'Yes,' said Domenica, 'but their skulls went quite a bit further back than ours do. They had a perfectly decent-sized brain.' She tapped the journal cover. 'And this article is all about their general level of sophistication. And their artistic abilities.'

Angus laughed. 'Artistic abilities? Are you suggesting they went in for flower arranging?'

'Feathers,' said Domenica. 'They probably used feathers as decoration.'

'Rather than wandering around with clubs?'

'They probably had clubs. But everybody did. *Homo sapiens* had clubs – still have, come to think of it. Big ones.'

'But what happened to them?' asked Angus. 'If they were by no means stupid and if they were good at feather arranging – why would they disappear?'

'Nobody really knows,' Domenica replied.

27. Glenbucket

Angus looked at his watch.

'I would love to discuss Neanderthals at greater length, but look at the time.' He sighed. 'If I'm to achieve anything today ... '

'It's Saturday,' Domenica pointed out. 'You don't need to drive yourself quite so hard, Angus. Your studio will still be there on Monday.' She added, *'Deo volente.'*

Angus raised an eyebrow. 'Saying *Deo volente* is like warding off the evil eye. Throwing salt over one's shoulder. That sort of thing.'

'Perhaps. But who amongst us is strong enough not to worry about tempting Providence?'

Angus glanced at his watch again. 'I know I don't have to, but I really would like to get some work done today. I'm at a crucial point in that portrait of ... ' He looked at her and smiled. 'That portrait of our tartan-bedecked friend.' He uttered the name with relish: 'Glenbucket. Robert Andrew Glenbucket of Glenbucket, the Glenbucket.'

Domenica rolled her eyes. 'How do you keep a straight face? Is that what he actually calls himself?'

Angus nodded. 'He's absolutely serious. And he's actually a rather charming man. Eccentrics often are, in my experience.' He paused. 'Lord Monboddo, for example. Nicholas

Fairbairn. Hugh Macdonald, who opined on the world from Kay's Bar in India Place and who could complete the *Times* crossword puzzle in under seven minutes. David Bogie, who was once overheard carrying on a lengthy conversation with the pygmy hippo in Edinburgh Zoo. All of these were wonderful people.'

Domenica smiled. 'They added a certain something to Scotland, I agree. But your man sounds obsessed, quite frankly. He's spent ages – not to say a fortune – working on genealogy, hasn't he?'

'People do,' said Angus. 'It's an extraordinary human preoccupation.'

Domenica frowned. 'Do you have the slightest interest in who your forebears were? I don't. It's not that I'm indifferent to them – I'm certainly not ashamed of them – all those faceless Macdonalds who came before me – it's just that ... ' She shrugged. 'It's just that I don't see the point.'

'I know what you mean,' said Angus. 'My Lordie ancestors were a very dull bunch. None of them is recorded as having done anything, or gone anywhere. They hung about Pitlochry for generations. One or two of them went to Dundee, but didn't stay long and headed back to Pitlochry. That's it.'

'But then this person you're painting, this ... '

Angus smiled. 'Glenbucket.'

'This Glenbucket: why does it mean so much to him?'

'He's half American,' said Angus. 'Americans like to know who they are. And who can blame them? They have that vast country with goodness knows how many people. That means a mass culture, and they want texture in their lives.'

He paused. 'And texture, I suppose, requires rootedness, requires history.'

Domenica looked thoughtful. 'Does it?'

Angus did not hesitate. 'Yes, it does. If you don't know how you started, your story is somehow incomplete. And we all want a story, don't we?' He asked the question rhetorically, but now that he had posed it, he was genuinely uncertain as to what the answer might be.

Domenica, though, was struck by something else. 'Those who have no history seem to acquire it,' she said. 'While those who have it seem to want to divest themselves of it.'

He looked at her quizzically. 'Meaning?'

'Well, we have rather too much history that we're uncomfortable about. We're keen to unburden ourselves of it, aren't we?'

'Scotland has too much history?'

Domenica hesitated. 'A bit. A lot of people in Scotland would like to get rid of the last few hundred years,' she said. 'Roughly the period after the Union. The British Empire. We were part of that, remember. And now we're embarrassed and like to say that it was a purely English enterprise. And the historical burden, therefore, is theirs, not ours.'

Angus saw her point, but then if you had something *imposed* on you, was it part of your story in quite the same way as if you had been the imposer? 'Well,' he said, 'nobody asked the people of Scotland whether they wanted a Union in the first place. And it wasn't *all* of us who did the Empire thing. It wasn't the crofters in the Highlands. It wasn't the men who went out in the fishing boats, or the shepherds, or the riveters on the Clyde, or the men who went down the pits in West Lothian, or ...'

Domenica shook her head. 'A class analysis gets everybody off the hook – everywhere. It puts the blame on a small number of people and exculpates everybody else. I don't think that will work. They rallied under the same flag, you know.' But then a thought occurred to her: did such an approach let off all the women? So much of history was *men's* history. They did the plotting and fighting and land grabbing. Women weren't allowed to vote, nor occupy crucial positions, and so none of what happened was their fault. That was tempting. And yet women, surely, condoned the things that men did; they egged them on and enjoyed the proceeds. It was a different sort of historical guilt, perhaps – the guilt of an accessory – but it was still guilt.

Domenica toyed with her copy of *Evolutionary Anthropology*. It was easier – far easier – to think about Neanderthals, rather than the eighteenth or the nineteenth centuries. Or to think about Glenbucket, and his desire to establish himself in some creaky and highly romantic vision of Scottish history. She looked at Angus. 'Does your man have a claim to be who he wants to be?'

Angus looked thoughtful. 'I suppose he does. He's gone into it very closely, and he says he's found he's descended from Old Glenbucket – through one of his sons, who went off to Jamaica. He had a mistress there, apparently – a Frenchwoman from Martinique – and he says that he's found a direct link between himself and the product of that liaison. Wrong side of the blanket, of course, but most of these interesting connections are.'

Domenica admitted this was colourful enough. 'Rather more interesting than my standard Macdonalds in their crofts on Skye. Or your Pitlochry people, for that matter.'

Angus agreed. 'But, look, I'd better go. I'll take Cyril.'

'And will Glenbucket be sitting?'

'Not today. I have photographic references for his outfit. I'll be working on those. Painting tartan is quite complicated – as you can imagine.' At every level, he thought. It was complicated because it was symbolic of such a complex story. A cloth of sorrow, he thought.

He looked down at Cyril, who sensed that a walk was imminent, but was not sure. The dog looked back up at him and Angus saw in his eyes that burning longing that was so characteristic of canine eyes. But a longing for what? What did dogs want that made them look so needy, so plaintive? Love? Like the rest of us? Was it as simple as that?

28. Our Inner Neanderthal

After Angus had left for his studio, taking Cyril with him, Domenica decided to have another cup of coffee and a further slice of toast. Her main breakfast was over: two boiled eggs, a single slice of toast, thinly spread with Dundee marmalade, and a modest slice of Loch Fyne smoked salmon. Toast was an important element in her breakfast, but was strictly controlled on carbohydrate grounds. The world was full of carbohydrates, paraded before weak humanity in the guise of things that most of us found so hard to resist: Danish pastries, marzipan, Dundee cakes, croissants, *pain au chocolat*, all the various varieties of pasta, potato crisps dusted with sea salt and cracked black pepper, chocolate unapologetic for its mere thirty per cent of cocoa solids – the list went on and on, and the weaker brethren (in which category most of us are numbered) fell for the enticement as eagerly as a lazy trout takes the fly. There were no carbohydrates in boiled eggs, nor in salmon, but toast, and the marmalade that accompanied it, was a different matter. Yet every now and then – and Saturday, surely, was a now-and-then day – she would allow herself a second slice, washed down by a cup of milky coffee. And if that could be accompanied by a leisurely read or a glance at the *Scotsman* crossword, then she felt content. It was not exactly nirvana, but, in an imperfect world, it was happiness of a rather profound sort. And it was, she thought, what so many women wanted: to get their man *out of the way* for the day and to have the house to themselves.

The slice of bread entrusted to the toaster, she pressed the button on her automatic coffee machine and heard the satisfactory grinding of the beans preceding the disgorging of the coffee. Then, sitting back, she picked up *Evolutionary Anthropology*. The entire issue of the journal had been devoted to Neanderthal matters, and for a few moments Domenica considered what was on offer. There was the article she had been reading by her friend from Berlin, *Neanderthal Art: A New Hypothesis*. Neanderthal art? Domenica had been surprised. She thought there had been only a handful of Neanderthal cave paintings discovered, which was hardly a school of art, let alone a retrospective Renaissance. Then there was a piece on animal bone sites around Neanderthal settlements – that could wait, perhaps. But then her eye fell on a piece entitled *Neanderthal and Homo Sapiens: Liminal Spaces, Interbreeding and Its Consequences for the Genome of Modern Man*.

That looked interesting, and, once her toast was made and duly spread with Dundee marmalade – not quite as thinly as it should have been, but one had to have some pleasures in life – she began to read the article. Neanderthals and *Homo sapiens* encountered one another somewhere between Europe and Asia sixty thousand years ago. Neanderthals appeared not to have survived the encounter and it had always been assumed that they had fallen victim to the superior technology and brain power of *Homo sapiens*. But it was not as simple as that, it seemed.

Domenica took a sip of coffee, and then a bite of her toast. Neanderthal man would have loved Dundee marmalade, she thought. And then she smiled at the ridiculousness of that thought. The Neanderthals never got anywhere *near* inventing Dundee marmalade.

She read on: interbreeding between *Homo sapiens* and Neanderthals means that modern humans have a certain amount of Neanderthal DNA in their genome. She paused, and read the relevant paragraph again. Could that be true? Could she really be two per cent Neanderthal, as this article was suggesting? But then it became more interesting: the amount of Neanderthal DNA in the genome of various individuals varied quite considerably, and there were people who had more than that small percentage.

She thought for a moment. Was she likely to know anybody who fell into that category, who had a larger quantity of Neanderthal DNA than was the norm? Anybody in Edinburgh – or Glasgow, perhaps?

It was at this point that the bell rang and thoughts of Neanderthals, of sloping foreheads and distant caves, faded. Domenica put down her coffee cup, wiped a trace of marmalade from her chin, and went to the front door.

Torquil, the young man from the ground-floor flat, the new neighbour she had met a few days previously, stood in the doorway, finger poised to press the bell a second time.

'I thought you might be out,' he said. 'I saw your husband and his dog and ...'

Domenica gestured for him to come in, but he shook his head.

'I've actually come to borrow something,' he said.

Domenica smiled. 'That's what neighbours are for.'

He returned her smile with his own, and she noticed he had a dimple on his left cheek, perfectly placed in relation to the corner of his mouth. That, she knew, was rare: dimples usually came in twos, one on each cheek, with the exception of the chin dimple, which cleaved the chin with a single indentation in just the right way to be suggestive of firmness of purpose. That dimple, commoner in men than women, had launched a hundred film and modelling careers, and here ... She shifted her gaze. Yes, Torquil had a slight chin dimple as well as a single dimple on his left cheek.

She stopped herself. Auden had written in 'In Praise of Limestone' that the blessed will not care what angle they are regarded from, having nothing to hide, which she had always thought was true, but any gaze could still be disconcerting. And so she waited expectantly to find out what he needed to borrow, trying hard not to look at the young man's chin, as difficult as affecting indifference to achondroplasia or a port-wine stain. Oddly, she found herself thinking about the implications of good looks of the sort with which Torquil had been favoured. How would one view the world if one contemplated it through the eyes of one who had his looks? Positively – because the world was kind to the good-looking? How many perfect monsters were perfect monsters because, through physical misfortune, they had repelled those they encountered? How many of the sweet and gentle were sweet and gentle because they got the attention we all crave, and were given it liberally from their first days as appealing infants?

He broke the silence, still smiling. 'I need to borrow a bucket and mop. It's our turn to wash the stair.'

29. Absolut

'But of course,' said Domenica. 'I'll get them for you.'

She left him on the landing and made her way to the cupboard where she and Angus kept their ancient mop and battered tin bucket. Torquil's request was, she thought, a promising sign. In Scotland, the rules on tenement living were deeply embedded and jealously policed: every house-holder, by immemorial custom, had to play his or her part in cleaning the common stair, a shared flight of stone steps linking landing to landing. That task was allocated on the basis of a weekly rota, with a small printed notice being hung on each doorway in succession: *It is your turn to clean the common stair.* There were no exceptions, although neigh-bours might deputise for the frail or incapacitated or, by mutual agreement, engage a cleaner to do the work for them. Students, of course, were known to be a problem and not infrequently had to be reminded of their duty. Domenica was well aware of that, and had half expected that the new occupants of the downstairs flat would need to be spoken to about their obligations; now Torquil had shown that concern to be pessimistic, and she was pleased.

She handed the equipment over to him with an apology for the state it was in. 'It's seen better days,' she said. 'But the bucket doesn't leak, and the mop just about does the job. I've been meaning to get a new one, but . . . '

'Life gets in the way,' said Torquil, with a smile. 'I know. I've been meaning to buy one for ourselves ever since we moved in, but haven't. I will, though.'

Domenica laughed. 'When you've finished,' she began, only to be interrupted by his saying, 'Of course, I'll return it straight away.'

'No, I wasn't going to say that. I know you will. I was going to invite you in for a cup of coffee.'

The invitation seemed to be welcomed. 'I'd love that,' he said.

'I have a coffee machine that makes proper coffee,'

Domenica said. 'I can do all the usual things. Cappuccino, latte, Americano . . .'

Torquil laughed. 'Any old how,' he said. He hesitated, and an anxious frown came over his brow. 'You didn't hear noise yesterday, did you?'

Domenica shook her head. There would be parties, she imagined: five young people in a New Town flat usually meant parties were in the offing. But she sought to reassure him. 'Noise doesn't travel very much in this building,' she said. 'We very rarely hear anything from our neighbours. Even from young Bertie – you've met him, I take it?'

'That little boy?' asked Torquil. 'The one who sometimes sits on the stairs?'

'That's him,' said Domenica.

'I saw him yesterday,' said Torquil. 'He was sitting outside his flat door, all by himself, his nose buried in a book. I asked him what it was. You won't believe the answer.'

'Oh, I'll certainly believe it,' said Domenica. 'Bertie's reading tastes are rather advanced – although he himself is not at all – how might one put it? – *trying*. Some highly intelligent children can be a bit exhausting, you know. Bertie's not. He's lovely.'

'It was a book about Kierkegaard,' said Torquil. 'I couldn't believe it at first, but I asked him to show me, and sure enough. There it was: *A Life of Søren Kierkegaard*. And he's only . . .' He looked to Domenica for guidance.

'Seven. He's seven.' She sighed. 'I remember his birthday. He's always wanted a Swiss Army penknife, and that mother of his gave him a gender-neutral play figure . . .'

Torquil raised an eyebrow. 'A doll?'

'Yes, but a gender-neutral one. You couldn't really tell what sex it was supposed to be.'

'I suppose dolls can be fluid,' mused Torquil. 'I mean, when they leave the factory they might be a bit uncertain.' He laughed. 'In the sense of it being left up to their owner to decide for them.'

'You're suggesting that dolls should be able to self-identify? So to speak?'

Torquil smiled. 'I don't see why not.'

Domenica thought for a moment. 'But what if you bought a doll that you believed was a girl doll, but then you discovered, when you opened the box, that it was a boy doll. Would you be able to go back to the shop and ask for an exchange?'

Torquil thought about this. 'I don't think so,' he said at last. 'I think people need to move with the times.'

'Oh, we all must do that,' said Domenica. 'And rightly so. Move with the times or you're history, as they say.'

Torquil nodded. 'My parents are history,' he said. 'I think their lives are actually in black and white – like an old movie.' The grin returned. 'Mind you, I rather like them for it. They belong to a generation that ... '

'That was less afraid to say what it felt?' prompted Domenica.

Torquil hesitated.

'But also tolerated all sorts of cruelty and discrimination,' Domenica went on.

'*Absolut*,' said Torquil, and added, 'Sorry. That's a bit of an affectation on my part. *Absolut* is *absolutely* in Swedish. I've watched too many Swedish films. In Scandinavian noir people say *absolut* all the time.'

Domenica stared at him. This was wonderful. They were

going to get on very well indeed, she thought: here was a young man whose taste in film was *Swedish*! 'So Bertie was reading about Kierkegaard? What did he have to say about it?'

'Oh, he told me that Mr Kierkegaard was Danish. He called him *Mr* Kierkegaard. He was terribly polite. He said that he wrote hundreds of books and liked to go for walks about Copenhagen.'

'Dear Bertie!'

'I could hardly believe it. Seven! Then he said something about trying to read the book to his friend, who couldn't read yet, but not getting very far with it.'

'That'll be a little boy by the name of Ranald Braveheart Macpherson,' explained Domenica. 'He lives over on the other side of town, but the two of them are to be seen running around Drummond Place Garden.

'It's his mother, you see,' Domenica continued. 'She's – how shall I put it? – ambitious for him. Which is fair enough – to an extent. Mothers need to be ambitious for their children otherwise ... well, nobody would ever learn the piano. Mothers have to be pushy. But there are limits and that woman is way beyond them.'

'*Absolut*,' said Torquil.

30. A Category Three Row

It took Torquil rather longer to clean the common stair than he had anticipated. He had thought he would finish within twenty minutes; in fact, it was a full three-quarters of an hour before he appeared once more at Domenica's door, the bedraggled and dripping mop in hand.

'That's your duty done for the month,' said Domenica, relieving him of the equipment. 'You've earned your coffee.'

He sniffed at the air. 'I can smell it,' he said. 'Coffee. One of my favourite smells. Alongside freshly cooked bacon. And the smell of a new shirt.'

'I go for dried lavender,' said Domenica, adding, 'À chacun son parfum.'

'Bay rum,' said Torquil. 'Do you like the smell of that?'

Domenica looked doubtful. 'Those are what I'd call masculine smells. Angus likes bay rum. He had a bottle of it in the bathroom but the cap was a bit loose and the rum part evaporated. It smelled of nothing in particular after that.'

'I sometimes use it as an aftershave,' said Torquil, rubbing his chin.

Domenica took the opportunity to glance at his chin again – at the strategically placed dimple. She thought: a few millimetres the wrong way, and a facial feature can be all wrong. That was not the case here.

They made their way into the kitchen, where Domenica poured their coffee.

'You said something about noise,' said Domenica. 'And then we were sidetracked by talk about young Bertie. Did you have a party? As I said, we don't hear much in this building.' She paused. 'Mind you, Bertie plays the saxophone from time to time. We get 'As Time Goes By' drifting up occasionally. He plays it rather well.'

'My favourite film,' said Torquil.

Casablanca, thought Domenica. The right attitude to cleaning the stair. Dimples. All very positive.

'Yes,' she said. 'It has wonderful lines.'

'About the day the Germans invaded Paris?'

Domenica nodded. 'Yes. What does Rick say? *I remember every detail: the Germans wore grey; you wore blue.*'

Torquil took a sip of his coffee. 'That's very funny.' He hesitated. 'It wasn't a party, you know.'

'No?'

'No. It was a row. A real screaming match, I'm afraid.'

Domenica said that she was sorry to hear that. 'Mind you, I remember how, in my student days – rather a long time back – we had a flat over in Marchmont. It was in Warrender Park Terrace – in one of those buildings that look down over the Meadows. We had a view of the Castle. There it was, on the horizon. I remember thinking: how lucky I am to be able to look out over a castle from my bedroom.'

'I think that living in Edinburgh is a little like living on an opera set,' said Torquil. 'You almost expect a window to be opened and an aria to burst forth.'

'Or a chorus of tobacco-factory girls to appear – as in

Carmen. Except, nobody has tobacco factories any longer. Or, rather, they're discreet about them.'

'A chorus of computer programmers doesn't have quite the same ring,' said Torquil.

'Modern life is inimical to opera,' said Domenica.

Torquil disagreed. '*Nixon in China*? Scottish Opera did that recently. I saw it. It was wonderful.'

'Oh, I think there are plenty of suitable themes,' said Domenica. 'For example, Mr Gorbachev would have made a wonderful opera. And Mr Obama too. Nelson Mandela. These would all be great operatic subjects.' She paused. 'No, I was thinking more of the accoutrements of modern life. That's the problem for opera, I'd have thought.'

Torquil looked puzzled. 'But *Nixon in China* had a plane ...'

'Planes are fine,' said Domenica. 'Flight is timeless. Icarus is an ancient story. No, I was thinking of antibiotics. Take *Bohème*, for instance. Mimi is ill for the entire opera, and then, of course, succumbs – as is only proper for an operatic heroine. Credible enough for the nineteenth century. But if it were set in modern times ... well, what could the librettist do? The obvious solution is antibiotics – and Mimi would be as right as rain.'

Torquil burst out laughing. 'No prolonged death scene.'

'No. You see? Modern technology ruins everything: our sense of the unknown, for example – because there's no longer any reason for anything to be unknown. If you don't know something, the internet is a few keystrokes away – and you have your solution. There are no secrets any longer.'

Torquil reached for his coffee cup. 'Is that such a bad thing?'

'I would have thought so,' said Domenica. 'It makes it rather difficult to escape your past – if you want to do that, of course – which some people may.' She took a sip of her coffee. 'But we're getting into profound issues here. What was this row you people had?'

Torquil sighed. 'All of us are good friends, you know. There's no fundamental problem. It's really to do with . . .'

He broke off, as if uncertain whether to continue. But Domenica's curiosity had been roused. Rows in shared flats fell into three categories, she thought: a row about food was category one (*Who ate my cheese?*); a row about mess was category two (*You're a real pig, you know*); and the third category was a row about sex (*I didn't know you felt that way . . .*)

'I shouldn't pry,' she said. She shouldn't, but she was still very interested. And she was an anthropologist, after all. '*Nihil humani mihi alienum.* Terence, I think.'

'It's about bedrooms,' said Torquil. 'It's about who gets which bedroom.'

Domenica nodded. *Category three row*, she thought. 'You don't have to tell me,' she said, somewhat reluctantly.

'No, I don't mind,' said Torquil.

She looked at him appreciatively.

'You see,' he began. 'As I think I told you, there are five of us: me, Rose, Dave, Alistair and Phoebe.'

'Yes, you did. You told me.'

'And the flat has three bedrooms. It's spacious enough, but there are only those three bedrooms.'

Domenica waited.

'So,' Torquil continued, 'everybody has to share – except one person.'

'And that person is?' prompted Domenica.

'Me, as it happens,' said Torquil. And then, in justification, 'I found the flat. I signed the lease. I'm the one who's responsible for everything.'

'Then it's fair enough that you should have the single room.'

He looked grateful for the recognition of his claim. 'Thank you. But then that means that Rose and Phoebe share, and Dave and Alistair share too.'

Domenica thought about that. 'That sounds reasonable.'

'Yes, but . . .'

Sometimes *but* conceals a whole hinterland of issues, decided Domenica, and this, she suspected, was just such a but.

31. Irene Reversed

It had been Stuart's suggestion that Nicola should abandon her flat in Northumberland Street and move into Scotland Street permanently – or at least for the foreseeable future. The arrangement that had been in place since Irene left for Aberdeen had been working well enough – Nicola looked after the children, often staying overnight if Stuart had to work late or wanted to go out – but it would be easier all round, he thought, if she moved in altogether.

'I know you like your own space, Mother,' he said. 'But we could clear out Irene's study and install you in there. It's probably the best room in the flat – with its view of Drummond Place Garden. It's very light.' He smiled. 'If one can possibly keep one's mother in south-facing circumstances one should do so.'

Nicola had received the proposal with interest. Irene's study? Cleared out? This was a delicious prospect, not only because of the attractions of the room itself – and she did prefer a room with a southern aspect – but for what this would represent in terms of victory over her daughter-in-law. She had done her best to like Irene – she really had; it was her Christian duty to like her – but years ago her patience had been exhausted and she had decided that Irene was simply *not possible*. That was a powerful term when applied to people: *not possible*. A person who was *not possible* was different from a person who was *impossible*. Being *impossible* involved having various behavioural quirks that made you difficult company; whereas being *not possible* implied that there was simply no chance of an ordinary human relationship, ever. To be *not possible* was to be beyond reach; a person who was *not possible* simply would not understand what the problem was.

Over the years, Nicola had bitten her tongue. She had put up with Irene's lectures, with her knee-jerk contradiction of any opinion she – Nicola – expressed; she had done her best to forgive her bone-deep condescension; she had turned a deaf ear to her recited catalogue of instances of male insensitivity, many of them imaginary or at least blown out of all proportion. And as each fresh Irene story came to light, Nicola had struggled to conceal her mirth or, in some cases, horror. She had heard from Domenica, who had heard from Angus, who had heard from Matthew, who had been told by Big Lou, who had had it from Stuart himself, that when Irene travelled to a Melanie Klein conference in Milan, flying by way of Amsterdam, she had asked the KLM captain why he was flying the plane. The captain, cap under arm, had strolled down the aisle in midflight to greet the passengers and had chanced to enquire of Irene as to whether she was being well looked after. Irene had taken the opportunity to ask him why men seemed to be in the cockpit while women were in the galley.

'Doesn't that strike you as wrong?' she demanded.

The pilot had done his best. There were many female pilots, he assured her, and they had a better safety record than men on the whole. That had not pacified Irene, who had then pointed out the visible cabin crew and announced that they were all female whereas there appeared to be three men in the nose of the plane.

The pilot had been tactful, but was still treated to a dressing-down. Eventually, he asked her whether she would like to fly the plane herself, and returned to the controls.

There were many other instances of Irene's insufferable behaviour, including, of course, her hijacking of the production of *Waiting for Godot* put on by Bertie's Primary Three class. That was just the tip of a bulky iceberg: Nicola had listened to accounts of episode after episode of Irene's posturing, of her virtue signalling on a positively semaphoric scale, and of her interdiction of any newspaper other than the *Guardian* appearing in the flat. Stuart actually enjoyed the *Guardian*, a good newspaper by any standards, but he also rather liked the *Financial Times* – especially the Saturday edition – the *Scotsman*, the *Herald* and the *New York Times*, which he read online. He thought it only reasonable to read more than one paper, so as to get a balanced view of the issues of the day, but in that open-minded stance he found himself at odds with his wife.

'I will not have the bourgeois press in the flat,' she said. 'Sorry, Stuart, but there are limits.'

'But is the *Scotsman* bourgeois?' asked Stuart mildly. 'I thought they were open to a wide range of opinion.'

'There's such a thing as repressive tolerance,' Irene retorted. 'I would have thought that even you knew that, Stuart.'

Even you is a wounding phrase at the best of times, but when said slowly, allowing for the full measure of its connotations of disparagement to sink in, it may have a devastating effect on *amour propre*.

Nicola, hearing of the newspaper ban, had gone out of her way to defy it. When she knew that Irene would be coming down from Aberdeen for one of her visits, she made a point of leaving other newspapers lying around, even placing two copies of severely interdicted newspapers, the *Daily Mail* and the *Daily Telegraph*, on the hall table, where Irene could not miss them. Irene had taken them and thrown them out of the window into the street below, unfortunately at precisely the time that the local community police officer was making his way to begin his shift at Gayfield Police Station round the corner. Noting the source of the litter, the policeman had knocked on the door of the flat and produced the gathered-up pages as evidence of the littering offence. Irene had been fined, much to the delight of Nicola and her friends to whom she told the story. Great was their pleasure on hearing the tale: 'You must be as terrible in her sight as an army and all its banners!' one remarked. 'Oh, joyous, happy prospect!'

'Such a pity it was one of those ticketed fines,' Nicola observed. 'It would have been so entertaining to be at the Sheriff Court and see her answer for her crimes. I would have issued invitations – edged in black – to attend her trial. What a pity!'

But here was an irresistible consolation prize indeed: the chance to pack Irene's books and papers into boxes, and then take over what she called her *space*. If challenged, she would stand up to Irene and say, 'Sorry, it's my space now. You've got a space up in Aberdeen, haven't you?'

What a delight that would be. And she would take down all of Irene's pictures, too, and put in their place the polar opposite of what had been there. Nicola did not like fox hunting, which she saw as an organised celebration of cruelty, but in view of Irene's previous history as a prominent saboteur of the Fife Hunt – the meetings of which she was happy to travel some distance to in order to pour invective on the huntsmen – in view of that she was prepared to hang a sporting picture on the wall, in exactly the spot where Irene's portrait of Gramsci had been. So it was that *Taking the Stirrup Cup Together: the Fife Hunt Prepares for a Day Out*, a sentimental and idealised Edwardian lithograph, found a home on that wall. Nicola did not like the picture at all, and would not have chosen for company any of those portrayed in it, but, in the circumstances, she derived great pleasure from its presence. After all, she thought, one could put up with any amount of aesthetic discomfort when the prospect of revenge was so delicious as to be positively exquisite.

32. *A Suitable Education*

Now, having settled Ulysses for the night and having read a chapter of *The Thirty-Nine Steps* to Bertie, who was always allowed a further half hour of private reading before lights-out, precious minutes that made him feel so adult, Nicola went into the kitchen, where she found Stuart browsing through a men's clothing catalogue.

'It's all about blue this year,' he said, pointing to a picture in the catalogue. 'Listen,' he said. *'Blue is the new you.* That's what this says. And then: *Blue is so much more than a mere colour – blue is a statement.'* He looked up from the catalogue. 'And then they have a picture of a man in blue – making a statement, I suppose.'

'That he likes blue?' Nicola was dismissive. 'That's the obvious inference. Mind you, I have no interest in whether or not I'm wearing this year's colours.'

'No,' agreed Stuart, tossing aside the catalogue. 'Nor do I. I'll wear ... well, the usual things.'

Nicola looked at her son. 'There's nothing wrong with your clothes, Stuart. They're a bit ...' She searched for a tactful adjective. 'Functional, perhaps. Of course, clothes *should* be functional. There are always those poor souls who have *wardrobe malfunctions* – a wonderful euphemism for one's clothes falling off or suddenly becoming too revealing.'

'I've been thinking of getting a new sweater,' said Stuart.

'Perhaps you should.'

'I was thinking of blue ...'

Nicola smiled. 'If it's you, why not?'

'And I might get Bertie some new clothes too. He still has those trousers that Irene bought him. Those pink ones. He seems resigned to them, but I know he doesn't like them.'

'I'll take him into town tomorrow,' said Nicola. 'I'll get him a pair of jeans. Denim.'

Stuart looked doubtful. 'Irene was very anti-denim.'

Nicola waited, but he did not explain. Of course, it would be obvious, if one thought about it, why Irene would not like denim. Denim was *faux* workwear for the bourgeoisie, who wore it ironically. But what about corduroy – a reactionary material, surely, in Irene's book: *corde du roi* – its alleged etymology gave it away. It was the sort of material even a monarchist might embrace.

'So, get him some denim jeans,' said Stuart. 'I'm sure he'd love a pair.'

Irene nodded. She would get Ulysses something too – perhaps a red bandana to tie round his neck. She had seen a baby wearing a red bandana a few days ago and had thought it very fetching.

But there were other matters she wanted to talk to Stuart about, and now she raised them. 'You may recall, Stuart,' she began, 'that we talked about Bertie's education.'

Stuart gazed out of the window. *I have not been a good father*, he thought. *I gave up, and left it to Irene. I've been weak.*

'Would you like a glass of wine?' he asked.

Nicola frowned. 'Do you not want to talk about this?'

He took a deep breath. *The days of being weak are over. Irene is in Aberdeen; I'm in Edinburgh. I can get into the water – it's safe.*

'No, I would like to talk about it. But sometimes a glass of wine helps.'

She agreed, and Stuart poured a glass of red for each of them.

'You know,' said Nicola, raising her glass to her lips, 'whenever I drink red wine, I think of Abril. I can't help it. It's a seemingly inescapable association. I see Abril. I hear him going on about his wine. I used to doze off sometimes when he started to talk about fermentation tanks and so on.'

Nicola had been married – it was her second marriage, after she had been widowed – to a Portuguese wine producer, Abril Tavares de Lumiares, who had left her for his housekeeper, on the alleged instructions of the Virgin Mary. Ever since then, she had had a poor opinion of both the Portuguese wine trade and the Virgin Mary.

'You need to get over Abril,' said Stuart. 'I never liked him. Not that I really knew him, but still.'

'The Cinderella Syndrome,' said Nicola. 'Stepmothers are never liked – I imagine there is a counterpart for antipathy towards stepfathers.'

'Possibly. I found him a bit ...' Stuart hesitated. He did not want to offend his mother, and he had rarely talked about his feelings for Abril, who had married Nicola well after

Stuart had become an adult and who therefore had played no part in his life. Of course, he had taken his mother away – to Portugal – and that might be a cause for resentment; but there was no point, Stuart thought, in exploring feelings that were now so firmly consigned to the past.

'You found him a bit what?' prompted Nicola.

Stuart swallowed. He might as well be honest; as his mother, Nicola had an uncanny ability to discern what he was really feeling: mothers, he thought, see through their sons. The sons don't notice it, but they can never fool their mothers.

'I found him a bit greasy,' said Stuart apologetically.

Nicola gave him an intense look.

'Which of course he wasn't really,' said Stuart hurriedly.

'But he was,' said Nicola. 'He used to leave greasy stains on the back of the chairs, where his head touched the fabric. And his nose was quite greasy too. If he peered through a window, he would leave a grease mark on it. You could always tell if Abril had been pressing his nose to the glass.'

'Was it dietary?' asked Stuart. 'What do the Portuguese eat? Lots of sardines. I've heard that pasta gives you oily skin. And sardines too, I gather.'

'Possible,' said Nicola. 'But then again, possibly not.'

Stuart shrugged. 'Let's not talk about Abril. You were going to say something about Bertie's education.'

Nicola took another sip of her wine. 'All right,' she began. 'I've been thinking, as you know, of how Bertie might benefit from a change. The Steiner School is wonderful, and it's been great for Bertie, but I think he might benefit from different surroundings – even if only for a short time.'

'For a term?' asked Stuart. 'A few months?'

145

'Maybe just a month or so,' said Nicola, 'as a sort of treat. To get him away from that dreadful Olive. And Pansy. And that ghastly Tofu.'

'All schools have kids like that,' said Stuart. 'They're a fact of life.'

'Oh, I know that,' said Nicola. 'But taking him out of their orbit for a while might provide him with a ... a breath of fresh air, I suppose.'

Stuart looked thoughtful. 'You mentioned a boys' boarding school when we spoke about this last time. You said something about Merchiston.'

'Yes,' said Nicola, 'I did. But since then, I've been thinking of something even more radical.'

Stuart waited. Then Nicola dropped her bombshell.

'Glasgow,' she said.

33. The Best News Ever

Stuart took a large sip of wine. He had not expected this.

'Glasgow?' he said. And then, 'Well, I must confess I hadn't ...'

'No, I'm sure you wouldn't have,' said Nicola. 'And nor would I have contemplated bringing Glasgow into the equation, but then ... Well, you know how Bertie goes on about Glasgow. You'd think he was talking about Shangri-La.'

Stuart smiled. 'He loves it.' He remembered their earlier visit to Glasgow – the first time that Bertie had been there. They had gone to retrieve the family car after Stuart had driven over to Glasgow for a meeting and then, absent-mindedly, returned by train. They had ended up spending time in the company of the late Lard O'Connor (RIP), a much-regretted Glasgow gangster, who had been impressed by Bertie and who had taken both him and Stuart to see the Burrell Collection. In Bertie's mind, Glasgow was a promised land, a shining city upon a hill, and the River Clyde, upon whose sylvan banks the city nestled, was a holy river, as compelling a source of pilgrimage, in Bertie's view, as any Ganges, Narmada, or Godavari.

'Well,' Nicola continued, 'I had a conversation yesterday with Ranald Braveheart Macpherson's parents. It was when I went to collect Bertie from his play date with Ranald. And over a cup of tea, Ranald's mother revealed that Ranald is going on an educational exchange for a month to the Glasgow Academy Primary.' She paused. 'And furthermore, she said that they have another place available in the same scheme, and that if we were interested, Bertie could possibly go as well.'

Stuart was silent. Then, 'Bertie? Go to school in Glasgow? The Glasgow Academy.'

Nicola inclined her head. 'It's a very good school. The Primary has various branches – this one is at Milngavie.'

Stuart gasped. 'Milngavie?'

'Yes. Of course, there would be fees involved, but I'd cover those.'

'But he'd have to board? I think he's far too young to

board. I mean, think of *Tom Brown's Schooldays* and *Lord of the Flies*, and all that. I'm no great fan of boarding schools.'

Nicola shook her head. '*Lord of the Flies* is hardly apposite, Stuart. We're hardly proposing to send Bertie to a desert island. And he wouldn't have to board at the school itself. Part of this arrangement is that the children stay *en famille* with a member of the Academy staff. One of the teachers, who lives in Bearsden, would have them staying with her.'

Stuart gasped again. 'Bearsden?'

'Yes. She has a slightly older daughter. She often takes children whose parents have to be away for one reason or another. Her husband is a cello maker and he works in a workshop at home, and so he's always in. According to Ranald's mother, it's a tried and tested arrangement, and is usually a great success. They had a Greek child from Corfu last time and it all went very well – a Greek father and a Scottish mother, so the child spoke quite good English. These exchanges can be wonderful for children – as long as they're robust enough to be away from home.'

'Well, Glasgow's not exactly at the other end of the country.'

'No,' said Nicola. 'And he could come back for weekends. So he would only be there Monday to Friday.'

'And if he became homesick I could pop over and collect him,' mused Stuart.

'Precisely. And remember – he'll have Ranald Braveheart Macpherson with him – so that will help.'

'A lot,' said Stuart.

He looked at Nicola. 'Do you think we should?'

'I see no reason why not,' said Nicola. 'It's only for a month and it could be a wonderful treat for him.'

'Of course, he's likely to discover that Glasgow is much the same as anywhere else,' said Stuart.

'But it isn't,' said Nicola. 'You know that, and I know it too, Stuart. Glasgow is *not* Edinburgh.'

'He's had his inoculations, though,' said Stuart. He paused. 'Shall we ask Bertie?'

'Yes. Will you do it?'

'Right away.'

He finished his wine and then left the kitchen and knocked at Bertie's half-open door. As he entered the bedroom, Bertie looked up from his book.

'What are you reading, Bertie?' asked Stuart as he sat down on the bed.

Bertie showed his father the cover of his book. *The Lighthouse Stevensons*. 'It's about the people who built all the lighthouses,' he said. 'They were all called Mr Stevenson, and they built all our lighthouses, Daddy. That's what they did.'

'Very interesting,' said Stuart. 'I suppose if you find you can do one thing rather well, you should carry on doing it.'

Bertie agreed. 'They built a lighthouse called the Bell Rock Lighthouse, Daddy. In the sea off Fife. It was jolly dangerous because it was just on a rock and the sea came up and covered what they'd built every day. They had to wait for low tide before they could start again.'

'They were very skilful,' said Stuart. 'And do you know, Bertie, that Robert Louis Stevenson was a member of that family? He wrote books rather than build lighthouses.'

'He wrote *Kidnapped*, didn't he, Daddy?'

'He did, Bertie.'

'It's a bit scary, that book. Ranald said that he doesn't want to read it, but then he can't read yet – and nor can Tofu. Tofu says that reading's old-fashioned and that he's not going to waste his time learning how to do old-fashioned things. He said you might as well spend your time learning Egyptian hieroglyphics.'

Stuart smiled. 'Tofu is wrong on most things, Bertie – as I suspect you've noticed.'

Stuart waited a few moments. Then he said, 'Well, Bertie, perhaps you might like to spend a few weeks at another school – without Tofu. Or Olive, for that matter.'

Bertie's eyes widened. 'Really, Daddy? Do you think I could?'

'How about Glasgow?'

Bertie dropped his book. 'Did you say Glasgow, Daddy? Glasgow?'

Stuart nodded. 'There's an exchange scheme, Bertie. And Ranald is on it. We wondered whether you might like to join him – and go to school in Glasgow for a month.'

Bertie leapt out of bed, tossing the bedclothes aside. 'I can get changed straight away, Daddy. Should I wear my new shoes? What will it be like? Will you write to me?' The questions came thick and fast. 'Will it be in the Gorbals, Daddy?'

Stuart caught his wrist. 'Hold on, Bertie. I didn't mean right now. These things have to be arranged, and I just wanted to check that you would be happy to go.'

Bertie leapt again – this time into his father's lap. 'Oh yes, Daddy. I can think of nothing better. Glasgow!'

'In that case,' said Stuart, 'I'll get in touch with the school – both schools – first thing on Monday, and find out what needs to be done. I can't guarantee it, Bertie, but Ranald's mother said that she thought they'd be happy to take you at the same time that Ranald goes.'

Bertie climbed back into bed. 'This is the best news ever,' he said. 'And you're the kindest dad in the history of the world.'

Stuart closed his eyes. *For years I failed you*, he said to himself. *For years.*

Bertie reached out to touch his father's forearm. 'Don't look sad, Daddy,' he whispered. 'It wasn't your fault that you married Mummy.'

34. Major Events

All that had happened on a Friday. And if Friday had seemed momentous, it was but as nothing compared with Saturday, a day that began with stillness and promise as a zone of high pressure drifted up from France, avoided England, and then, finding just the right atmospheric conditions, settled over Scotland and Norway, generously promising both northern countries at least four days of balmy, almost sultry conditions. It was still very early summer, not a time at which anybody in Scotland, other than the most incorrigible optimists, could even think about putting their overcoats away until autumn. But now, as Edinburgh looked forward to a day of uninterrupted sunshine, Montesquieu's observations on the association between climate and disposition were everywhere laid out for ratification: in the spring in the step of the city's early morning walkers, in the appearance of bright, short-sleeved clothing, in the figures in Princes Street Gardens, sprawled out on the grass, careless of latitude, feeling – or almost feeling – the very blades of grass beneath them beginning to perk up with the challenge of summer.

Major events lay ahead that Saturday morning. Bertie, still exhilarated at the prospect of Glasgow, was due to go into town with his grandmother and his younger brother. Nicola was to purchase a pair of jeans for him and a red bandana for Ulysses, if one were to be available.

'We may be unsuccessful in that search,' Nicola warned. 'Bandanas are not the sort of thing one sees these days, but we shall try.'

'Yes,' said Bertie. 'And Ulysses won't mind, Granny. He doesn't really know what's going on.'

For Stuart's part, the morning had the particular promise of a meeting – for coffee – with Katie. This was to take place at the Scottish National Portrait Gallery, and then they planned to go for a walk at Cramond, followed by lunch in South Queensferry. Stuart was excited by the prospect – so much so that when he shaved that morning, he traced a heart on the bathroom mirror, using shaving cream. It was a childish thing to do, he thought, but it had been spontaneous, and if you ever reached the stage in life, he told himself, when you could not be bothered to draw hearts on mirrors, then surely your life would be the flatter for that.

Out at Nine Mile Burn, Elspeth and Matthew had quite

separate plans, at least for the first part of the day, and these plans were significant. Elspeth had recently made a new friend in Alice, a young woman she had met at the West Linton Mother and Toddler Group. That group had been formed by various members of a local National Childbirth Trust prenatal class, who had stayed in touch with one another after the birth of their children. Elspeth had got on particularly well with Alice, who lived in a nearby village. She was married to an architect, and had herself completed several years of her architectural training at the Glasgow School of Art before she had decided that she wanted to do something different and had set up a small business making silk flowers. That had proved successful, and even after she started a family – she had a daughter slightly younger than Elspeth's triplets – she had been able to establish a small workshop in the grounds of their house. There she employed – on a part-time basis – a Syrian woman whose husband had a job in a laboratory at the Veterinary School at Easter Bush and a young woman who had previously been a motorcycle mechanic but who had decided to abandon that career and move back to live with her parents in West Linton. 'I was trying to prove something to myself,' she confessed to Alice. 'And to others, I suppose. Anyway, I hate motorcycles now. I'm more into flowers and stuff. Much more.'

Elspeth had arranged to visit Alice that morning and then to have a picnic with the boys and with Alice's daughter, Wee Alice. Alice knew of a burn down near Peebles where the children could play safely in the water and where she and Elspeth could catch up on each other's news. Their friendship was an easy one: they agreed on most subjects, and those on which they disagreed were never raised. They liked the same films and books, and exchanged boxed sets of DVDs. Alice had offered to teach Elspeth how to make silk flowers, and had said that she might even be able to use her at times when they had large orders to fulfil. 'We're beginning to send them to France,' she said. 'They go to Lyon. Apparently, there's a lot of interest in silk flowers in Lyon.' But then she stopped. 'Of course, you don't really need to work. I was forgetting. Matthew's not short of money, I gather.'

Elspeth was tactful. 'He doesn't flash it around. And everyone has to be careful.'

'Yes, but you don't actually *need* to work, do you?' She sighed. 'Architecture's odd. Colin's really good at his job, but he ends up doing rubbish work half the time. Kitchen extensions and so on. He'd like to design concert halls and airports.'

Elspeth looked away, embarrassed by Alice's remark about Matthew's circumstances. Matthew was discreet, and not at all showy; they lived simply enough. Of course, the house was large, but it had not been all that expensive, and was not in very good condition. The problem was envy – not that she was accusing Alice of that – but it was a problem with an awful lot of people. 'Everyone wants to feel useful,' she said. 'And I think you should work if you can.'

They had left the subject there, and if Elspeth were to learn how to make silk flowers, it would be for her own enjoyment rather than to participate in Alice's business.

For his part, Matthew had agreed with James that he

would drive him over to Single Malt House to check up on his uncle, the Duke of Johannesburg, whose behaviour was causing James some concern.

'I don't want to go by myself,' James said. 'If you wouldn't mind coming with me ...'

Matthew had readily agreed. 'I hope everything's all right,' he said.

'I don't think it is,' replied James. 'In fact, far from it.'

That outing promised to be revelatory, and it was, but, as it happened, it was considerably less dramatic than the experience ahead of Angus, and indeed of Cyril, on a planned walk to the Moray Pleasure Gardens, to which Angus had an informal key. Calling in on India Street, Angus proposed to invite his friend, James Holloway, to accompany him and Cyril as their walk continued in the gardens between Moray Place and the Water of Leith below – a wild spot within the city, a noted example of *rus in urbe*, where cliffs descended to the river bed, and where groves of trees, clumps of shrubs, and meandering paths provided plenty of challenge and olfactory entertainment for Cyril. Angus wanted to sound out James about an exhibition he was curating at the Scottish Arts Club, and they could discuss it as they walked while Cyril, free of his leash, heady with freedom, ran in circles, endured the taunting of nimble squirrels, and generally behaved as nature had designed dogs to behave.

35. *A Walk to Stockbridge*

'Cyril seems in fine fettle,' remarked James Holloway as he and Angus made their way down India Street.

Hearing his name mentioned, Cyril glanced up appreciatively. A dog's name is, to a dog, mood music of the most desirable sort. While we might tire of the constant iteration of our names, dogs did not, as Angus now explained to James.

'The point about these creatures,' he said, gesturing to Cyril, 'is that they have very simple word association capabilities. They have a vocabulary, of course, but it's usually relatively small. Some dogs have no words at all, other than their name – Cyril has a bit more than that, but his name, obviously, is the most important word in the world – for him.'

The second mention of his name brought another appreciative glance from Cyril. This time he smiled, his gold tooth flashing briefly in the sun.

'Yes,' continued Angus, 'the best thing for him would be to hear a constant refrain of *Cyril, Cyril, Cyril* – sung by a mass choir, if you will, but uncomplicated by further words. That would be heaven.' He paused. 'Of course, human beings tend to assume our divinities are similarly pleased by our recital of their names. Perhaps it's the same thing. Why engage in the endless repetition of the same few words? What if God were to say: *I heard you the first time. No need to go on and on*?'

James smiled. 'But the purpose of prayer, surely, is to remind *ourselves* of something. *Om* is rather interesting in that respect.'

'*Om*,' muttered Angus.

'Yes. People say it at the beginning of a yoga class, for example. They take a deep breath and say *Om*.

'Of course, it has a broad meaning,' James continued. 'It's meant to be the sound of the universe, isn't it? It brings together mind, body and spirit.'

'That's a lot of work for a small word,' Angus said. He looked down at Cyril. 'Do you think that the canine equivalent is *woof*?'

James laughed.

'No,' said Angus. 'That's a serious suggestion. When a dog says *woof*, does he actually mean anything?'

James said he thought that would depend on the context. The bark of a guard dog might be a warning, for instance. It was reasonable to give such a bark the meaning *Look out!* or *There's something going on over there!*

'Or *I want my dinner*,' added Angus.

'Precisely. And in that case, surely, a bark becomes language.'

'On the other hand,' Angus went on, 'a lot of barks are simply expressions of an emotional state – excitement, anticipation, sheer joy. Those barks, I would have thought, are getting close to *Om* – the canine variety of *Om*, that is.' He paused. 'Have you ever heard a wolf howl, James?'

James shook his head. 'I can imagine it sends shivers up the spine.'

'It does,' said Angus. 'Rather like *Mist-Covered Mountains* played on the pipes. Or *Highland Cathedral*, too, I suppose.

When you're at Murrayfield Stadium and the rugby is about to begin and the pipe band plays *Highland Cathedral*, well . . . ' A thought occurred; wolves had been forgotten. 'It's actually what one might call an *Om* moment, isn't it?'

'Perhaps the whole crowd might chant *Om* before kickoff,' suggested James, with a smile.

'It might help,' said Angus. 'As long as the Scottish side knew it was for them. And *Om*, I fear, doesn't lend itself to partiality. One can hardly say *Om* and then add, to the other team, *But not for you, actually*. No, I don't think *Om* works that way. *Om* is inherently universal. Just as *Peace be with you* is intended universally, and without the qualification *But not with you, or you, or you . . . seriatim*, so to speak.'

Angus warmed to his theme. 'We're very lucky to have the pipes,' he said. 'They're one of Scotland's greatest assets, you know. We don't necessarily talk about them as such, of course, but they are. The sound of the pipes binds us – gives us a sense of identity.' He paused. 'Does that sound corny? Or even dangerous?'

James shook his head. 'I would have thought we wanted a sense of community. I would have thought that we wanted to care for one another.'

'We do,' said Angus. 'Or, shall I say, most of us do. And other people have similar things that make them feel *Yes, this is who we are. This is something that we all share.* German slap dancing, for example. That's hilarious to an outsider – these men dressed in *Lederhosen* stamping their feet and slapping their thighs while an oompah band plays away in the background. Priceless, but look at the faces of the people watching, and you see something else – a sort of cultural recognition;

a sort of *this is ours* look. And ...' He hesitated. But then he thought, yes, one could extrapolate from that. 'And that surely is the basis of the feeling that we're all in this together; that we must share with one another and try to treat one another well.'

'Nobody would argue with that,' said James. 'Unless one were a radical individualist, and they're somewhat tiresome, as a rule ...'

'Profoundly tiresome,' said Angus. 'And they're on very shaky ground philosophically. If they were consistent, they couldn't rely on anybody for anything. They couldn't phone the police if they needed help; they couldn't expect anybody to empty their rubbish bins on alternate Fridays; they couldn't go to the dentist, because dentistry involves a commitment to co-operative effort at some point – there have to be people who train dentists and so on. Life becomes nasty, brutish and short, as Hobbes said, I believe ...'

'Unless he's being misquoted,' said James. 'Perhaps he said that life in the state of nature was nasty, *British*, and short.'

They both laughed.

Cyril, looking up, barked.

'Cyril has a great sense of humour,' said Angus.

He barked again.

'That sounded a bit like *Om*,' said James. 'Do you think that Cyril's learning?'

They had reached the junction of India Street and Gloucester Place. As they rounded the corner, Cyril tugged at his lead. He had realised now where they were going, and he was particularly fond of the Water of Leith, in which Angus would allow him to splash and retrieve sticks at the end of a walk.

'We need to talk about this exhibition I'm getting together,' said Angus. 'It's at the Scottish Arts Club. We're planning a little show, as I think I mentioned to you, and I wanted your advice on a selection issue. The idea is that the show is of paintings in members' private collections – not their own work, of course, but stuff from their collections.'

'Nice,' said James.

'Yes, but we've been offered rather too much, and we have to decide which works to choose. It's delicate, and as curator I'm going to have to justify my selection.'

'That's what curators do,' said James.

'And the trouble is that one of the paintings I'm being pressed to show is, in my view, simply not by the painter the owner claims it's by.'

'Oh,' said James. 'Awkward.'

'It's a portrait, you see,' said Angus. 'And you know about portraits.' He paused. 'And it's also not *of* the person it claims to be of.'

'What a rotten painting,' said James.

36. A Speluncean Entrance

From the junction of Gloucester Place and Doune Terrace, the road dropped precipitously the short distance down to Stockbridge. Within a few minutes Angus and James were down by the banks of the Water of Leith, the river that runs from its Pentland source to the basin at the port of Leith. It is not a deep river, but it is a fairly fast-moving one, and when there has been heavy rainfall it has its share of tiny rapids where it dances with boyish enthusiasm. For the most part, it is a well-behaved river, rarely breaking its banks and never stagnating. Its water is clear, as it has a relatively short journey from the hills and its banks are unburdened by industry.

A short walk beside the river brought them to St Bernard's Well, a stone temple erected at the end of the eighteenth century, complete with small pump-room for the taking of the waters, and presided over by a statue of the goddess Hygeia.

As he bent down to release Cyril from his leash, Angus looked up at the goddess, who was standing in assured pose beside a column around which a snake had been entwined. 'I assume that she got the snake from her father,' he said. 'She was the daughter of Asclepius, wasn't she?'

James nodded. 'She was. As I recall, she had a number of sisters, including Panacea, who was in charge of remedies for everything . . . '

'Broad-spectrum antibiotics,' said Angus.

'Yes. And another sister was Aglaea, who was goddess of beauty and adornment.'

'Probably the less serious sister,' suggested Angus, tucking Cyril's lead into the pocket of his jacket. 'There's always one. Asclepius, of course, came to a sticky end, did he not? Hades had taken a dim view of the number of people he was bringing back to life. That rather defeated the point of dying, he thought. He persuaded Zeus to remove Asclepius with a bolt of lightning.'

'Zeus needed no encouragement to do that sort of thing,' said James.

Angus looked thoughtful. 'Imagine living under gods who were quite so prone to temper tantrums. We're so used to a belief in the benign: a benign deity, a benign government, a benign system of justice. Imagine if we had none of that – if we felt at the mercy of the irrational and the malignant. Imagine if we felt that those in authority actually hated us.'

James shrugged. 'Plenty of people have had to live like that.'

'I suppose so,' Angus conceded. 'And still do, if one thinks about it. There's no shortage of people who are oppressed by their own government. Minorities of one sort or another. It's a familiar story, isn't it?'

'Yes. And a bleak one.'

Angus watched Cyril race along the path. He called out to him, and the dog stopped and came trotting back towards him.

'How obedient,' said James.

'Well brought up,' said Angus. 'Dogs need to be disciplined. They're pack animals who instinctively need a leader.' He pointed at his chest. 'Me, in Cyril's case. I suppose he thinks of me as Zeus – in a way. Zeus could put him on short rations. Zeus might not have heard of the smacking ban. Zeus has immense power – in his eyes.'

'Which I'm sure you exercise with restraint.'

Angus laughed. 'I try to. And I think that dogs do have a sense of fairness, somewhere, deep down.' He paused. 'But, going back to people being oppressed ... Does it make a difference, do you think, if people who are on the receiving end of that sort of treatment have some idea in their head of the ultimate *wrongness* of what is being done to them?'

James looked doubtful. 'Possibly.'

Angus explained. 'You see, if you are being treated badly, you must feel a bit better if you know that the people who are doing that to you are offending something bigger than themselves – if you see what I mean. You must feel a bit better if you can say to yourself: what they're doing is wrong according to some . . . ' He searched for the right word. 'Some form of natural justice. Or, I suppose, some ultimate value. In other words, if you think you've got right on your side. Would it make things easier to bear if you thought your persecutor would be judged – and punished – in due course?'

James thought it possible. 'I suppose there's some satisfaction to be had at the thought that the person tormenting you will be punished – by *somebody*. And the courts do that, don't they? People are publicly sent off to their punishment, and the victims, or the victims' families, watch from the public benches. They seem to need that, don't they? That's what they mean when they ask for justice. They want that satisfaction.'

'*If* it's satisfaction,' said Angus. 'And I'm not sure whether it really is. They think they'll feel better when the wrongdoer is punished, but I don't think they necessarily do. They might even feel better if they were able to forgive.'

They resumed their walk, heading towards the gate that would admit them to the wild gardens sloping up to their left. Angus, though, was still thinking about the problem of ultimate authority. 'What worries me,' he said, 'is relativism. I've often discussed this with Domenica, you know. If you say that morality is a matter for the individual to decide upon – if you abolish all imposed codes, for instance – all religious commands and precepts – if you say there really is no ultimate just figure in the universe who watches what we do – and that's what most people in this country believe, of course – then how do we deal with the emptiness of knowing that bad behaviour – oppression, exploitation, whatever – will go unpunished? Or, indeed, that it may even get away with *not being identified as such*? It's all very well saying that people can work that out for themselves, but there are plenty of people who need some sort of structure for those matters.' He paused. 'They may need some *bigger tune*. They need to be able to point to something – to some tradition, some moral flag, in a sense – some band of others who say, *Yes, we're with you!*'

They reached the entrance to the Gardens before James could answer. Angus, having fished the key out of his pocket, opened the gate to admit them, and Cyril rushed through, tearing off up a path on which some cold scent of squirrel could still be detected. They watched as he disappeared into a heavy thicket, and then reappeared and made his way further up the slope. Then he was lost to them.

'I think we'd better try to keep an eye on him,' said Angus. 'Dogs can get over-excited and go off for miles if you let them.'

They left the path and clambered up towards the bushes into which Cyril had dived. Parting the branches with a stick he had picked up off the ground, Angus revealed Cyril halfway down a large hole in the side of the cliff, a small cave that had appeared with a fresh fall of rock.

'Has he found something?' asked James.

'A speluncean entrance,' said Angus, adding, 'Gorgeous word, that.'

37. *Homo Neanderthalis*

Angus called out, 'Cyril, Cyril! Get out of there! Immediately!'

He was addressing the dog's hindquarters, though, and the metronome of Cyril's tail, set at an excited *prestissimo*, continued to wag at an impossible rate.

'I don't think he can hear you,' said James. 'With his head down that hole ...'

Angus agreed. 'Like many dogs, he suffers from selective deafness anyway. If he's doing something he's enjoying, he pretends not to hear. Some men are like that with their wives, I believe.' He was aware that one should not make such observations, but he made it anyway, because he thought it was true. In fact, he knew an elderly member of the Scottish Arts Club who had a setting on his hearing aid that could cut out the frequency of his wife's voice. That vision of marriage, though, was very old-fashioned and stereotyped: the persistently nagging wife was a stereotype who no longer existed, just as the irresponsible, domestically inadequate husband had become an outdated caricature. And yet, just as one abolished an outdated persona, one met, in real life, its perfect embodiment . . .

If Angus's train of thought was heading off in that direction, it was abruptly brought to a halt by a bark from Cyril, muffled by the surrounding earth into which he was burrowing.

'He's after something,' said Angus. 'This might be a fox's den.'

He decided to act. If Cyril had driven to earth a fox or some other creature, then he should be stopped. It was hard enough for wild animals to survive in cities, even in small areas of wilderness like this one, and if they were harried by people's dogs, then life could become impossible. Edinburgh, like most cities, had its population of urban foxes, and Angus rather enjoyed encountering them. From time to time, if he woke up early enough on a summer morning, he saw a local fox trotting down Scotland Street, stopping from time to time to sniff at some prospect, an abandoned chicken bone here, a luckless mouse there. He found himself wondering where that fox had its home – how it found sufficient privacy amongst all the urban clutter, a bolthole where it could bring up its cubs. Perhaps this was that place, and now here was Cyril rudely breaching the peace, terrifying the cubs in their chambers.

He bent down and grabbed Cyril's tail, tugging on the protesting appendage. Cyril gave a yelp, and started to reverse out of the hole in the ground. As his head emerged, Angus seized his collar, pulling him free of the fankle of exposed roots and clumps of earth that he had been so eagerly investigating.

James peered into the hole. 'It doesn't go very far,' he

said. 'But I think there's a very small rockfall. It's created a sort of cave.'

Angus pushed Cyril away and instructed him to sit. Looking rather disconsolate, Cyril obeyed.

'If you put him back on his leash,' said James, 'I'll hold him while you have a better look.'

With Cyril back under control, Angus went down on his hands and knees and looked into the small cave. It was not a fox's den, nor, it seemed, the home of any other creature; if it was, then its occupant was nowhere to be seen. What was visible, though, was a largish round object that had been buried and was now half exposed as a result of Cyril's burrowing.

'He's certainly found something,' said Angus.

James looked over his shoulder. 'That thing in the middle?'

Angus reached inside. The earth smelled rich and dry, and was warm to the touch. This was the earth, he thought, to which we all return ... And this, he thought, is how home feels to a fox, or to a mole perhaps: roots, soil, rock. He touched the object, and it moved slightly. He tugged at it, and his fingers went into some sort of cavity. Instinctively, he let go, because there could be anything inside whatever it was he was tugging: spiders, perhaps, and Angus, like most people, had a healthy measure of arachnophobia. But then he conquered his distaste, and pulled again at what seemed to him now to be a large clump of earth attached to a rock or perhaps a bolus of roots.

Suddenly the object became detached from the earth around it and came away in Angus's grasp. Now he could scoop it out, and bring it to the mouth of the opening. He stood up and surveyed the exposed object.

James bent down to get a better look. He turned to Angus, who was rubbing the earth off his hands. 'That,' said James, 'looks like a skull.'

Angus very gingerly lifted up the earth-covered object. It was certainly skull-shaped, but then it was also the shape of a small football, or a round vase, or any number of other things. He turned to James and smiled. 'We are not in a Scandinavian noir,' he said. 'So one doesn't discover skulls in New Town gardens.'

James laughed. 'Well, it looks a bit like it to me.'

Angus put the object down, and dusted off his hands once more. 'If it were a skull,' he said, 'what would we do?'

'Contact the police,' said James. 'They'd come over and erect some of that tape they use to protect crime scenes. Then they'd go away.'

'But I don't think it's a skull,' said Angus. 'It could be anything under all that mess.'

'It could,' said James. 'Why not take it back to Scotland Street? Play the amateur archaeologist. Dust everything off and see what you end up with. A Roman religious figure statue, perhaps? Didn't they find a rather marvellous Roman lion not far away? Something like that?'

Angus always carried a plastic bag with him when he took Cyril for walks, in case he needed to clean up after him. This now proved just large enough for the discovery, and it was duly placed in it. Then, deciding that the walk had taken long enough, he began to head home, saying goodbye to James at the foot of India Street and promising to let him know what emerged once he had the chance to examine Cyril's find more closely.

That examination took place on the kitchen table in the flat, where the object was placed in the middle of a large baking tray and then, under Domenica's guidance, scraped clean of surrounding mud, earth, and vegetable matter.

Slowly it emerged, and slowly their excitement mounted. Then, when they had finished, Domenica turned to Angus. Her expression was one of wide-eyed astonishment.

'Perfectly Neanderthal,' she said, her voice lowered for the momentous announcement. '*Homo neanderthalensis*, Angus.' She reached out to him, her voice dropping to a whisper. 'Look at the forehead.'

Angus smiled. 'No need to whisper, Domenica.'

'But this is dynamite, Angus. Tell me again: where did you find this?'

'I didn't,' said Angus. 'Cyril did.'

Cyril, at their feet, looked up. His gold tooth flashed. He vaguely sensed that he had done something exceptional, but he had, of course, no idea what it was.

38. Generic Guilt

While Angus wrestled with the implications of finding himself in possession of what appeared – in Domenica's view, at least – to be a Neanderthal skull, Stuart was leaving the flat below to make his way to the Scottish National Portrait

Gallery on Queen Street. He felt gloriously unencumbered. Bertie and Ulysses were off shopping with Nicola, who was proposing to take them for a lunchtime pizza after she had bought Bertie his jeans and Ulysses his bandana. Thereafter, she had promised to look after the children for the rest of the day, in order to allow Stuart and Katie time to have their walk at Cramond and their lunch at South Queensferry. No mother, it seemed, could be more encouraging of a son's extramarital liaison: Nicola felt that Stuart deserved every moment of love and affection he could find after years of marriage to Irene. That woman, she thought, that woman . . . But she stopped herself thinking about her, as whenever Irene came to mind, she felt her blood pressure rising. Irene was extremely bad for blood pressure – every bit as bad, she suspected, as large helpings of salt. Irene had *health warning* written all over her in large, Scottish Government-approved lettering. No, she would not think of her; she would simply *deny her mental time*. And yet, whenever she went into the room that had been converted from Irene's *space*, as she called it, to her own study, Nicola felt a surge of sheer delight – as might a territorial usurper, some seeker of *Lebensraum*, some covetous surveyor of another's property, feel when contemplating the fruits of a successful land grab. Of course, she was the usurper in this case, not that that detracted in the slightest from the sheer pleasure she had derived from bundling Irene's possessions away and replacing them with her own.

The packing away of Irene's possessions – her books and papers – had been particularly satisfying. Nicola had unceremoniously dumped these items in cardboard boxes and then written on the boxes: ASSORTED RUBBISH. She had not thrown the boxes away, of course, but had stored them in the cupboard off the hall, where they would be available for Irene to collect, should she want to take them up to Aberdeen. The labelling had been an intensely pleasurable moment, although on noticing it Stuart had raised an eyebrow. 'Isn't that a bit childish, Mother?' he asked.

'Very,' Nicola replied, unapologetically. 'Very childish. But then we all need the occasional moment of childish pleasure, Stuart – whatever age one happens to be.'

He was doubtful. 'I don't know ... What's that famous line? *When I became a man, I put away childish things ...* ?'

Nicola smiled. 'Yes, yes, Stuart, but I happen to know what C. S. Lewis said about that.'

Stuart waited. If somebody threatened to quote C. S. Lewis to you, there was not much one could do but wait.

'C. S. Lewis said, "When I became a man, I put away childish things, including the fear of childishness and the desire to be very grown up." She looked at Stuart unflinchingly. 'And all I would add to that is *mutatis mutandis* in relation to the *man* bit.'

Stuart sighed. 'All right, Mother. But don't antagonise her unnecessarily, please. We still have to see her from time to time.'

'As I'm only too painfully aware.' Nicola sighed. 'But yes, I shall avoid occasions of conflict. We don't want Bertie to pick anything up.'

Stuart thought that Bertie already understood how difficult Irene made it for practically everybody. He was loyal to his mother, but there was no doubt in Stuart's mind that a great weight had lifted off Bertie's shoulders since Irene had gone off to Aberdeen to pursue her PhD.

But now, as he made his way up Dublin Street to the Portrait Gallery, he put out of his mind any thought of Irene and concentrated on the prospect of seeing Katie. She had been pleased by his invitation, and when he had suggested that they should meet for coffee at the gallery, she had said that this would suit her very well. She had planned to go to Valvona & Crolla and that was only a ten-minute walk from the gallery. She was going to buy Parmesan cheese, she said – and how it excited him to imagine her eating Parmesan, crumb by delicious crumb; such an evocation would not work with Cheddar, but Parmesan was different ... He looked about him, as if anxious that somebody would be watching him and would somehow detect the concupiscence pervading such thoughts. How disturbing it would be if others could read what went on in our minds, could imagine what we were thinking, for all the innocence of our outward appearance; that another could look at somebody like him, walking innocently up Dublin Street, and know that he was thinking of an attractive young woman eating Parmesan cheese, while all about him was the classical architecture, the order of the Edinburgh New Town

Stuart arrived a good quarter of an hour in advance of the time they had agreed upon. The café on the ground floor of the Scottish National Portrait Gallery, a popular meeting place, was already busy, and he had to hover for a few minutes before he was able to stake a claim to a table. It was the usual mixture of people: retired teachers from Morningside, book groups on outings connected to their next historical novel, people from the country doing a day of museums in Edinburgh, young people thinking of writing a novel but struggling for ideas, sixth formers from local schools gossiping with one another on their study days, people killing time before a meeting in St Andrew Square, people not sure at all what to do and doing this because they could think of nothing else. He looked about him. Were there others, he asked himself, who were here, as he was, to meet a lover? Perhaps even clandestinely, snatching at shared moments with somebody in an unhappy marriage or relationship of habit, guilty, furtive, a little bit afraid? As he was – if he were to be honest with himself – because he was still technically a married man.

He looked at the portrait hung on the wall behind him. It was one of the gallery's most popular pictures, Guy Kinder's brooding portrait of the crime writer, Ian Rankin, sitting in the Oxford Bar, the haunt of his fictional Edinburgh detective. Ian Rankin was looking directly at Stuart, making Stuart avert his gaze. *He sees through me*, he thought. *And yet, and yet . . . And yet he understands. Because I'm entitled to this. I'm entitled to a bit of romance after all those years with Irene. Why should I feel guilty about that? Why?*

And the answer came to him quite suddenly: *because this is Scotland, and guilt, historically, is what we feel – about so many things. You are not French, Stuart – if you were, there would be no problem. You are Scottish – and there it is.*

39. Skinny Latte, No Vanilla

He saw Katie the moment she came through the gallery's front door. He waved, but she did not see him, and was busy, anyway, taking off the light mackintosh she had been wearing; rain had been threatened, but not materialised. Once she had done that, she made her way purposefully past the gallery shop towards the café. Stuart was now standing to attract her attention, gesturing to the table he had secured.

'Have you been waiting for ages?' she asked. She leaned forward and planted a kiss on his cheek; he blushed.

I must get used to this, he thought. *There's nothing wrong – now – in being kissed by another woman.* And then he thought: *when did Irene last kiss me? Or I her?*

He shook his head in answer to her question. 'A few minutes. I was a bit early, but not all that much.'

She took the seat opposite his, and as she did so, she reached across the table to lay her hand upon his. 'I was at Valvona & Crolla. I think I told you.'

'Yes, you did. You were going to buy Parmesan cheese.'

She pointed to the bag she had been carrying. 'I get it there because it's much nicer than the stuff you get in supermarkets. I think that the supermarket cheese is younger. Parmesan cheese should be aged in those great big wheels. For years, I think.'

Stuart had seen segments of wheels, but never the full three hundred and sixty degrees, or at least not in the flesh, or in the curd, as one might say. Did one buy cheese in degrees? *Five degrees of Parmesan, please . . .*

She looked at him and smiled. 'One of these days I'll make you some Parmesan ice cream. Have you ever tasted it?'

'Parmesan ice cream?' It seemed unlikely to him.

Katie kissed her fingers in a gesture of gourmand satisfaction. 'Savoury ice creams are all the rage, you know. And it's not hard to make.'

'It just seems a bit unlikely.'

Katie smiled. 'There's more to life than vanilla, Stuart.'

He looked at her. Her remark had taken him by surprise. *Vanilla* had a code meaning; Stuart was worldly enough to know that, but surely Katie would not mean it in that sense. Perhaps *vanilla* could be generalised to embrace conventionality in cuisine. Fried chicken, spaghetti bolognese, pizza margarita – all of these were vanilla, in the sense that they were completely standard fare of the sort to be found on the menus of countless restaurants, whereas Parmesan ice cream was redolent of a much more exotic culinary life.

He laughed nervously. 'Oh, I know that.'

She was staring at him. He met her gaze, and then looked away. 'May I tell you something?' she said. 'I'm realising that you and I hardly know one another. I don't know what you like, for example. Just for example.'

He caught his breath. Once again, he was not sure how to interpret this remark. Was she talking about ice cream, and by extension his more general likes and dislikes when it came to food, or was this some other sense of *like*.

'I'm not sure what you mean,' he said. 'What I like . . . what I like about what?'

She shrugged. 'Nothing in particular. Or, rather, everything, I suppose. What music you like. What food. What you like to drink. I know that you like beer – you had that when we were in the Wally Dug. I know that at least. And I know you like brown leather deck shoes because . . .' She glanced down at his feet.

He was relieved. He did not want the conversation to drift into intimate areas, and of course that was not what she had meant at all.

'Music?' he said. Music was safe. 'I like music. I like music – I like it a lot.'

'I could tell that,' she said. 'You like poetry, and therefore you like music. *Post hoc, propter hoc.*'

He loved that. How many young women in their twenties could use Latin like that? Very few, he thought. It was just not what one expected . . . but *hic abundant leones*, he thought. Why should such a person *not* use Latin expressions? Were Latin expressions just for dry-as-dust male classicists, for whom nobody these days had any time? Such people were *history* – *historia*, even, and nobody needed to bother about them any longer, not according to the contemporary *Zeitgeist*.

'I know that you like poetry,' she continued, 'or you told me you do . . .'

'I do. I do like poetry.'

'That's great. It's just that I've found that when I mention that I'm doing a PhD in Scottish poetry, people say, "Oh, I love poetry," and you ask them to tell you who their favourite poet is, and then they look blank. Or after a while they say Burns, or William Wordsworth. You'd be surprised at how many people can't name *any* poets – other than Burns or Wordsworth.'

Stuart smiled. 'Fergusson,' he said. 'Henryson. Frost. Heaney. Longley. MacDiarmid. MacCaig. Kathleen Jamie. Liz Lochhead.' He beamed at her. 'Of course, Wordsworth is a bit ... a bit *vanilla*, wouldn't you say?'

Katie laughed. 'Definitely. Although there are poets who are far more vanilla poets than Wordsworth.' She paused. 'I wonder why nobody's ever published *An Anthology of Vanilla Poetry.*'

'Who would be in it?' asked Stuart.

Katie held up her hands in alarm. 'It would be an invidious business editing that. A minefield.'

Stuart pressed her. 'But there must be the usual suspects.'

Katie looked thoughtful. 'It might be easier to identify the vanilla poems themselves,' she said. '*Ode to a Nightingale, Fern Hill, If, Adlestrop, My Love Is Like a Red, Red Rose ...*'

'So you would include Burns?'

'Burns as a poet isn't vanilla,' Katie said. 'He doesn't belong there at all – as a poet – but what counts, you see, is what is *made* of the poem. So a very heartfelt, moving poem – one of great depth – can be made to be vanilla in the mouths of its proponents.'

Stuart nodded. 'I've always loved *Red, Red Rose.*'

'Of course you have. It's a beautiful, profound poem. A great poem. And it speaks to everyone.'

'So please take it out.'

She laughed. 'You're probably right. Okay, it's out.'

'And there's another one in your list,' said Stuart. '*Adlestrop* doesn't belong there. It's not vanilla poetry.'

'It isn't, I agree. And yet, if the test of vanilla is whether it's going to *offend* anybody, then *Adlestrop* won't offend. Who's going to take exception to a poem about stopping at a village station and hearing the steam hiss and birds sing? Nobody I know.'

Stuart pointed towards the service counter. 'There's no queue. Shall I get you a cup of coffee?'

'Please,' she said. 'Skinny latte.' And then she added, 'No vanilla.'

40. The Discomfort of the Past

Stuart came back with their coffee: her skinny latte and his cappuccino. Resuming his seat, he said, 'The problem, surely, with poetry – as with any of the arts – is working out how you defend a distinction between good and bad. We were talking about vanilla poetry in the sense of stuff that is, well, bland, I suppose.'

'Yes,' Katie said. 'We were. Poems that may be easy on the ear but don't really say very much. Or, if they do say something, say it in a way that doesn't *linger*.'

'And by *linger* you mean make an impression?'

'Yes, because they've stimulated our imagination. Or

because they raise an issue of importance. Or they make us weep, or gasp, or think *yes, precisely.* There are all sorts of ways in which poetry can escape being banal.'

Stuart nodded. 'Yes, I suppose there are. And we have to be able to say *this is a good poem* or *this is a bad poem*, don't we?'

Katie agreed that we did. 'There's a big difference between McGonagall, say, or his equivalent today, and a serious work of art.' She smiled. 'We have to be able to distinguish, otherwise we put the greeting card verse – the doggerel – on the same level as one of Shakespeare's sonnets. We know that there's a difference . . . '

'Of course there is.'

'But we have to be able to say *why* there is a difference,' Katie continued. 'It isn't just personal preference – it has to be something more than that.'

'And what is it?' asked Stuart.

'Depth. Profundity. Moral significance. That special quality that real art has of lighting up the world.' She paused. 'You know it when you see it – and then you have to have the courage of your convictions and say, outright, that the *jingles* are shallow and impermanent, of no lasting significance. People will hold up their hands and say, *Elitist!* And you have to be able to say, *No, you're wrong.* You have to be able to say that defending real art is *not* being elitist or, if it is, then there's nothing wrong with elitism. As long as your elitism is an *open* elitism – in other words, as long as it extends an invitation to everybody to come to the intellectual feast. You're not stopping anybody from enjoying art – you're saying, *Come on in. This is for all of you.*'

Stuart was inclined to agree. But he had been married to

Irene long enough to be aware of the forces ranged against that approach. 'I think you're right,' he said. 'But the problem is that there are plenty of people who judge art not by what it is, but by who made it.'

'There are,' said Katie. 'And if an artist's face doesn't fit, then bad luck. Or if the artist holds views that don't accord with what people are expected to believe.'

'Like the old Soviet Union,' said Stuart. 'If you didn't toe the party line, then you were silenced.'

He was not sure, though. Was that not a bit extreme? Was it really like that?

'Of course it's more subtle than that,' said Katie. 'The language of enforced conformism is different, but I think one would have to be naïve not to see it in operation right under our noses.' She sighed. 'In the past, men silenced women. We didn't hear women's voices because everything was dominated by men. People fought against that – thank goodness – and women's voices came to be heard – were given their proper place. But we have to be careful, I think, that we don't drift into the other position of discounting something because it happens to have been created by a man. That's just one example. There are others.'

Stuart thought about that. 'Are we in danger of doing that? Do you really think that's happening?'

'You tell me,' said Katie.

'I'm not sure,' said Stuart.

Katie looked at her watch. 'Have we got time to go upstairs?' she asked. 'There's an exhibition of portraits by Virginia Crowe. I'd rather like to see it.'

'Of course we have,' said Stuart. 'We have all the time in

the world. We don't have to go to Cramond. We can stay in town. We can have lunch here, or walk along to The Chaumer at the other end of the street and get lunch there. Why don't we do that?'

'I'd like that,' said Katie. 'Cramond can wait.'

A small group of young children walked past, having finished an early lunch at a nearby table under the supervision of several parents.

Katie asked, 'How old is your little boy again? Bertie? How old is he?'

'Seven,' said Stuart. And then he smiled as he remembered something. 'He told me that he came here with his class from the Steiner School. The teacher brought them all down to look at the paintings. She's called Miss Campbell.'

Katie smiled. 'Sweet.'

'Bertie said that they were looking at a portrait of Mary, Queen of Scots, and there was a heated discussion about what happened to her. One of the children said that she had had her head chopped off.'

'Well ...'

'There's a horrible little girl called Olive in Bertie's class. Apparently, this was the signal for her to go into gory detail about the execution, and about how Mary's little dog was hiding under her skirts. Awful details.'

Katie shuddered. 'Our history's full of cruelty.'

'But one of the boys came to the rescue and said that her head hadn't been chopped off – it *fell off.*'

Katie laughed. 'What a wonderful way of protecting children from grim reality. Presumably that child had been told this by a parent who didn't want him to be frightened.'

'I imagine so,' said Stuart. 'A benevolent rewriting of history.'

'Bertie asked me if it was true,' Stuart continued. 'He said, "Daddy, is it really true that Mary, Queen of Scots' head *fell* off?"'

'And you answered?'

Stuart looked into his coffee cup. 'I so wanted to protect Bertie. I so wanted to protect him from the cruelty of the world. I was so tempted.'

'I can understand why,' said Katie. 'The idea of chopping another person's head off is so abhorrent, so barbaric.'

'Yes, it's barbaric,' said Stuart. 'Yes, that's just what it is. But what's the difference between that and executing in any of the other ways on offer? Hanging, injecting them with poison, electrocuting them, gassing them. What's the difference?'

'None,' said Katie. 'They're all barbaric.'

'So I changed the subject,' said Stuart. 'I started to talk about something else. I just couldn't face telling him.'

'I understand,' said Katie.

He looked at her. He felt a sudden surge of tenderness, and knew that what he felt was love. He was sure of it.

Then Bruce Anderson arrived.

41. Behold Bruce Anderson

Bruce Anderson, property surveyor; alumnus of Morrison's Academy, Crieff; *aficionado* of a particular brand of clove-scented hair gel (no longer widely available); owner of a well-appointed flat in Abercromby Place (south-facing); breaker of hearts; narcissist … There were so many ways of describing Bruce, just as there are so many ways of describing virtually any of us, although in Bruce's case, each description concealed a hinterland of complications. Yet at the end of the day, a pithy description might be as apposite as any: *very good-looking – and knows it.* Now here was Bruce coming into the café of the Scottish National Portrait Gallery where his eye fell on Stuart, whom he knew, of course, from the Cumberland Bar. And then he saw who Stuart was with – noting, with interest, that it was not Irene, *that unspeakable woman*, as Bruce described her, but some rather attractive – no, *very* attractive – young woman who could hardly have anything to do with Stuart, of all people, who was such a thoroughly *hauden doun* husband.

The Scots expression, Bruce thought, said it perfectly, as Scots expressions so often did: *hauden doun* caught the nature of oppression under which Stuart had for many years laboured: held down, in English, which somehow made the subjugation seem less vivid and hopeless – and Stuart's life under Irene had been just that, thought Bruce. I would never have put up with that woman, he said to himself, although she would never have tried it with *me*. Women didn't, of course, he went on to think, because *I* have *them* in my thrall. They don't try that sort of thing with me because I can make them go weak at the knees just like *that* – and here Bruce imagined himself clicking his fingers – that's all – and Irene, or any other woman for that matter, going weak at the knees and gazing at him with that look that he so effortlessly evinced in women – that indefinable but unmistakable look that said, 'I'm yours.' *Hah!* thought Bruce, and then *Hah!* again: biology, pheromones, whatever – the trump card. Of course, it was all the more pronounced if he wore his kilt, he reminded himself; that sent them *wild*. Funny that, but it just did.

Now Bruce ignored the very strong convention – one that is written down nowhere, but that most people intuitively understand and observe: that if you go into a café or bar, or even more so, any restaurant, and you see somebody you know already seated, you do not go up to them and simply seat yourself at their table without first asking. What you do is that you approach and then say, 'Do you mind if I join you?' It is as simple as that. Or you might say, if the person already seated is alone, 'Are you waiting for somebody?' And then if – and only if – the person whom you know says, 'Please do,' or words to that effect, you sit down.

Of course, if the person whom you know is already with somebody, you are hesitant about approaching in the first place. People go to such places to talk, and may not want to involve others in their conversation. If you feel that, then you say, 'Don't let me interrupt,' and you then read the response. 'No, you're not interrupting – please join us' is usually enough to make it clear that you are welcome to do so, whereas a silence, even slight, will send the opposite message. Bruce ignored all this, drew up one of the two spare seats at the table and sat down.

'Crowded,' he said. 'This place is popular, isn't it?'

Stuart bit his lip.

'So,' Bruce continued, 'are you going to introduce us, Stuart?'

Stuart looked down at the table. He did not like Bruce; he never had. How was it possible, he had wondered, to be so pleased with yourself? What did it feel like to think there was no room for any possible improvement?

'This is Katie,' he said. And then, 'Katie, this is Bruce Anderson. He ...' He stopped. What could he say about Bruce? 'He lives in Abercromby Place.' It was lame, but it was true, and better than uttering the word that had come to mind: *Lothario*.

Katie looked at Bruce. She smiled at him. 'But I think we've met before, haven't we?'

Bruce shrugged. 'Yes, maybe ...'

Katie remembered. 'You weren't at Morrison's, were you? Crieff?'

Bruce's face broke into a smile. 'Morrison's? As a matter of fact, I was. And you?'

She did not let him finish. Now she remembered. 'You were two years ahead of me. You were the Bruce Anderson who used to live on the road that goes round to the Hydro. In that house near the golf course.'

'Yup,' said Bruce. 'That's me.' He paused. 'Grown up

now – as you may have noticed.' He laughed. 'And you know what? I think I remember you too. Yes, I think I do.'

'And you were friendly with that guy who became a helicopter pilot, weren't you?'

Bruce's smile broadened. 'Bobby Macleod? Yes, I was. We were great mates.' He turned to Stuart. 'Did you ever meet Bobby Macleod, Stuart? He played rugby. Winger. Boy, he could run.'

Stuart shook his head. This conversation was beginning to irritate him. It was not Bobby Macleod's fault, of course; he may well have been a distinguished rugby player and a good helicopter pilot too, for that matter, but Stuart did not want to go into any of that. He wanted to continue talking to Katie about poetry and art; they had only just started their conversation and then Bruce had turned up, and . . .

'I knew Bobby's sister,' said Katie. 'Jean – remember her?'

'Yes,' said Bruce. Jean had been in love with him, of course, but they all had been. She was a few years younger than him and had been beneath his notice, but there had been little doubt about it. When you were Bruce, you recognised *the look*. It was unmistakable.

Bruce looked at his watch. 'You know, I was going to have coffee here, but look at the time. How about lunch? Have you got any plans?'

Katie did not hesitate. 'No,' she said.

Stuart had been staring glumly at the portrait on the wall above their table, at Ian Rankin, who was staring back at him. They did have a plan – they were going to walk along Queen Street to have lunch at The Chaumer. He looked back sharply. 'Actually . . . '

He did not complete the sentence, as Bruce now said, 'Good, well, let's go to that place on the corner of Dublin Street, the Magnum. Know it? They do lunch.'

And Katie said, 'That's a great idea.' And then turned to Stuart and said, 'Stuart? Is that all right by you?'

Stuart took a moment to reply. Then he said, 'I'd forgotten. I have to be back to look after the kids. You go.'

42. Matthew and James Set Off

While Stuart was having his meeting with Katie in the café of the Scottish National Portrait Gallery – a meeting brought to such an unfortunate end by the arrival of Bruce Anderson and by his tactless and intrusive invitation to lunch – Nicola, along with Bertie and Ulysses, was being shown a choice of large spotted handkerchiefs in Stewart Christie's on Queen Street. And at that very time, Angus Lordie, with Cyril curled up on his studio blanket, was looking critically at his nascent painting of Glenbucket, while Domenica, almost alone now in 44 Scotland Street, was poring over an article on Neanderthal skulls. The Neanderthals were not of particular interest to Domenica; she regarded them, in fact, as somewhat dull country cousins – not people with whom one would look forward to spending the entire afternoon should they present themselves on one's doorstep. She was, however, now planning to compose an email, with pictures, to be sent to one of the authors featured in the latest issue of *Evolutionary Anthropology*. She was proceeding with caution: no finder of a skull should ignore the melancholy story of the Piltdown Man hoax, and she was not proposing to fall into that trap. She was not a palaeontologist; nor was she even a palaeoanthropologist, or an anthropopalaeontologist (if such a thing existed). She knew the limits of her *Fach* and would stick to them, but that did not preclude her from taking an interest in what might prove to be a very significant find.

If this did turn out to be a genuine early skull, it would undoubtedly attract wide attention. For a few moments, she allowed herself to imagine what name might be given to the find: there were the obvious descriptions of such things, of course: *Homo erectus, Homo habilis, Homo rudolfensis* and so on, and if this specimen were to be distinguished in any way from other examples of early man, then it too might be given a name of its own. That was a delicious prospect: *Homo angusus* would be a nice tribute to Angus, even if a slight mouthful, but then she thought that Angus's well-known modesty might preclude that. That was a pity, but one would not wish to saddle anybody with an eponymous fossil unless they willingly signed up to it. Professor Higgs, of course, had his Higgs Boson, but a boson was a rather different thing. It was no burden, she imagined, to have an invisible particle named after one. And then she remembered Pope Pius XI who had a South American glacier named in his honour – the Pio XI glacier in Chile – a dubious compliment, Domenica had always thought, bearing in mind the essentially chilly nature of glaciers. Had Pius XI been a cold personality? Had his normal manner been *icy*? Did he mind being a slow-moving river of ice?

No, if the skull were sufficiently distinguished to merit a name, then it would have to be something that reflected its Edinburgh origins. *Homo edinburgensis*, perhaps? *Edinburgh man* ... That was a possibility, but was not very imaginative. *Homo urbe novo – New Town man*? A bit of a mouthful, perhaps, and she was not sure about the locative case, which was a tricky case; in third declension nouns it was the same as the dative – or she hoped it was. *Homo watsoniensis*? Watsonian man? Domenica smiled. That had possibilities; yes, that had distinct possibilities.

And while all this was going on in Edinburgh, just outside town, at Nine Mile Burn, Matthew and the au pair, James, were setting off on a mission they had discussed and decided upon the previous evening. They were heading for Single Malt House, the home of James's uncle, the *soi-disant* Duke of Johannesburg and previous owner of the house now occupied by Matthew, Elspeth and their three sons.

'Tell me again why you're worried,' Matthew said as they drove past the encroaching rhododendrons.

As he asked the question, rhododendron branches, springy and lush in leaf, seemed to wrap the car in their embrace.

'I must do something about these wretched rhodies,' Matthew muttered. 'They're all over the place.'

'Let me try,' said James. 'I was reading an article about them in *Scottish Field*. There's a way of controlling them.'

'I'd appreciate it,' said Matthew. 'If you need to get any chemicals or anything, just let me know.'

'I don't approve of that,' said James. 'Let's stick to the

Geneva Convention. I think you have to do something to their roots.'

Matthew brought the conversation back to the Duke. 'So, what makes you think there's something wrong?'

'I haven't seen him,' said James. 'I used to go round there once a week. He used to phone me and invite me round. He usually had some work he wanted done in the garden or the steading or whatever. Then he stopped calling me.'

'Did you try to contact him?'

'I got his answering machine. I left messages, but he never got back to me.' He paused. 'I sent him an email.'

'And did that get a response?' asked Matthew. 'Or was he away?'

They were now at the road end; traffic shot past, liberated from Edinburgh, heading on the undulating road for the freedoms of West Linton and Biggar and the blue hills beyond.

'People drive far too fast here,' said Matthew.

'They're stupid,' agreed James.

'And rude,' added Matthew.

'Not everybody, though,' said James. 'I'm not saying everybody's stupid.'

'No, of course you aren't.' Matthew thought: particularly you. You have the nicest manners and you're bright and everybody loves you because you give every appearance of loving them. Matthew allowed his mind to wander: the loved are loved because they love; the hated are hated because they hate ... That was true, but only to an extent: there were many who did nothing to provoke the hate that came their way.

He glanced at James. 'Did he reply to your email?'

'Yes and no.'

Matthew frowned. 'What am I to make of that answer?'

'I had an email from his address,' James answered. 'It was definitely from *dukeofjohannesburg@whatever dot whatever* ... That's his address, all right, and it was signed by him, but there was something about it that made me suspicious.'

Matthew was intrigued. 'All right,' he said. 'You were suspicious. But why?'

James hesitated. 'You've heard of Bletchley Park?'

'The place where they decoded signals? Where they had the Enigma machines?'

'Yes, there was a film about it. Did you see it? It was about that guy who worked there who was a seriously good mathematician, and he invented a machine – the first computer actually – and he managed to crack the Enigma code.'

Matthew knew about that. 'Him and the Poles,' he said. 'People forget to give the Poles the credit they deserve.'

'Okay, and the Poles. But there were people there who did all sorts of things with the messages they intercepted, not just Enigma transmissions. They could tell who was operating a Morse key, for instance, from the style that was used, from the pace, the gaps. It was like listening to an accent. They could tell.'

'I've read about that,' said Matthew.

'Well, it's the same with email. People have a particular style – you get to know who's at the other end from their choice of words, their greeting, and so on.'

Matthew nodded. 'I suppose so. And?'

'Well, my uncle never says *Hi James*. He just doesn't.'

'And this email did?' asked Matthew.

'Almost,' said James. 'This one said *Hi Seamus.*'

Seamus, thought Matthew. *Seamus.*

43. At Single Malt House

They arrived at Single Malt House, the principal, indeed the only, seat of the Duke of Johannesburg. It was not a comfortable-looking house – the sort of house that would, in the country, and in the past, have been described as a *tacksman's house*, a house suitable for one who took a lease on a substantial piece of land but who was not considered the social equal of the local laird. Such houses were serviceable as farmhouses, but would have, in addition, a few good rooms that could be used for entertaining. A tacksman might even have a library and a gunroom, but could take family meals in a simple, rather than a formal dining room. Single Malt House had long since slipped out of that antique social order, and would now be just as likely to be in the hands of a lawyer or accountant who wished to live out of town but who could not be bothered with fields and livestock. Such a household would be on nodding terms with mud, with certain breeds of dogs, and with pheasants, of course, but would be well heated and draught-proofed – both features markedly absent from real working farmhouses.

Matthew parked the car under an oak tree at the end of the drive. Not far away, under a lean-to built against an old steading, was the car that he and James both recognised as the Duke's. This was the car that the Duke had bought from a man at Haymarket Station – a strange, canoe-sterned vehicle of no recognisable make, although there was a possibility that it might be Belgian.

'At least your uncle's car is here,' remarked Matthew, as he switched off the ignition. 'He must be in.'

Matthew looked doubtful. 'Sometimes he goes off in an ancient Land Rover,' he said. 'I don't see that around. But then the farm manager uses that a lot to go into Penicuik. He may have it.'

'What about that Gaelic-speaking chauffeur of his?' asked Matthew. 'What was his name again?'

'Pàdruig,' answered James. 'He never drives the Land Rover: he only drives the ... the ... '

'The Belgian car?' prompted Matthew.

'Yes,' said James.

Matthew began to get out of the car. 'Where does Pàdruig live?' he asked. 'Does he stay here?'

James shut the passenger door behind him. 'He has a small flat at the back of the house. He lives there, I think. He comes from Stornoway. He's the real McCoy. And before that, his people came from St Kilda. My uncle told me that. He said Pàdruig's grandfather had been one of those people who were lowered on ropes down the cliffs to harvest sea-birds' eggs.'

'It was a hard life,' said Matthew. 'I went there once, you know. When I was at school. A friend's father had a boat that

193

he kept at Ardfern. We sailed over to Barra and then on to St Kilda. It took us ages, but we managed to get into Village Bay. I found it really moving – the thought of all those people – the whole community – being taken away, off the island. A whole culture ended.' He paused. 'That wouldn't happen today.'

They began to follow a path that, skirting a somewhat unkempt lawn, led to the front door.

'Does your uncle normally cut his lawn?' asked Matthew.

James glanced at the uneven sward. 'He usually does,' he said. 'Sometimes it gets a bit long, but he usually cuts it. Or he gets the stockman to do it.'

'Well, he hasn't done that for a while,' said Matthew.

They approached the door; this dominated a small porch built out from the main façade of the house and of a different, lighter stone. On either side of the porch there was a large window, with astragals. Sun-blanched curtains were evident at the sides of these windows, but these were drawn back, affording a view of the rooms within. One was a drawing room, the other contained a large table on which papers and books were spread, as if to serve a working session that had suddenly ended. That's how it must have been on Hirta, out at St Kilda, Matthew thought: tables left with the things still upon them, the interrupted notes of a song still hanging in the air.

James pressed the doorbell, glancing at Matthew as he did so, giving a shrug, as if he already expected no response. The bell was surprisingly loud, and could be heard from somewhere within the house.

'Give it two rings,' suggested Matthew. 'Two rings always show you're serious.'

James pressed the bell again, but once more there was no response. James tested the door handle: it was locked. 'He never locks the door,' he said to Matthew.

Matthew looked up. On the floor above, a window was open. He pointed to it. 'Somebody's in,' he said. 'Look up there.'

James shrugged again. 'I don't know ...' He stopped. 'There's a window at the back, you know. The catch is broken. Once my uncle locked himself out and we crawled through the window. It's quite large.'

Matthew was not sure. 'I don't know about breaking into people's houses. I'm not sure that we should go that far.'

'He could be ill,' said James. 'He could be lying on the floor somewhere.'

Matthew hesitated. James was right, and there were times when people had to get into houses without the owner's consent. This, he decided, was probably one of those.

He had an idea. 'Have you got his phone number?' he asked.

James nodded. 'It's on my phone.'

'Well, why don't you phone him – just on the off-chance? See what happens.'

James took his mobile from his pocket and tapped at the screen. Almost immediately they heard a phone ringing within the house. And almost immediately the ringing stopped.

'Uncle?' James said, in a surprised tone.

There was a silence, and then a click as the receiver at the other end was put down. James turned to Matthew in astonishment. 'He's inside.'

Matthew made up his mind. 'Show me this window,' he said.

They walked round to the back of the house, the gravel crunching beneath their feet. They disturbed a bird that had been perching on a windowsill, a thrush, in a speckled waistcoat, thought Matthew. It swooped off into the foliage of a garden shrubbery.

'That's the window,' said James, pointing to a window that was a good eight feet above the ground.

'I'll give you a leg-up,' said Matthew. 'Then you reach down and give me a hand.'

He thought, as he crouched, his hands cupped to provide a lifting stirrup for James: when did I last do this? Did I *ever* do this before?

44. *Something Very Odd*

As James had predicted, the window, unsecured by a working catch, had opened at the merest touch. Once he had manoeuvred himself inside, he turned round and leaned over the sill to extend a hand to Matthew. With one hand grasped by James and the other scrabbling for purchase on the sill, Matthew managed to pull himself up to join his cohousebreaker. Then, with a squeeze and a certain amount of pulling and pushing, they were both safely in a small scullery. This room, lined with shelves, had a Belfast sink and several stacked and unopened wooden cases of claret.

Matthew felt his heart racing within him. This was, technically, a criminal intrusion. The fact that you were in a house with the permission of the occupant's nephew presumably made no difference to the fundamental illegality of the entry. Of course, you could claim that you were only in the house in order to check up on the householder, but Matthew suspected that such an excuse might be difficult to assert. The Duke could reasonably point out that he had not answered the door simply because he did not want to admit anybody to the house. You were entitled to do that, after all, in your own house.

James picked up Matthew's nervousness and sought to reassure him. 'Don't worry,' he said. 'My uncle won't mind. I regularly let myself in.'

'But,' said Matthew. 'But ...'

He did not finish. James had touched him on the forearm and placed a finger to his lips: he had heard a noise within the house, although he was unsure what it was – the clearing of a throat, perhaps; the scraping of a chair against a floorboard; the tapping of a branch against a windowpane. No house is entirely silent: the small sounds of a building's respiratory system, its circulation, the creaking of its bones, are there to be heard if one stops to listen for them. But this was more than that – this was the sound of human presence, and now it was repeated.

Signalling to Matthew to follow him, James walked quietly towards the door that linked the scullery to a corridor. Then he pointed to another door, at the end of the corridor. 'That's my uncle's study,' he whispered to Matthew. 'We should go and take a look.'

They made their way along the corridor. The study door was pulled to, but not closed, and James had simply to push gently to open it.

Matthew gave a start. There, seated in an armchair, his legs up on a table, holding an open book across his stomach, was Pàdruig, the Duke's driver. As the door opened, he remained where he was, only moving his head slightly to stare at the two intruders.

'Well,' said Pàdruig. 'So it's yourselves.'

It was not a statement with which Matthew felt he could disagree. Nor could James.

James managed a smile. 'I thought we'd give you a surprise, Pàdruig,' he said breezily. And then added, 'Where's my uncle?'

Pàdruig shrugged. 'Out.'

James hesitated. He glanced at Matthew. 'Out where?'

'Just out,' said Pàdruig. 'He doesn't always say, you know. He goes out.' He paused. 'And then he comes back.'

James glanced at Matthew again. 'Has he gone into Edinburgh?' he asked.

Pàdruig shrugged again. 'Could be. Sometimes he goes in for lunch on a Saturday.'

'You don't drive him?' asked Matthew.

Pàdruig had been looking at James; now he shifted his gaze to Matthew. 'Sometimes he likes to drive himself. He takes his car.'

'But that's parked outside,' said James. 'I saw it.'

Pàdruig moved the book from his stomach to a nearby table and then rose to his feet. He was a large man with the colouring and bearing of an extra from one of those films of Highland warriors. A claymore, Matthew thought, would not be out of place. 'I can tell him you were here,' he said, his tone businesslike. 'When he comes back, I can tell him. I'm sure he'll be sorry to have missed you.'

James bit his lip. 'I've tried to phone him,' he said. 'I've phoned twenty or thirty times. He always used to return my calls.'

'Perhaps his mobile's battery is flat,' said Pàdruig. 'I'm always telling him to recharge it, but he doesn't, or doesn't do it often enough, and then he can't pick up calls. You know how it is.'

'But I've phoned him on the landline,' said James. 'I get nowhere with that as well.'

Pàdruig affected nonchalance. 'Your uncle's a busy man. He has the estate to manage – and the cattle are always getting out. They lead him a merry dance, and he's only got one stockman. I think things may get on top of him.'

James did not respond. He moved towards his uncle's desk and looked at the papers on top of it. There were several envelopes, one of them lined in red and bearing the legend, *Final Demand*.

'There's one thing you can never criticise my uncle for,' said James. 'That is – paying his bills. He makes a point of paying on the nose always. The day he receives a bill, he pays it.'

Pàdruig tensed – and Matthew noticed that. He decided to take the initiative. 'I think we should wait, James,' he said. 'We should wait here until your uncle comes back.' He turned to Pàdruig and smiled politely. 'You won't have any problem with that, will you? You must have work to get on with.'

Pàdruig's eyes narrowed. 'He's not coming back for a

long time,' he said. 'He's often not in until eleven at night. I wouldn't want you to wait that long.'

James looked uncertain, and so Matthew said, 'We'll come back tomorrow. Sunday. I take it the Duke will be in then.'

Pàdruig smiled ingratiatingly. 'That's much better. But remember: phone beforehand to see if he's in. I wouldn't want you to waste your time.'

James nodded. 'We'll do that. But I'm very anxious to see my uncle. Please tell him we were here.'

Pàdruig nodded quickly. 'Of course. Of course.'

They left, this time using a door rather than a window. Once outside, James looked over his shoulder, before saying to Matthew, 'That was positively creepy.'

Matthew agreed. He was worried, but he wanted to be tactful. 'Do you think something's going on?'

James shook his head. 'Who knows? I hope not, but I don't think my uncle is in town. I think he's ... he's ...' He trailed off. He was not sure what he thought.

Matthew now made an important observation. 'Did you notice,' he said, 'that there were cardboard signs on some of the things in the study? On the bookcase (*preasa*), on the door (*dorus*), on the telephone (*fòn*), and so on? Cardboard signs with Gaelic on them. Gaelic names for the things?'

'As if somebody's trying to teach my uncle Gaelic,' said James.

Matthew nodded. 'That's what I thought,' he said. 'I assume that's Pàdruig.'

'But my uncle never expressed any interest in learning Gaelic,' said James.

'That's what makes it a bit suspicious,' said Matthew. He thought for a moment. 'Do you think ... Do you think he might be being *held*? Held, and *made* to learn Gaelic?'

It was a preposterous idea. This was the twenty-first century: why would anybody force anybody else to learn Gaelic, he wondered – useful though Gaelic would be. Matthew had often regretted not learning it at school, where it had been an optional subject. He liked Gaelic poetry, which he had read in translation; he liked Gaelic song; and he was all for the survival of threatened languages. But he was not sure why anybody should *force* anybody to learn a language. Surely it was impossible that the Duke was being held against his will – held in *Gaelic* immersion – at the behest of his driver? It was far more likely that he had been spirited away for reasons that would become apparent, but only when – and if – they found him.

45. *Drawing and Grammar*

That Saturday, Angus did not make the progress he had hoped to make with the Glenbucket portrait. He was working from photographs in between live sittings, and he never felt entirely comfortable with that. It was good enough for minor passages in the painting – for work on the detail of cloth, or buttons, or for general background – but when it came to painting the human face, there was no substitute for a live encounter between artist and subject. That was not only to do with light, and its unpredictable vagaries, but it was a question of life itself – the presence that one detected in an animate object, the pulse, the breath, the soul: there were so many terms that could describe it. It was the *atman* and the *jiva* of the *Bhagavad Gita* and the *Upanishads*, the soul of Traherne and Eckhart; it was the same thing, and although most of us never stopped to think much about it, or even to find a name for it, let alone a theological structure, we could tell when it was there and when it was not. Angus remembered his father telling him of how he had been present at the death of an elderly relative, a sheep farmer from Lochaber, and of how he had known the precise moment when he had ceased to be. 'The very transition was clear,' he said. 'A light went out. There was nobody there any longer. It was, well, it was a passage.' That description had impressed itself upon him even though he was only ten at the time, an age when the whole issue of death is entirely academic, having nothing to do with oneself. The memory returned to him in life-drawing classes at art college, when the model sometimes lay in repose, and on a warm day might even drop off to sleep. The human body in sleep is not motionless: slight movements, brief flickers, proclaim personhood, reveal the presence of life; but it is not just these that tell you there is a soul within the physical envelope, it is something else altogether – an electromagnetic field perhaps – that is unmistakable.

Life-drawing classes ... As he worked on the portrayal of a tablecloth behind his subject, he remembered those classes, compulsory in those days for all art students: drawing, it was believed, was a basic skill expected of any artist. Drawing is to art as grammar is to language: you can speak without any knowledge of grammar, but do not expect to be understood, and certainly do not expect to become a poet. And as a poet, even equipped with grammar, you will be severely limited in the creation of poetry if you do not understand how a language is put together, how the flesh of sentences conceals a skeleton of rules underneath. You may not use techniques of stress and metre – you may write nothing but free verse – but if they are not there in the background, the music of language will not come; the prose will never ascend to the level of poetry. So Angus believed, and nothing he saw in contemporary conceptual art persuaded him otherwise. Without rigorous training in the fundamentals of the craft, a pedestrian, inarticulate banality prevailed.

At those life-drawing classes, starting three mornings a week at nine o'clock sharp – a punishing hour for the bohemian ranks of art students – they sat in the echoing, cavernous studios of the Art College, with the light flooding in from the north; the Castle their background, stern, forbidding, redolent of ancient conflicts, its ramparts and the sheer drop of the Castle Rock a reminder of the days when burning oil might be dropped on unwelcome visitors below – Scotland in those days was most decidedly a non-inclusive place; sitting there, slightly cold, surveying the goose-pimpled model – in spite of the two-bar radiator that the college thoughtfully provided for the naked – conversing occasionally, and *sotto voce*, so as not to disturb one's fellow students, one's thoughts might wander from the task in hand. But that was no bad thing: the aim, after all, was to develop such a facility in drawing that the movements of the hand holding the pencil became automatic, guided by inner brain pathways that were laid down by constant practice, habilitating themselves for our human demands, as are our everyday movements, our walking, our gestures, our ways of conducting ourselves as physical beings.

His thoughts wandered to the circumstances in which he found himself, a newly fledged art student, living in Edinburgh away from the confines of home – not that home was in any sense particularly confining, but it did represent a whole world from which Angus wanted to detach himself. That world might glibly have been described as a bourgeois milieu – and that was certainly how his fellow students spoke of their predominantly middle-class backgrounds, disparaging, even if with a degree of fondness and humour, the attitudes of their parents, their work ethic, their petty concerns over the avoidance of debt and noise and messy relationships – but that description of the world from which Angus had migrated to Edinburgh did not capture the essence of the Perthshire circle whose dust he had brushed off his heels in going to the Art College. Angus came from something different from bourgeois suburbia; he had been brought up in an extended family of substantial farmers, against a background of large, rambling houses, where a hazy romanticism rubbed shoulders with a feeling for a Scotland of the past, where people were known by the name of their lands, or their clan; where the rugs on which one picnicked were always tartan – though nobody's tartan in particular – where the name of the whisky you drank was important, and where there was a bone-deep conviction, never articulated, that Scotland was a place to which everywhere else could only be compared adversely. England, Ireland, France were all very well, but they were not Scotland; the English were tolerated, but not necessarily loved; the Irish were amusing, but different in a subtle way; the French were admittedly good players of rugby and artistically and gastronomically admirable, but the Auld Alliance, wheeled out at sentimental dinners, was a long time ago, remembered in Scotland perhaps, but forgotten in France. From that world, with its quaint certainties, Angus had escaped at the age of eighteen, with his A grade in Higher Art, a portfolio of drawings and watercolours executed in the art department of Trinity College, Glenalmond, and a belief that he had embarked on a journey that would lead to his becoming not only an artist but a great artist. In that spirit, he arrived in Edinburgh and took up the accommodation arranged for him in digs run by a Mrs Anna Symanski, the seventy-year-old widow of a Polish airman who had escaped to Scotland at the age of twenty, had married within months, and survived numerous aerial engagements, only to fall from the skies over Germany a few months before the end of the war. His young widow, from Dunfermline, had spent a total of fourteen weeks with her husband, but never remarried. She learned Polish to honour his memory – they had never conversed in his native tongue – and converted to Catholicism for good measure: touching acts of homage to a brave and good man.

These digs were far from comfortable, but Angus reminded himself that art students traditionally lived in garrets, and that being in a Georgian house off Leith Walk was a distinct improvement, especially if one pretended that the other residents were not there.

46. *An Art Student's Digs*

For long decades Mrs Symanski took students, and other lodgers, into the house she had inherited from an aunt, who, like her, was a widow; in the aunt's case, of a Leith general practitioner. The aunt had gone off to live in Troon with her sister, and had made the house over to her niece to give her a livelihood. It was an act of great generosity, motivated not only by family affection, but by an awareness of what the country owed to the unsung heroes of the Polish air force, who lost their own country, but helped to save that of so many others.

'Take lodgers,' the aunt had said. 'You have five rooms to let out. Put two students in each. That makes ten altogether. You could live quite comfortably on the income from that.'

Mrs Symanski had followed this advice. Although she had a preference for students, she also took in the occasional junior civil servant or struggling office worker. Sometimes men from the bonded warehouses of Leith came to stay for a few months when they were turned out of their homes by their wives; occasionally nurses from the Eastern General took a room while they were waiting for something better.

There were rules that were strictly enforced: nobody was to come in at night later than eleven-thirty, at which time Mrs Symanski locked the front door against all comers; nobody was to consume alcohol in their bedrooms or in the bathroom; guests of the opposite sex were to be entertained only in the front parlour, where a small television, permanently switched on, made conversation difficult; and finally, there was to be no shouting or swearing in any circumstances. A young man from Ayrshire, who had littered his conversation with profanity, had lasted one week before he was asked to go elsewhere, as Edinburgh, Mrs Symanski explained, was not a place in which such language was welcome. They were, in fact, in Leith, but the point still stood.

She was an astute businesswoman and did not hesitate to make maximum use of the space she had. A box room at the back of the house was converted to a single bedroom, even though it had no window and was large enough only for the shortest of available beds. In Angus's time, that was occupied by the shortest of the house's tenants, a young man from Dundee, who was barely five feet tall, a junior clerk in the offices of the City Council, whose main interest in life was yodelling. Mrs Symanski had been at school with this young man's mother, and had made an exception to her rules to allow him to yodel in the house, but only in his room, and with the door closed. That did not prevent the yodelling from being heard elsewhere, and there were complaints, but they were never acted upon.

Behind the house there was a small garden. Somehow or other, Mrs Symanski had contrived to have a caravan placed in this garden, possibly by having it lifted by a crane from the lane behind the house and then deposited immediately outside the kitchen. Angus, and others, had asked her how the caravan got there, but she had never provided an answer, simply tapping the side of her nose and saying, 'There are ways of doing anything if you know the right people.' This caravan, which had permanently flat tyres and a film of green algae growing up its side from where the rainwater dripped off the roof, had been procured to house an extra tenant. He was called Richard, and he worked as a draughtsman in a civil engineering firm. 'I'm saving to go to Canada,' he said to Angus. 'That's why I endure the humiliation of living in Mrs S.'s caravan. She charges me half of what you inside people pay. When I get the money, that's me off to Toronto. Goodbye, caravan.'

Breakfast was provided by Mrs Symanski, as was an evening meal. These were served in the largest room in the house, which had been the doctor's drawing room, and into which a four-leaf dining-room table had been moved. This managed to seat everybody, with a chair at one end being reserved for Mrs Symanski, although she rarely sat on it. She was busy in the kitchen, where, assisted by a maid, she prepared the food. Breakfast was an indeterminate cereal, cardboardy in consistency and taste, thin slices of toast, and fried egg, bacon and sausage. The evening meal was soup, followed by a fish or meat course served with mashed potatoes and a green vegetable, often cabbage, but sometimes spinach or tinned peas. For a surcharge added to your monthly rent, you could entitle yourself to a slice of cake at the end of the meal.

Baths were fifty pence, payable in advance, and booked with Mrs Symanski. 'Hot water is very expensive,' she said.

'I would like to make baths free, but that is not the world we live in.'

Mrs Symanski quickly took a shine to Angus.

'That boy has manners,' she said to a friend. 'He's a gentleman, you see. He's trying to be an artist, but at heart he's a gentleman.'

He showed her his work, including his life drawings. She raised an eyebrow at the nudes. 'You wouldn't see that sort of thing in Dunfermline,' she said.

She asked him whether he might paint a picture of her late husband. 'I can show you photographs,' she said. 'I can show you photographs of Anton in his air force uniform.'

Angus was happy to oblige. He chose a large canvas and painted his subject standing at the edge of an airfield, with two Spitfires in the sky behind him, performing an aerial ballet. It was a good likeness, as even then Angus's ability as a portrait painter was showing itself. Mrs Symanski looked at it and then leaned forwards and kissed the portrait, kissed the lips of the husband she had lost all those years ago, and wept.

'I think of him every day,' she said, wiping her eyes with her handkerchief. 'Every day, I think of what my Anton might say to me, if he were still with me.'

'Of course you do,' said Angus. 'Of course you do.'

'And now you have painted him so well. It will bring him back to me even more powerfully.'

'I'm glad,' said Angus.

'These days nobody knows what it was like,' she continued. 'They don't know what it was like for those brave boys – your age, Angus. They stared death in the face every single day, and they knew that they had not to care, or to pretend not to care, because if you started to think about it you would be unable to get on with what you had to do.'

'I can imagine,' said Angus.

She kissed him, in gratitude, as she had kissed the painting. After that, for the entire year he spent in that house, Angus was allowed a free bath every day, much to the annoyance of the other lodgers, whose egalitarian sentiments were somehow offended by this sign of favour. That reaction provided a lesson for Angus that subsequent experience proved time and time again: that most people were, at heart, envious of what others had, no matter how hard they tried to control their envy. That explained so much: from widespread willingness that more tax should be paid by everyone with an income greater than one's own, to the satisfaction felt when those we know lose their money through misfortune. We love Nemesis when her radar picks up those in the public eye; we are, understandably, less enamoured of her when she turns to those such as ourselves, the innocent, the deserving.

47. Unauthorised Biting

That was long ago, and now the callow art student was an established portrait painter, in demand for portraits of husbands, commissioned by wives, of wives, commissioned by husbands, and of various public figures – the provosts of burghs, long-serving politicians, successful financiers – as well as those who had done nothing in particular with their lives but whose vanity was tickled by the thought of a portrait. Angus painted with moral attention: he did not conceal or distort, but he understood ordinary human sensitivities. So, undictated to by his sitter, he instinctively found his or her best side, minor imperfections were dealt with charitably or made to seem a badge of character, and noses, if necessary, were slightly straightened or made less prominent. All of this was done out of kindness, that quality that eclipses all the other virtues, and that of itself is a perfectly adequate guide to the living of a good life.

There may have been little progress made on Glenbucket's portrait that Saturday, but on the following Monday Angus had arranged for his subject to come to the studio at ten in the morning for a two-hour sitting. This would allow for sustained work on the face, particularly on the brow – Glenbucket's most prominent feature. His was a strong face, one quite capable of bearing several centuries of genealogy, even if the genealogy involved tenuous and unconfirmed connections. The eyes were piercing, hawk-like, thought Angus, and the generous moustache, of the sort sometimes referred to as a walrus moustache, could only be sported by one who was confident in who he was. If you passed Glenbucket in the street, you would certainly notice him, and speculate perhaps on who he was and what he did: he was a farmer, perhaps, or an army officer who had allowed himself to expand a bit in the mid-section, or a captain in the merchant navy, on shore leave.

You would not guess his provenance. You would not know from his clothes or his overall look that this was the joint owner, along with a French businessman, of a small distillery on Speyside. You would not guess that this was a man who had a pilot's licence; who read Ronsard and Apollinaire; who had invented a hot pepper sauce that was stronger than Tabasco and was produced for export in Baton Rouge, Louisiana. Nor would you guess that this was a man whose emotional life was dominated by a single consuming passion – not for another, but for a country, for Scotland.

Of course, his kilt, and the associated band of tartan draped across his shoulder, might have pointed in the direction of patriotism. And it was in this garb that he now stood before Angus, looking out, as instructed, past Angus, at a fixed point on the wall behind, where Cyril's lead hung on a peg, along with the fob on which the key to Drummond Place Garden was secured.

Cyril himself lay on his studio blanket, feigning sleep but gazing, with a certain fascination, at the two sturdy, tartan hose-clad ankles that supported Glenbucket in all his Highland finery. Ankles, for Cyril, were a major moral challenge – perhaps the only moral challenge with which he had to wrestle. A dog is never tempted by the possibility of disloyalty or betrayal – such concepts are completely alien to the canine view of the world. A dog is never troubled by guilt if he succumbs to the temptation of discovered food, or if he chews on something that he knows he is not meant to chew upon. A dog may learn to expect punishment if he does any of those things, but he does not regard them as a moral issue. What is a moral issue, for a dog, though, is the question of when it is legitimate to bite a human. An authorised bite is one thing; an unauthorised one is quite another. Such a bite transgresses a term of the ancient compact between the canine and the human worlds, and dogs know it. And yet ankles for a dog are a target so tempting that it is sometimes impossible to do anything but break the terms of that old social contract and sink one's teeth into an irresistible ankle. Cyril had done that from time to time in the past – particularly when confronted with Matthew's ankles under the table at Big Lou's coffee bar. The last time he had done that, giving Matthew a quick and hastily disengaged nip on the right ankle, he had been immediately punished by Angus – but it was worth it. The sheer pleasure of biting somebody's ankle is something of which many dogs can only dream, but Cyril had done something to realise it, and he knew that it was every bit as satisfying as it might be imagined to be.

'Your dog,' said Glenbucket, 'is watching me. I suppose I'm in his territory here, and he feels he has good reason to keep an eye on me.'

Angus glanced at Cyril from behind his canvas.

'I hope you don't mind his being here,' he said. 'He always keeps me company when I'm working in the studio. But I suppose I should ask people whether they mind.'

'I don't mind in the slightest,' said Glenbucket. 'I was raised with dogs. We had Dandie Dinmonts – you know those funny little dogs that Sir Walter Scott was so keen on. They were named after his character in *Guy Mannering*.'

'Of course,' said Angus. 'One of Scott's nicest characters, I think.'

'They've become quite rare,' said Glenbucket. 'People

are being encouraged to breed them in case they disappear altogether. My mother was very keen on them. She had four at one time, when we lived near Bridge of Earn. They were given to her by one of her lovers.'

Angus raised an eyebrow, but continued to paint.

'Your mother had lovers?' he asked, and then, realising this was an intrusive question, added, 'Not that I should ask that sort of thing.'

'Oh, she had lovers all right,' said Glenbucket. 'She was infinitely alluring to men. They took one look at her and became weak at the knees. I saw it happen time and time again.' He paused, and smiled at a memory. 'I remember when she was stopped for speeding in Italy once, on the road out of Perugia. I was in the car with her – I was about four-teen at the time, and embarrassed, as all fourteen-year-olds are, by my parents. I knew she had lovers, you see – I called them uncles – and I realised that none of the mothers of any of my friends strayed from the straightest and narrowest of paths in that respect. But mine did, and barely tried to con-ceal the fact from me.

'The policeman flagged us down and came up to speak to my mother. He was wearing one of those Carabinieri uniforms – you know, dark blue jodhpurs and shining boots, mirror-like in the intensity of their polish – and a cap that peaked in a jaunty manner, sporting that Carabinieri symbol of a flaming torch.

'I imagined that all was lost and that a heavy fine would be imposed, or that my mother would be dragged off to some medieval Italian prison, full to the gunnels with Mafiosi and ferrety Sicilian pickpockets, sent from the South to pick the pockets of the North, but no, my mother simply smiled at the policeman and then complimented him on his uniform. He was clearly pleased, and they spent the next twenty minutes discussing the cut of his trousers and jacket, before he waved us on with a recommendation of a restaurant in Assisi, near the Basilica of Saint Francis, where Giotto portrays Saint Francis feeding the birds, in which the speciality of the house was, by unironic coincidence, roast partridge and various little birds – swallows and the like – done to a tee on the spit.'

48. *Little Hans, the Wolf Man, etc.*

Elspeth had wasted no time in putting into effect the plan upon which she and Matthew had agreed with James. The essence of the scheme was that James should be relieved of some, although not all, of his duties as an au pair, by the engagement of an assistant. The major part of these duties consisted of looking after Matthew and Elspeth's energetic and highly demanding triplets, Fergus, Tobermory, and Rognvald. That was a job at which he had excelled, effortlessly managing these rambunctious toddlers, involving them in physical activities designed to use up their endless capacity for rushing around – although they never did completely deplete their stores of energy – and somehow marshalling them so that they could be clothed, fed, and washed, and then – twelve hours later – read a bedtime story before being returned to bed. In her more despairing moments, Elspeth reflected on how the whole regime seemed to be an exercise in containment aimed at stopping the boys from destroying too much, from climbing and then falling out of trees, from running off into the mists of the Pentland Hills, and from falling foul of the ill-tempered Highland cattle that grazed a field adjacent to their garden. It was a task that she felt, quite frankly, she was unable to perform unaided, and James had been a godsend. His rapport with the boys, established within minutes of his arrival, had meant that they listened to him and, for the most part, did his bidding. Neither parent knew, or even suspected, that although James had a natural ability to win over anybody, including small children, he had made it clear to the triplets that they were to obey him and cause no trouble. This he had done by whispering in the ear of each of them, 'If you are naughty, you know what will happen? One of those Highland cows out there will come and bite you. Hard!'

It had worked perfectly. Whenever there was an outbreak of tantrums or even a surly refusal to do as bidden, James would simply mutter *Highland cows!* and the child in question would immediately comply with whatever was asked of him. James had not thought of the psychological consequences that can follow upon threatening a child with a vivid sanction, nor of the power that a fear of being bitten by an animal may hold. He was unfamiliar with the *locus classicus* of such a question, Freud's extraordinary case of Little Hans, the small boy whose analysis at one remove – Little Hans's father reported to Freud what his son said and asked his son the questions that Freud suggested he ask – was to become a landmark case in the Freudian movement. Little Hans was worried that the dray horses he saw in the street would bite him, a fear that Freud quite reasonably interpreted as being in reality a fear that his father would castrate him for desiring his mother. It is difficult, of course, to see what else the basis of such a fear could be, other than that horses are large creatures occasionally known to bite people. Such a naïve view, of course, ignores the glaring fact that the horse represented the father and the black hair around the horse's mouth clearly stood for the father's moustache.

Little Hans survived to become a successful producer of operas in Europe and America. He left his childhood phobias behind him and led a happy and constructive life. By contrast, Pankejeff, another of Freud's famous patients, did not fare so well. Pankejeff became known in Freudian literature as the Wolf Man, a sobriquet derived from a very important dream he had in which he saw wolves sitting in trees. Freud decided that this dream was the result of the Wolf Man's having witnessed, as a child, parental intimacy – known in Freudian terms as the *primal scene*. This is something best not seen by small children, or indeed by larger children, or by anybody else really. In Pankejeff's case it led to six decades of psychoanalysis – one of the longest analyses on record. Freud had declared the Wolf Man to be cured, but this appeared not to be the case, and years later he might be seen standing in the street staring into a mirror, convinced that a doctor had drilled a hole in his nose. Most noses do, in fact, have two holes, but this, presumably, was a supernumerary one. Pankejeff wrote a memoir, *The Wolf Man*, in which he discussed his condition and his prolonged engagement with psychoanalysis; he was never very happy, and interminable analysis did little to relieve his angst.

Sixty years of analysis seems a long time during which to contemplate one's psyche. In one case, though, the analysis might be seen as lasting for eternity. This is suggested by the history of the psychoanalytical movement in Morocco, not the most receptive territory for Freudian ideas. Very few psychoanalysts have practised in Morocco, although for a brief period after the fall of the Vichy regime, French analysts who had been compromised by their association with a collaborationist school of analysis retreated to Casablanca, where they opened a psychoanalytical institute. Their patients might have remained in France, but did not, such is the dependence that might develop between analyst and analysand. They accompanied their analysts into exile, and when, in due course, both patients and analysts died, they were buried side by side. So the patients lie for eternity, on an earthly couch, silent beside their equally silent analysts.

James thought of none of this when he discovered this convenient way of ensuring good behaviour on the triplets' part. And it is entirely possible that the boys were unscarred by the whispered threat and developed no phobias relating to Highland cows. A Highland cow, after all, features on the wrapper of a well-known brand of Scottish toffee, and James was liberal in distributing sticks of this toffee to his young charges. The association of Highland cows with the pleasure of a mouthful of McCowan's Highland Toffee probably outweighed any negative association, or any incipient Oedipal issues, and thereby avoided any need for future analysis. Toffee, of course, confers an additional benefit in childrearing: a child whose teeth are stuck together with toffee for long periods is unlikely to girn or ask interminable questions, giving an exhausted mother a few moments of peace. Such a fix might help parents at the end of their tether, but is frowned upon in the enlightened circles in which Matthew and Elspeth certainly saw themselves moving. But there are many things disapproved of in enlightened circles that actually work rather well in the real, even if unenlightened, world.

49. Scandinavian Affairs

The whole point of relieving James of some of his responsibilities for the triplets was to allow him to spend the time so freed working with Big Lou in her coffee bar – a business in which Matthew now had a considerable financial stake. This suited James, who was a keen and exceptionally talented cook, as well as suiting Matthew, who felt that something had to be done to revitalise the coffee bar and attract a few more customers. Lou herself, of course, was indifferent to that objective. 'If people want to come to my coffee bar, that's up to them,' she said. 'I don't want to be pestering them.'

'It's not a question of pestering, Lou,' Matthew had explained. 'It's a question of enticing them. If you have a good menu, people will flock to you. There's quite good footfall going up and down Dundas Street.'

'Footfall?' asked Lou. 'You mean: people walking by – on their ain twa legs?'

Matthew smiled. 'Footfall is a technical term that you hear in the retail sector, Lou.'

This brought another snort from Big Lou. 'Retail sector? You mean *shops*, Matthew?'

Matthew grinned. 'You're right, Lou,' he conceded. 'There's a lot of circumlocution around.'

'You mean *havering*?' Like many Scots words, there was no English word that did quite the work of *havering*.

Matthew realised that although Lou had acquiesced to the broad shape of the plan – the freshening up of the coffee bar's décor and the creation of a new menu – she was luke-warm about having James as her new assistant. 'He's just a laddie,' she said.

'We'll see,' said Matthew, and then, becoming more formal, he added, 'And remember, Lou, this place has a management board now, and I'm on it. In fact, I control it – not that I wanted to make much of that, but there you have it.'

Big Lou looked momentarily taken aback, but then she added, 'I'm sure he'll be fine – if he's what you make him out to be.'

'He is,' Matthew reassured her. 'You wait and see, Lou.'

Of course, before James could begin to work at the coffee bar, the new au pair had to be found, and that, Matthew was concerned, could take time. But then Elspeth found herself in the nearby village, West Linton, talking to a fellow member of her mother and toddler group. This woman mentioned that she had just visited a friend in the village whose husband, a helicopter pilot, was being sent by his company to Dubai, and would have to leave more or less immediately. His wife and two young children would be moving too, and the husband was keen that they should all go at the same time. They employed, however, an au pair who could not get a work permit in the UAE and who would therefore have to find another job in Scotland, or go elsewhere.

Elspeth asked for details.

'She's Swedish, I think,' said her friend. 'Or maybe Danish. I get these places mixed up. Which is the one at the top?'

'That's Finland,' said Elspeth. 'At the top, on the right. Sweden is in the middle, but it goes quite a way up.'

'This doesn't go very far up.'

'You mean Denmark then?'

'I think so.'

It had been an unsatisfactory conversation from the geographical point of view, but it promised to be a quick and easy solution to the au pair issue. Having been given the telephone number of the helicopter pilot's wife, Elspeth called her and was told that the family was already packing up and that Josefine, the young Danish woman who had been with them for four months, would probably leap at the chance of the job of helping with the triplets. 'She adores children,' Elspeth was told. 'She has them eating out of her hand.'

'And she wants to stay in Scotland?'

'Absolutely. There's a boyfriend, I believe.' There was then a slight hesitation. 'In fact, perhaps more than one.'

'They may be the same boy.'

Again, there was a slight hesitation. Then, 'I hope so. But why don't you come and meet her? She's in right now, and it would be a great relief to her to know that something's been fixed up.'

Elspeth lost no time in making her way to the helicopter pilot's house. This was in a small estate of new houses built just outside West Linton, intended for commuters into Edinburgh.

There, she was greeted warmly by Jenny, the helicopter pilot's wife, who appeared to be flustered. 'I don't know how we're going to do it,' she said. 'I have to get this place under control and pack up all our things by next Tuesday. Next Tuesday, can you believe it?'

'They haven't given you much notice,' Elspeth said.

Jenny shrugged. 'The man my husband's replacing out there left them with no warning. He lost his nerve, apparently, refused to take off.'

Elspeth asked whether that was unusual.

'Harry says he's seen it once. A fixed-wing pilot got out of his seat and said, *I just can't do it.*'

'While they were in the air?'

'No. They were still on the ground. But look, come in and meet Josefine. She's very keen to meet you and to hear about this job. I've told her it's not definite, but I think she's moved in mentally.'

They went inside, where they found Josefine waiting for them in the living room. Elspeth drew in her breath. The young woman was a grace from Botticelli's *Primavera*; there was the same effortless, flowing beauty. But then Elspeth thought, *I have triplets in the house, but I also have a husband,*

and she thought those thoughts, usually unexpressed but often entertained by any wife admitting a young au pair to her house. Men were only human, and there were two men in her household: James, in respect of whom she was surely *in loco parentis*, and Matthew, in respect of whom she was, in a real sense, *in loco uxoris*. Just a thought, she thought.

Josefine smiled at her. 'I can start tomorrow,' she said, before Elspeth was able to open her mouth. 'Or today, if you like.'

Elspeth was not sure how to respond. She needed an au pair, and she needed one quickly. But she knew nothing, or next to nothing, about Josefine, and she would have liked to spend at least a few minutes talking to her before taking her on. But even as she wrestled with this dilemma, Josefine asked her, 'Doesn't James live with you? That nice Scottish boy? The one who . . .' She did not finish. The helicopter pilot had come into the room, looking harassed. His packing up had revealed that something was missing, and he needed to locate it.

Elspeth thought: how does Josefine know James – and how well?

50. Cheese Scones

When Angus Lordie returned to Scotland Street after his sitting with Glenbucket, he found Domenica in her study, talking on the telephone. She beckoned to him, and he sat down in the chair on the other side of her desk, waiting for her to finish her call. There was always something slightly discomfiting, he thought, about listening to one side of a telephone conversation; one may affect indifference, but one is inevitably drawn into speculation as to what the voice at the other end – the voice one cannot hear – is saying.

'No,' she said to the person at the other end of the line, 'I have not phoned about any of the registered sites for which the authorities have responsibility. This is something quite different.'

The voice said something that Angus could not make out. Then Domenica said, 'Yes, of course.'

A further unintelligible, crackling sound was all that Angus heard in response to that.

'Neanderthal,' said Domenica.

This was greeted with silence. Then, after a few moments, 'In a cave. Near the Water of Leith. My husband's dog.'

Angus smiled. It would be gratifying if Cyril were to get the credit for the discovery; how many dogs have made significant palaeontological finds?

'No,' said Domenica, in reply to a further enquiry at the other end. 'We haven't.' She sighed. 'The reason why we are approaching you, is that we want to do everything by the book.'

Angus made out a clearing of the throat at the other end of the line. Domenica looked at him, as if in a silent plea for sympathy.

There were a few more brief exchanges before the call came to an end.

'Well, really,' exclaimed Domenica. 'They were perfectly polite, but it was clear they didn't believe me.'

'Who?' asked Angus. 'Who didn't believe you?'

'The National Museum of Scotland,' said Domenica, rising to her feet. She moved to the window and looked out over the street. A brief shower of rain, unexpected, a passing thought from an innocent sky, had left the setts glistening. The figure of a young man came around the corner at the top of the street and glanced up at her window. Instinctively, she drew back. It was Torquil, the student from downstairs. He transferred his gaze to the window of his own flat and she saw him open his mouth to shout something. Then he cupped his hand to his ear in an effort to make out what was being said.

'That young man from downstairs is shouting out something to one of his flatmates,' said Domenica.

Angus joined her at the window. He glanced at what was happening down below, and then turned back to face Domenica. 'What did the museum say?' he asked.

'They wanted to know where we found the skull,' she said. 'They asked me whether I was sure it was a skull.'

Angus shrugged. 'You told them because it looked like a skull, I take it.'

'More or less,' said Domenica. 'But they said that they very much doubted that it was Neanderthal.'

'How do they know?' asked Angus.

'They don't,' replied Domenica. 'That's the point. So they're coming to take a look.'

'Here? To the flat?'

'Yes. This afternoon. At three-fifteen. They said that was the only slot they had.'

Angus laughed. 'What did Jean Brodie say of the school principal who had summoned her at such a time? *She thought to intimidate me by the use of quarter hours?*'

'Something to that effect,' Domenica said. 'But I shall not be intimidated. We've done nothing wrong. They seemed to imply that we were ... well, grave robbers, I suppose.'

Angus raised an eyebrow. 'Burke and Hare,' he said.

'Exactly. Anyway, somebody from the Department of Neanderthal Affairs of the Chambers Street museum will be here this afternoon to take a look at the skull.'

Angus clapped his hands in delight. 'The Department of Neanderthal Affairs!' he cried. 'What a splendid conceit. Are they serious?'

Domenica shook her head. 'They are, but I'm not. I think it was really the Department of Brochs and Early Pictish sites – that sort of thing. But I'm just assuming that the people who do all of that are also in charge of Neanderthal finds, of which there have been none in Scotland – thus far.'

He smiled. 'I take it that Neanderthal affairs are a devolved matter? I assume that Westminster has no jurisdiction over Scottish Neanderthals.'

'I imagine so,' said Domenica. 'London is slow to let go of powers, but they're probably quite happy to give us Neanderthals.'

'Shall I make some cheese scones?' asked Angus. His cheese scones, which he baked with a good dose of cayenne pepper, were popular, and he often prepared a batch if there was to be an important visitor. And what more important occasion could there be, he asked himself, than the visit of an official palaeontologist – if that was who was coming that afternoon at the very precise – not to say intimidating – time of three-fifteen?

'Cheese scones would be ideal,' said Domenica. 'After all, this is a fairly important occasion.'

Angus nodded. 'Of course it is.' He paused. 'But I must confess: I fear a resounding rebuff.'

Domenica did not share his anxiety. 'We're not trying to mislead anybody, Angus,' she said. 'We're not making any ridiculous claims. It's not as if we're coming up with anything like . . . ' She searched her memory for examples of historical hoaxes – they were common enough, but the only one that came to her was the case of Piltdown Man.

'Piltdown Man?' Angus prompted.

'Precisely.'

Angus smiled. 'People were more gullible then, I suppose. What did they do again?'

'It was a fraudster,' said Domenica. 'He wanted to establish the so-called Missing Link between apes and *Homo sapiens*. So he got hold of an orang-utan jaw and combined it with a bit of modern skull. People fell for it for years.'

Angus shook his head. 'Presumably wishful thinking played a part?'

'Of course. People believe what they want to believe – in so many respects. Look at our human beliefs about a lot of things – from economics to cosmology. You find something that appeals to you – some notion – and then you construct a supporting rationale for it. Astrology, for instance. People actually believe in that – they really do. But you don't even have to resort to such fanciful territory to find examples of human wishful thinking.'

Angus was quiet. 'I should hate to be lumped in with those Piltdown people,' he said.

Domenica sought to reassure him. 'All that we've said is that we've found a skull that looks Neanderthal. That's all. And when this museum person comes, that's the first thing I'll tell him.' She paused. 'I suggest you make your scones now.'

Angus went to the cupboard. He took out the cayenne pepper.

51. A Cayenne Kick

'Very tasty scones,' said Dr Ruaridh Colquohoun, senior Neolithic curator of the National Museum of Scotland. 'People usually offer us shortbread – at best. Scones are a distinct improvement, if I may be permitted to say so.'

Domenica nodded towards Angus. 'Don't thank me, Dr Colquohoun. The scones were made by my husband.'

The curator made an apologetic gesture. 'An assumption on my part,' he said. 'Please forgive me.'

Domenica smiled. 'Quite understandable. I'm not one to blame people for making assumptions that are based on their experience. I suppose it's still the case that there are more women making scones than there are men.'

'But we shouldn't assume that,' said Dr Colquohoun.

'These automatic assumptions – even if based on statistical probability – can confirm stereotypes.'

'Well, possibly,' agreed Domenica. 'But people should not be frightened to open their mouths … We'll soon be scared to say anything at all.'

Angus joined in. 'I don't like stereotypes,' he said. 'Although one might add that the assumptions go the other way too. There are those, I imagine, who assume that men can't bake scones.'

'Indeed,' said Dr Colquohoun. He examined the remaining fragment of scone on his plate. 'I must say, that was extremely delicious. There's something in them … something you don't normally encounter in a scone. Is it the sort of cheese you use?'

'That's not all that important,' Angus replied, but then qualified what he had just said. 'Actually, I suppose it is. You don't want to use soft cheese.'

Dr Colquohoun shook his head. 'No, of course not.'

'And the cheese should be strong if the flavour is to come out.'

Dr Colquohoun agreed. He picked up a crumb and sniffed at it. 'Parmesan?' he asked.

'You could use Parmesan,' Angus said. 'Any nice hard cheese like that would probably do. But Parmesan has a good, strong flavour. Parmesan has that special heartiness … '

'Kokumi,' Domenica interjected. 'That's what they call that special sensation you get when you taste Parmesan.'

'As it happens, I haven't used Parmesan,' Angus said. 'I used a strong Cheddar. Pretty standard stuff. But I add a good pinch of cayenne pepper. That's what gives a scone a kick. Cayenne pepper.'

'Well, I must say that they are very delicious as a result.' Dr Colquohoun picked up a further crumb and placed it on the tip of his tongue. 'Very delicious, I'd say.'

'I also use eggs,' Angus volunteered. 'Some people make scones without eggs, but I find they add something.'

'Undoubtedly,' said Dr Colquohoun. 'You can taste the richness.'

'I also put in a bit more butter than the recipe advises,' added Angus.

'I'm all for creativity in the kitchen,' said Dr Colquohoun.

'Would you care for another scone?' Domenica asked.

Dr Colquohoun was quick to reply. 'I wouldn't mind,' he said.

Cyril watched from his position on the floor. He liked the smell of cheese scones but he was wary of their taste. Angus had once given him half a scone left over by a visitor and he had been quick to spit it out. That was the cayenne pepper. Now, though, there was something else about this meeting that interested him – Dr Colquohoun's ankles. These were encased in a pair of light blue socks that left a small line of exposed flesh before the curator's trouser leg began. It was not much, but it was enough to attract Cyril's attention. A quick nip was always possible, and might, if he were lucky, not even be noticed. But then he saw Angus, and he realised that retribution would be swift and painful. So he turned away, and the moment of temptation passed.

With another scone on his plate and his cup of tea refreshed, Dr Colquohoun turned to the reason for his visit.

'When I heard about your telephone call,' he said, 'I must admit I was inclined to dismiss it and suggest no action.

But . . .' He hesitated. 'I still think it is impossible that whatever you found is a Neanderthal skull, but it could still be something. People are always finding Neolithic settlement sites, and these often reveal human bones. It occurred to me that you might have stumbled on one of these. That would be perfectly feasible.'

Angus scratched his chin. 'Forgive me, but I've forgotten when the Neolithic age was.'

'It came after the Mesolithic period,' said Dr Colquohoun. 'Mesolithic people were hunter-gatherers. In the Neolithic period they were settled communities – they farmed. They lived in villages. There's a very well-known one up in the Orkney Islands.'

'And the Neanderthals?' asked Angus.

'Oh, they were far earlier,' said Dr Colquohoun, gesturing to indicate the distant past. 'They became extinct about forty-two thousand years ago.'

Angus tried to envision forty-two thousand years. How many human generations would that be? 'Could they have lived in Scotland? In Moray Pleasure Gardens, for instance?' he asked.

Dr Colquohoun shook his head. 'Scotland was covered in ice then. And joined to continental Europe, of course.'

Angus glanced at Domenica. She had been so excited about the skull, and now the fundamental possibility of its being anything really interesting was receding. Neolithic skulls, it seemed, even if not exactly two-a-penny, were still not anything exceptional.

'And another thing,' Dr Colquohoun continued, 'is this: the range of the Neanderthals did not extend this far north, even if they coped with ice. They probably made it into England, but only in the south. They were probably most common in Spain. There are a lot of Neanderthal sites at that latitude.'

'I hope we haven't wasted your time,' said Domenica.

'Not in the slightest,' said Dr Colquhoun. 'Part of our job is to look at things people find. We get all sorts of things. And you never know ... although in this case, I'm afraid, we can definitely exclude at least one possibility. This will not be a Neanderthal skull.'

'Would you like a third scone?' asked Angus.

Domenica laughed. 'You don't have to say *third scone*, Angus,' she upbraided him.

'It would be my third,' said Dr Colquhoun. 'But this is a temptation, I'm afraid, that I am ill equipped to resist. I find scones are irresistible.'

'Then why fight it?' said Angus, passing another scone to their guest.

'I take it that Neanderthals would not have baked,' said Domenica.

'Certainly not scones,' said Dr Colquhoun. 'They did not have wheat, you see. Cultivation of crops came much, much later.' He paused as he took a bite of his scone. 'After the beginning of agriculture in Mesopotamia. But the Neanderthals were far more intelligent than people used to give them credit for being. Do you know they had art?'

Domenica mentioned the articles she had read in *Evolutionary Anthropology*.

'Then you'll know about those Spanish cave paintings,' said Dr Colquhoun.

Domenica nodded.

Turning to Angus, Dr Colquohoun said, 'I know you're an artist, Mr Lordie. You'll be interested in those Spanish finds. There's a very famous set of abstract symbols that is astonishingly old – well before *Homo sapiens*. Sixty-four thousand years ago.' He paused. 'And they really were abstract. Early cave paintings tend to be figurative – little pictures of hunters, and so on. Animals running away from a pursuer – that sort of thing. Neanderthal art, by contrast, is abstract. It's symbolic. Lines, dots.'

'Turner Prize stuff,' said Angus.

'Oh, far more subtle than that,' said Dr Colquohoun.

52. *Akratic Action*

Dr Colquohoun did not take a fourth scone, although he was offered one, but continued to address the subject of Neanderthals. He was sure that the skull that Domenica and Angus were proposing to show him would be a let-down – perhaps that of some unfortunate Victorian, set upon by footpads and then hastily buried in a shallow grave in the Gardens – but he was enjoying this visit. Domenica and Angus were exactly the sort of company he liked: intelligent, interested in the arts, and prepared to discuss – or at least to listen to him talking about – the Neolithic period. There were so many people now who were simply incurious about the past, who did not think about the echoes of ancient times that were all about us, even in the language we used in our everyday life. How many of our words were based on languages that had long since stopped being spoken? How many people talking of their *clan* would know that in Etruscan that meant *son*? Or that *three* in Etruscan was *ci*, which sounds so like three, whatever etymological caution might be sounded. Our words were ancient, handed down over thousands of years, linking us in our indifferent modernity with distant forebears who herded animals on obscure steppes, or who sailed their ships across ancient oceans. And even if one did not think back that far, how many people remembered that their not-so-distant ancestors spoke Pictish or Gaelic, lived in fear of Vikings, and devils, and pre-scientific threats of every description, and were surprised to survive to their thirtieth birthday? He thought about that every day, as he pored over pictures of mute stones, of flints, of patterns in the ground, of symbols that were now indecipherable but nevertheless once recorded somebody's whole world.

'The interesting thing about Neanderthal art,' Dr Colquohoun said, 'is that it exists at all. That's what counts. It doesn't matter that it consists of a few marks on the wall, or decorated stalactites. What matters is the fact that those ancient cousins of ours actually made the cognitive leap to expressing themselves. If you paint or draw something, you are recording an event or feeling *outside* yourself. That's what other animals simply cannot do. They don't see it.

'So this art attributed to Neanderthals suggests that they were capable of language. If you can draw something, then you should be able to associate sound with intention or feeling – or perception, perhaps. That means you can speak.'

'Did they?' asked Domenica.

'They had tongues and vocal cords. So yes, they should have been able to.'

'But we don't know?' asked Angus.

'That's right,' said Dr Colquohoun. 'We don't know, but we can surmise a great deal on the basis of what we *do* know. And I imagine that they had language – undoubtedly a simple one, if they had it at all. Perhaps just nouns and a few simple verbs.'

'Me Tarzan, you Jane?' suggested Angus. 'That level of sophistication?'

'Yes. I like to imagine a Neanderthal saying something like *Deer go hill*. The deer have gone to the hill. It doesn't take much intellectual power to make that sort of observation. Two nouns and one verb, and the verb may have a single tense. You have to be a little bit more savvy to wrap your mind around the past tense.'

Domenica smiled. 'How exactly did we get these Neanderthal genes we're meant to have?' she asked.

'Interbreeding,' said Dr Colquohoun. 'It appears that members of *Homo sapiens* and Neanderthals came into contact with one another. So there would have been children who were a cross between the two, but as time went on and the Neanderthals became extinct, their genes would have been diluted further and further until modern man ended up with really rather few of them.'

'I see,' said Angus. 'So somewhere way back we might have Neanderthal ancestors?'

'Indeed. Very early Lordies. Very early Colquohouns.' He paused and added, smiling, 'And very early Macdonalds.'

'It reduces our pretensions,' observed Domenica. 'Reminding ourselves of our hairy precursors cuts us down to size, don't you think?'

'It does,' said Dr Colquohoun. 'Although we don't really need the Neanderthals for that. A moment's contemplation of the higher primates might help to do that, I've always thought. Go and stand in front of the monkey cages at Edinburgh Zoo and reflect on your cousins. We're just primates – for all our airs and graces.'

Angus laughed. 'I often think that,' he said. 'When I watch the television news and see images of human conflict – people fighting one another on disputed borders, groups throwing rocks at one another, you know the sort of scene I'm talking about – I think: these territorial disputes are exactly what the primatologists observe. One troop of baboons chases away another when it encroaches on its territory.'

'Oh yes,' Domenica said. 'I know it sounds reductionist, but that's exactly what's going on.'

'The fundamental impulse,' continued Dr Colquohoun, 'is to control territory. To defend it against those who are seen as others.'

'And you could analyse so many contemporary conflicts in those terms too,' said Angus. 'Isn't it all a matter of whose territory it is?'

Domenica nodded. 'I would have thought so.' She paused. 'And yet, people rise above those disputes.'

Dr Colquohoun agreed. 'Of course, we're not stuck in that mode. There's always the ideal of co-operation that stresses a broader interest. There are plenty of precedents for that. The *Risorgimento*, for example. The creation of the modern German state. The United States of America. And so on. People find a common interest in co-operation. *E pluribus unum*, and all that.'

Angus looked thoughtful. He wondered where that left Scotland, a small state that had been absorbed into a larger state but had never forgotten that it was a country – a nation. And he loved that country, and the idea behind it. He did not want Scotland to disappear. He wanted local control – not control from London or Brussels, because he believed that people should have their own government, close, immediate, answerable; and yet … He sighed. 'I suppose people attach themselves to what they have, or what they have had recently,' said Angus, 'and believe that it's the ordained position. But it's just one stage in a process of evolution.'

Dr Colquhoun thought about this. He mentally repeated Angus's statement, and then looked at it from both sides, and from the middle. He turned it upside down. He was not at all sure what Angus meant – if anything: people often gave voice to meaningless remarks and it was a mistake to believe that they always made sense. He stared at the plate on which two cheese scones remained. Noticing his gaze, Domenica said, 'You really should have another one.'

Dr Colquhoun glanced at the scones. '*Akrasia*,' he said. 'That's what the Greek philosophers called weakness of will. If I have another scone, I shall be acting akratically.'

'But you'll enjoy it,' said Domenica. 'And therefore it's in your best interests to yield to temptation. It's what you want, after all, and surely it's in your best interests to get what you want.'

Angus remembered the Neanderthal skull, and he now

rose to retrieve it from the cupboard in which they had placed it for safekeeping. Unwrapping it carefully, he showed it to their visitor.

Dr Colquohoun drew in his breath. 'I'm astonished,' he said, as he lifted it gently to make his inspection. 'At first blush – and I emphasise that – at first blush this looks distinctly Neanderthal.' He laid the skull down gingerly. A fragment of earth fell off it onto the floor below – the *mool* of a grave, thought Angus, and for a moment he felt a pang of sorrow, for this skull had been a person once, and how could one ever not be sorry for a person?

'I shall take it back to the museum without delay,' he said. 'We must photograph it. We must notify Historic Environment Scotland. We shall call in further experts. There's a professor at the University of Glasgow who will be very interested in seeing this.'

Angus frowned. The University of Glasgow? What did this have to do with them? This was an Edinburgh Neanderthal; if Glasgow wanted a Neanderthal, then they should look for one of their own.

53. *Lobster à la Édimbourg*

Bruce Anderson, property surveyor, alumnus of Morrison's Academy in Crieff, where the girls voted him, three years in succession, the Best-Looking Guy in Perthshire – with virtually no dissent, apart from those few whose hearts he had broken; sole user in Edinburgh of a proprietary clove-scented hair gel; owner of a desirable three-bedroom flat in Abercromby Place in the Georgian New Town; close follower of Scottish rugby: this same Bruce Anderson now stood in his kitchen and dipped his brand new red silica ladle into the lobster bisque he was preparing for his dinner guest.

'Lobster bisque,' he muttered, taking a sip from the ladle. Smiling, he added, '*Lobster à la Édimbourg*, prescription-only.'

It was a private joke, made all the more private by the fact that there was nobody else in the kitchen, or indeed in the flat. The reference was to something said by his university friend, Freddie Carruthers, a dab hand in the kitchen, who used to refer to the dishes he cooked up for various girlfriends as *prescription-only aphrodisiacs*. Freddie had been a great favourite of the girls, but had fallen into matrimony, as Bruce put it, earlier than any of the others in their immediate student circle. Freddie had married Cholestrola Lupo, a member of a highly regarded Italian-Scottish family, and had soon become the father of three children. He had changed his name to Federico Lupo, and had been set up by the family in a prosperous restaurant business on the Ayrshire coast.

'I swear it was lobster bisque that got me where I am,' Freddie said to Bruce when they met for dinner in the Ubiquitous Chip in Glasgow. 'I gave it to Cholestrola and she was like, *Wow!* Never fails.'

Freddie had passed on the recipe, and Bruce had made it three or four times since then. It had been well received by those for whom he had made it, although not always with the results that Bruce had anticipated. In every case, though, it seemed to trigger a release of emotion, whether through olfactory resonance or through some undiscoverable hormonal effect. One guest, a young woman whom Bruce had met in the Wally Dug and had then invited back to his flat for dinner, had been moved by the bisque to start talking about her last boyfriend, whom she hoped to recover. For a good half hour Bruce had listened to a long and intimate exposition of her relationship that included detailed discussion of strategies to get him back. The evening came to an end when she broke down in floods of tears and was only calmed by Bruce's assurances that the former boyfriend was highly likely to grow tired of his new girlfriend.

'That's what guys are like,' said Bruce. 'They're fickle.'

After that, the romantic possibilities of the evening were more or less destroyed, as was the case with the next guest for whom he made the bisque. She made short work of her first bowl of it and readily accepted a second. It was only towards the end of this second helping that she asked, quite casually, 'What do you put in this soup? It's terrific.'

Bruce grinned. 'Actually, it's not soup, it's what we call bisque.'

'So, it's bisque. But what's in it? Lots of cream, obviously, I love cream. I seriously love cream.'

'It's lobster. Your actual lobster. You know – those big critters with the claws. You have to watch the claws. My friend, Freddie Carruthers, although he's Lupo now, he almost lost his middle finger when a lobster got hold of it. No, I'm not making this up: those claws are like giant nutcrackers.'

Bruce's guest had paled. Her spoon dropped into her bowl.

Bruce noticed. 'Sorry. I shouldn't talk about fingers being crushed. He was all right, as it happens, because the lobster thought better of it, let go of his finger, and went for his nose – missed it, though – fortunately. You wouldn't want a lobster to get your nose . . . '

He stopped. The young woman had brought her hands to her mouth.

'Are you all right?' Bruce asked.

She brought her hands down. 'I can't eat lobster,' she said, her voice wavering. 'I can't eat any seafood.'

And with that, she was copiously ill.

Bruce attended to the emergency as best he could, and she recovered after she had divested herself of the bisque. After that, Bruce busied himself in calling a taxi for her to be taken home to rest and drink the substantial quantity of water that she claimed would remove the last trace of lobster from her system.

It was best not to remember these incidents, he decided, and he put them out of his mind as he added the last ingredients of the complicated and time-consuming recipe with its call for Cognac, *mirepoix*, rice, tarragon, and stocks and pastes that needed to be prepared in advance. As he worked, his mind went to Katie, who would be arriving at seven-thirty, with a view to their sitting down to lobster bisque an hour later.

Bruce had enjoyed his lunch with Katie, and had asked her to dinner that evening. She had hesitated; she had regretted leaving Stuart in the National Portrait Gallery. She was not sure why she had done so, but had decided that it was a momentary revolt against being *corralled*. That's what she disliked, she felt: being obliged to do things that she did not want to do simply because that was what a man wanted to do. So when Bruce had suggested lunch, she had, on impulse, accepted his invitation. She was not a chattel. She could do what she wanted.

And then, when he suggested dinner, she had said to herself, *I shall say no*, but somehow it had come out as *yes*. This was something to do with the way Bruce looked; that was the only possible explanation. There are some men, she thought, who are *irresistible*. That's the only way of putting it. It was his eyes, perhaps. Or his skin, maybe. He was very slightly olive in colour; not quite, but a bit, and she loved olive. And then there was his hair, which stood up at the front in a sort of wave that went nowhere because it was cut shortish, and he wore something in it, a gel of some sort, that made her remember her grandmother's cupboards in her house in Ullapool, where you could sit in the front window and watch the ferry going out to the Outer Hebrides.

I have to stop thinking like this, she said to herself, as she made her way to Abercromby Place. *I shall tell him that Stuart and I are . . . well, whatever we are, and he'll understand, I'm sure. I shall bring this to an end before it's started.*

But then, as she climbed the stairs to Bruce's flat, she smelled something in the air: lobster bisque, and the effect of lobster bisque is to weaken the resistance. She struggled, but failed, and knew that she was failing.

It was not until she was directly outside the door, though, that she remembered. She had been at Morrison's Academy, and although she was a few years younger than Bruce, she had been there when he had been voted the Best-Looking

Guy in Perthshire. That had been Bruce Anderson – of course it had! And she had voted for him.

54. Martini Time

While Bruce was preparing his lobster bisque in Abercromby Place, Sister Maria-Fiore dei Fiori di Montagna was mixing a martini for her flatmate, Antonia Collie, in their Drummond Place flat, only a few doors away from where Compton Mackenzie, Jacobite, spy, author of *Whisky Galore* and President of both the Siamese Cat Society and the Croquet Association, had lived with his two MacSween wives, *seriatim*. Sister Maria-Fiore and Antonia had taken to the regular consumption of a martini at six-fifteen in the evening, when the evening sun, slanting in from the western end of Drummond Place, shone at such an angle through their large front windows as to illuminate the right half of their carved wooden mantelpiece with its figure of Demeter dispensing sheaves of wheat to worthy recipients. The previous year, Antonia had made an extraordinary discovery: she had found that at the summer solstice, a beam of evening sunlight, entering the flat by their principal Drummond Place-facing window, fell on a point of salience in the mantelpiece carving, and then directly shone through a gap in the carving of Demeter onto a half-concealed surface.

There, on that surface, had been carved the words *My journey starts afresh*.

Antonia had pointed out her discovery to Sister Maria-Fiore dei Fiori di Montagna, who had peered at the inscription in fascination. 'I assume that this is meant to be the sun talking,' she said.

'Indeed,' said Antonia. 'There is no doubt in my mind about that. This is undoubtedly the Scottish equivalent of Newgrange in Ireland.'

Sister Maria-Fiore looked blank, but only momentarily: she did not know much about Ireland, and had no idea where Newgrange was, yet even in such circumstances she was able to find a suitable aphorism. 'One place,' she pronounced, 'is often a reminder of another place. And that place may, in turn, bring to mind a third place. So it is that we find our place – among places.'

'Yes,' said Antonia. 'Quite possibly.' And then added, 'Of course, Newgrange allows the sun to enter the chamber in the mound at the winter solstice, whereas the light falls on our mantelpiece at the summer solstice.'

'Summer and winter are two sides of the same coin,' said Sister Maria-Fiore. 'Summer says to us the things that winter says, but in a different voice.'

Antonia did not disagree with that. She found Sister Maria-Fiore's observations charming, and had even been thinking of compiling them into some sort of book, once she had finished her current work on the lives of the early Scottish saints. Perhaps Sister Maria-Fiore's book of aphorisms might have the same measure of success as had been enjoyed by Kahlil Gibran's *The Prophet*. The

Lebanese mystic had been immensely successful with that compilation of utterances on all sorts of subjects including, she recalled, the eating of apples. Had he not said something about what you should say in your heart when your teeth sank into an apple: 'I, too, am an apple ...' Or was that about something else? It was difficult with mystics to work out what they were talking about, which, of course, was one of the things that made being a mystic relatively easy. If you were a mystic, then the more obscure your observations, the better – or the more mystical. The most successful mystics were those whose sayings and writings were quite impenetrable, tantalising others with a shifting allusiveness that promised enlightenment, even if not just yet.

But now, as the sun reached the mantelpiece, Sister Maria-Fiore handed a martini to Antonia. The nun was the one who mixed the drinks, using gin and dry vermouth, and adding, to Antonia's glass, but not to hers, an olive and a small amount of olive brine, the key ingredient of a dirty martini.

'Dirty,' said Sister-Maria, raising her glass.

'Dirty,' replied Antonia. It was their private toast, one of the little things that cemented their friendship.

'Where did you learn to make martinis?' asked Antonia. 'Did you have them in the convent?'

Antonia liked to get Sister Maria-Fiore to talk about her convent days, as she had fond memories of the time she had spent there herself, after the sisters had taken her in for recuperation. Antonia's attack of Stendhal Syndrome had been towards the more serious end of the condition's spectrum, and it was the kindness of the community of nuns in their remote Tuscan house that had brought about her recovery.

'It was one of the things we learned as novices,' replied Sister Maria-Fiore. 'One of the senior nuns was in charge of our training in routine tasks. She had been a waitress in Harry's Bar in Venice before she received the call. Many of the nuns brought with them the skills they had acquired in the outside world. Sister Beatrice, for example, was a very good mechanic, and there was another sister who had been a glassblower in Murano. There was usually somebody for whatever task required to be done.'

Antonia sipped at her martini. 'Do you have many regrets, Maria-Fiore?'

Sister Maria-Fiore frowned. 'About what?'

'About leaving all that behind you.'

The nun looked into her martini glass. 'Life,' she said, 'is a bit like a martini. You take a sip – and then you take another sip.'

Antonia nodded. 'I suppose so. But I just wondered whether you miss the routine of that other life you had. You know what I mean – getting up at the same time every morning, going to morning prayers, having the same breakfast. Going off to work in the dairy ...'

'I never worked in the dairy,' Sister Maria-Fiore corrected her. 'I mainly worked on the lettuce farm. And I helped with the bee-keeping.'

'Yes, but it was a routine, wasn't it? And everything was provided. You didn't have to worry about where your next meal was coming from.'

Sister Maria-Fiore looked thoughtful. 'That's true. But we weren't passengers, you know. The convent earned its crust of bread.' She paused. 'I valued the routine – yes, I did. But I felt a strong call to come to Scotland. I felt that there was a place somewhere, where I could realise my potential, if you see what I mean. And so when you suggested that I might come, it seemed to me that this was a message that I was destined to receive. You never know when a call will come. You might be doing something very ordinary – brushing your teeth, for instance – when a call arrives. The important thing is to receive those things that are sent to you. Do not send away things that are brought to your door. Embrace them. Nothing comes without first having been sent.'

'No,' mused Antonia. 'That's probably true.'

'Speaking of which,' said Sister Maria-Fiore, 'I was on the 23 bus earlier today. I was coming back from a meeting at the National Gallery.' Sister Maria-Fiore had recently been appointed to the Board of Trustees of the Scottish National Gallery, and had attended her first meeting earlier that day. It had been an important meeting, at which the trustees had discussed a proposal that all the gallery's paintings should be hung at a slightly lower level in order to ensure their accessibility to shorter people.

Antonia sipped at her dirty martini. 'And?'

'And I found the most extraordinary thing. Somebody had left something on the bus – it looked like a skull of some sort.'

'A human skull?'

Sister Maria-Fiore nodded. 'It couldn't have been, though.

You don't find human skulls on Edinburgh buses – at least not on the number 23.'

Antonia laughed. 'You're a hoot, *carissima*!' And then, 'So what did you do?'

'I threw it in the bin.'

'Our bin?'

'Yes.'

Antonia shrugged. 'People leave all sorts of things on buses. Trains too.'

'What we leave behind, others find,' said Sister Maria-Fiore.

55. Getting Ready for Glasgow

The arrangements for the Glasgow Academy exchange were made jointly by Nicola and Ranald Braveheart Macpherson's mother. Nicola did most of the negotiating with the school authorities and with the teacher with whom the boys would be boarding, while Ranald's mother made lists of what would be required to support two boys for the four weeks they would spend in Glasgow. A clothing list was drawn up and lists of food preferences were compiled: Ranald was mildly intolerant of certain forms of Brie although he liked hard cheese, especially Parmesan. 'It's important to tell them,' said Ranald's mother to her husband. 'Ranald would probably be too polite to say anything.'

'I doubt very much whether they would be offering the boys Brie over in Glasgow,' said Ranald's father, smiling. 'Brie's more of an Edinburgh thing.'

His wife looked at him disapprovingly. 'I take it you're joking,' she said.

He was unrepentant, and smiled again. 'Just saying.'

A further look was flashed in his direction.

'At least don't forget to tell them that he doesn't like asparagus.' He paused. 'Like me. Although, strictly speaking, I do like it – I like it very much, but there's the issue of its side-effects.'

'I'll tell them,' Ranald's mother replied.

Bertie and Ranald could barely contain their excitement. Bertie had the advantage of Ranald Braveheart Macpherson in that he had been to Glasgow before, which meant that Ranald turned to Bertie for guidance on what to expect of their Glasgow sojourn, and Bertie was only too pleased to give his friend the benefit of his knowledge.

'Do they eat the same food as us over there, Bertie?' Ranald had asked. 'Or should we take sandwiches?'

Bertie assured Ranald that there would be no need for sandwiches. 'The food in Glasgow is pretty good, Ranald,' he said. 'They don't have Valvona & Crolla, of course, but they have got a few shops of their own, I think.'

Ranald absorbed the information. 'But what do they actually eat?' he asked.

'Pies,' replied Bertie. 'They like pies over in Glasgow. I think they have pies every day.'

'They're really lucky,' said Ranald.

'Yes,' agreed Bertie. 'They often have a pie for breakfast,

and then another for lunch. And they drink Irn-Bru too. They drink lots of that.'

Ranald Braveheart Macpherson's eyes widened. 'And we'll be able to do that, too, Bertie?' he asked.

Bertie nodded. 'Sure to, Ranald. You're allowed to do lots of things in Glasgow that you aren't allowed to do in Edinburgh.'

Of course, the joy that Bertie and Ranald felt over their impending trip was not unalloyed. In particular, they were both given pause to reflect by Olive, who had heard of the proposed exchange and was determined to do all that lay in her power to undermine the two boys' delight in what lay ahead.

'I hear you're going to Glasgow, Bertie Pollock,' she said in the playground at the Steiner School.

Bertie was guarded in his reply. 'Maybe,' he said. And then he added, 'How do you know that, Olive?'

Olive tapped the side of her nose. 'Don't think people don't know what you do, Bertie. I know all about your movements – and so does Pansy.'

Pansy, Olive's faithful lieutenant, nodded knowingly. 'Everybody knows what you're planning, Bertie. Don't think you can get away with anything ...'

'Because you can't,' supplied Olive. 'We know all about your plans, Bertie. Everybody knows.'

'I don't care if people know,' said Bertie defiantly. 'I'm going with Ranald Braveheart Macpherson.'

Olive made a face. 'Oh, that's really sad, Bertie. In fact, it's tragic.'

'Yes,' agreed Pansy. 'It's truly tragic, Bertie. You and Ranald going off to Glasgow together. It's really tragic.'

'I don't think so,' said Bertie. 'I don't see what's tragic about that.'

Olive shook her head. 'That's because you've got no insight, Bertie. Most people who are tragic – like you – have at least some insight into how tragic they are. You don't though. You seem to have none.'

'None at all,' said Pansy.

Olive changed tack. 'Be careful that you don't get head-butted,' she warned. 'That's what happens to people who go to Glasgow. They arrive at Queen Street Station and before they know it, somebody comes up to them and head-butts them. The hospitals in Glasgow are full of people who have come from Edinburgh and been head-butted.'

'Full of them,' said Pansy.

'And there's not much you can do about it,' Olive went on. 'Some people think you can reason with people from Glasgow, but you can't, you know. People have tried, but nobody has ever succeeded.' Olive sighed. 'I feel very sorry for you, Bertie Pollock. I wouldn't be in your shoes for a hundred pounds.'

'Or even more,' said Pansy.

Bertie glowered at Olive, but this seemed to have no effect. Now crowing, Olive went on: 'I could go to Glasgow if I wanted to, but I don't. I have no need to go to Glasgow, Bertie, and so it doesn't worry me at all that you are going. All I ask is that you remember that I warned you. I don't want you to come crying to me afterwards and demanding why I didn't apprise you. I have warned you. Glasgow is full of Campbells.'

Bertie waited.

'And you know what the Campbells did at Glencoe, Bertie,' Olive whispered. 'Well, there are still plenty of Campbells about, and they're planning to do something like that again. They love doing things like that. Over in Glasgow, mostly – that's where they're planning to do it.'

Bertie closed his eyes. In theory, he knew how to deal with Olive. In theory, he knew that it was best to ignore her, but she had a way of needling others that made that very difficult to do. He sighed deeply. It seemed to him that he had many burdens in this life that other boys did not seem to have. He had to put up with Olive, and with Pansy too. Then there was his mother who, although she was now in Aberdeen, was always there in the background, ready to make him speak Italian or go to psychotherapy or yoga or do any of the other things that she seemed to enjoy imposing on him. But now there was the prospect of Glasgow, and that thought made it much easier to bear all these vicissitudes: Glasgow, the shining city on the hill, that place of laughter and friendship, and something that he had once heard Glasgow was famous for: great *craic*. He thought that *craic* meant fun, and if it did, then there was plenty of *craic* in Glasgow, and in a matter of days he and Ranald Braveheart Macpherson, loyal Ranald, his friend through thick and thin, would soon be there for a whole wonderful, exhilarating month, enjoying all the great *craic*. A month in Glasgow! At long last. *Glasgow! Glasgow! Glasgow!* He intoned the name much as a Buddhist might say *Om* and it made him feel a current of sheer excitement. Rarely had Bertie felt such a thrill at the prospect of anything. This was the summation of his hopes: the gates of freedom, until now only imagined, were now before him, beckoning him to enter.

56. Ossian, etc.

Nicola offered to drive the boys over to Glasgow in her recently acquired beige estate car. She was keen to try the new vehicle on a long-ish run, and taking Bertie and Ranald Braveheart Macpherson over to Bearsden was a trip of just the right length. She had been meaning to get over to Glasgow anyway, as she had business interests there – or rather, one business interest – and it occurred to her that she could make her business call first and then go on to the home in which the two boys would be staying while on their exchange. This was the house of one of the teachers at the Glasgow Academy Primary, a Mrs Edwina Campbell, to whom Nicola had spoken on the phone several times and whom she was eager now to meet. Once Bertie and Ranald were settled, she could drive back to Edinburgh in time to help Stuart put Ulysses to bed.

She was worried about Stuart. She knew that he had been seeing somebody, and she had wholeheartedly encouraged him in that, even if she knew very little about Katie. But that did not matter: anybody – anybody at all – would be better than Irene, as far as Nicola was concerned. And yet she did not want to pry into Stuart's private life – she was not that sort of mother – and so she refrained from asking him whether the fact that he was now down in the dumps, as he currently appeared to be, had anything to do with difficulties in his nascent romance. She suspected it was. She had overheard him talking to somebody on the telephone – she assumed it was Katie – and she could not help but hear him say, 'Of all people to go off with – Bruce! How could you?'

Nicola did not have much trouble in working out what was happening there. Bruce could only be Bruce Anderson, whom she had met once and had immediately judged to be a card-carrying Lothario. And a conversation with Big Lou that she had had over coffee one morning had confirmed her assessment. Lou, who had known Bruce for years, was in no doubt as to his habit of making advances to other men's girlfriends. 'It's happened so many times,' she had said. 'And it always ends in tears. He's like a tup that cannae leave the ewes alone.'

An opportunity to tackle Stuart about this tactfully would no doubt present itself in the future, but for the moment she could concentrate on the trip to Glasgow and getting Bertie launched on the exchange to which he had been looking forward with such relish. Now, at last, the day had arrived, and Bertie had woken up at five in the morning, such was his excitement. After knocking timidly at his grandmother's door, he crept into her room and whispered into her ear, 'I think it's morning, Granny.'

Nicola looked myopically at her watch. 'Is it, Bertie? I'm not so sure, darling – it's only five o'clock. That's not the real morning.'

Few parents or grandparents have the heart to send children back to the bed at that hour, and so Nicola lifted up a sheet and invited Bertie to try to get a further hour or so of sleep in her bed. He needed no second invitation, and soon she had her young grandson snuggled up to her, his breath upon her shoulder, his entire being shivering with excitement at the thought of what the day would bring.

'Try not to think too much about Glasgow,' Nicola murmured. 'Glasgow always comes to those who wait.'

'I can't help it, Granny,' Bertie said.

'I know, Bertie,' said Nicola. 'But try to think about something else. Then, before you know it, it will be time for us to pick up Ranald and start our journey.'

'Will you tell me a story, then?' asked Bertie. 'That will help me not to think about Glasgow.'

'A story?' said Nicola drowsily. 'I'm not sure if I can think of a story at this hour, darling. You know how it is ...'

'What about Fingal?' asked Bertie. 'Could you tell me about Fingal?'

Nicola struggled. She was ready to slip back into sleep, and she had hoped that Bertie would do the same, but this unanticipated request for a story about Fingal, of all people, was having the opposite effect.

'Fingal?' she muttered.

'Yes,' said Bertie. 'He was Ossian's father, I think. Ossian wrote all those poems about him.'

Nicola was now wide awake. 'Have you been reading about him, Bertie?' She had ceased to be surprised by Bertie's reading, which was as unpredictable as it was prodigious. There were few seven-year-olds, she imagined – no, there were *no* seven-year-olds in the length and breadth of Scotland who could converse on the subject of Ossian and Fingal. And yet Bertie was so modest, so innocent, that this extraordinary knowledge that he seemed to possess did not seem to be worn on his sleeve. Quite the opposite, in fact: Bertie wore his knowledge with a charming and completely inoffensive modesty.

'I'm not sure that Ossian actually existed, Bertie,' said Nicola. 'And I don't really know all that much about Fingal, I'm afraid.'

'Do you think that Mr Macpherson made him up?' asked Bertie.

Nicola stared up at the ceiling. *I am so ignorant*, she thought. *And it's too late, really, to do anything about it.*

'I'm not sure,' she said. 'Was he the man who collected the poems?'

'Yes,' said Bertie. 'He said that he collected ancient poems from a very old man called Ossian. He had a long white beard, I think, and he sat on a stone up in the Highlands and recited poems about battles. Just like Mr Homer.'

'Men with long white beards,' muttered Nicola, and thought, for a moment, how convenient it would be – for some at least – if *all* male authors were, like Ossian, discovered to be *imaginary*. She did not think that way, of course, but she knew that there were some who did, who disapproved of men on principle, Irene being one, she suspected. How sad; how sad to feel antipathy towards half of humanity, whether male or female, simply because of what they were. How did this happen? How did misogyny and misandry come into existence? Was there a *need* to hate – some dark ally of an old malevolent god that drove people to this lack of charity towards others?

Bertie, though, appeared to have lost interest in Ossian. 'Where will we go when we arrive in Glasgow?' he asked. 'Will we go straight to that lady's house? The one we're going to be staying with?'

Nicola yawned. It was too late now to snatch any further sleep. 'No,' she replied. 'I think we'll go first to the place where I have to do a bit of business. You remember that I own a little factory in Glasgow. You remember about that?'

Bertie did not say anything, but she heard him catch his breath.

'Yes,' she said. 'I still have that little business. Of course, I don't run it myself – there's a manager to do that. But I like to drop in from time to time.'

She felt Bertie quivering again with excitement. 'Your pie factory?' he asked, his voice seeming far away, as if to utter the question might be to close off the possibility it raised.

'Yes,' said Nicola. And then, 'Would you like to go there, Bertie? I've always promised you I'd take you.'

Bertie was too overcome to give voice to his reply. Instead, he gripped Nicola's hand under the bedsheet and pressed it to his chest, to his heart, in a gesture of complicity and love.

57. Inclusive Pies

Breathless with excitement, strapped into the rear seat of Nicola's beige estate car, Bertie and his friend, Ranald Braveheart Macpherson, saw Glasgow begin to material-ise before them, viewed over the rim of the car window. Unlike Edinburgh, with its ordered classicism, or Paris, with Haussmann's broad boulevards, this was a lived-in cityscape, like a pair of comfortable trousers hung up to dry beside the Clyde estuary. Sunlight was upon the buildings and the low green hills that embraced them, sunlight like attenuated gold, descending in shafts. No painter, steeped in the roman-tic Scottish landscapes of the nineteenth century, no Horatio McCulloch attempting to capture Loch Katrine or some other scene of mists and mountains, could have done better than Glasgow herself as she revealed herself that morning.

'I think that's Glasgow, Ranald,' said Bertie.

Ranald nodded. 'I think so too, Bertie.'

Bertie sighed with pleasure. Turning to Ranald, he said, 'I'm glad we came, aren't you, Ranald?'

Ranald nodded again. 'It's the best thing we've ever done, Bertie. And you're my best friend in the whole world. Promise.' And with that, Ranald crossed himself in a gesture intended to underline the seriousness, and honesty, of what he had just said.

Bertie inclined his head. He felt that about Ranald, too. And he thought of his good fortune, that he should be here in Glasgow with his friend, and with a whole, uncharted month ahead of them. He reached out for his friend's hand and squeezed it briefly – a gesture returned by Ranald in a small ceremony of devotion. It was a brief moment, but its timing was perfect, as they were now approaching a turn-off on the motorway and from the front seat Nicola announced that the pie factory was only half a mile off to the left and that they would be there within minutes, traffic permitting.

Her prediction was correct, and very soon the beige estate car rolled into a parking place at the side of a rather shabby industrial building proclaiming itself to be the headquarters of Inclusive Pies.

'That's us,' announced Nicola as she switched off the car's engine. 'This is the pie factory, boys.'

Inclusive Pies was a firm that Nicola had inherited from a childless Glaswegian aunt. The solicitors administering the estate had advised her to sell it, but she had declined, as she had met the staff, took to them immediately, and did not like the thought of casting them adrift to face an uncertain future. She would keep the factory going; another owner could easily strip the firm of its principal asset, the site it occupied, and bring pie production, and the jobs that went with it, to an untimely end. If I am to be a capitalist, Nicola said to herself, then I shall be an enlightened one. This had led her to institute an employee share participation scheme, that had diluted her holding to sixty per cent of the shares, but had markedly raised the morale, and the productivity, of the firm. There were five employees, including the manager, and all of them had been there for years, pleased with their growing stakes in the company and proud, too, of the Scotch pies they produced. These had won several prizes at food festivals, including, most recently, an award for the greasiest pie at the annual Scottish Food Convention in the Scottish Event Campus on the Clyde.

The firm had been founded by Nicola's late uncle, who had set it up under the name of Pies for Protestants. It had been successful, and the name, if anything, had either not been noticed by purchasers, or had been positively approved of. However, changing times, and a certain embarrassment over the perhaps unintended connotations of the title, had prompted a relaunch as Inclusive Pies, which had resulted in new markets being opened up and a sustained rise in profits. This was considered to be all the more of an achievement, given the public campaign that had been waged for some time against the Scotch pie in general. This had been triggered by research revealing the total weight of Scotch pies consumed by the average adult Scot each year: fifty-six pounds. That, together with the figures for the volume of Irn-Bru drunk by that same average Scottish adult (sixteen gallons), had led to calls for health warnings to be attached to each Scotch pie. These moves had become bogged down in disagreements over the wording of the warning: there had been strong support for *These pies will kill you sooner than you think*, but the alarmist tone of that message had put some people off. *This pie will damage your health* was thought to be too similar to existing warnings for tobacco and alcohol, while *Dinnae put this stuff in your gob* was thought to be too self-consciously demotic and perhaps a touch vulgar. The debate had been long and acrimonious, and as a result the initiative fizzled out. The Scotch pie continued to be sold to its consumers in rising numbers.

None of this was in the minds of Bertie and Ranald, and indeed Nicola, as, noses quivering at the delicious smells emanating from the factory, the Edinburgh party made its way up the front steps to be greeted by the manager, Mr Hen McQuoist.

'Well, here you are!' Mr McQuoist exclaimed. 'Come away in.'

Hen and Nicola were old friends, and they embraced warmly at the front door.

'Is he your Granny's lover?' whispered Ranald Braveheart Macpherson.

Bertie shook his head. 'I don't think so, Ranald,' he replied.

Ranald was not convinced. 'He kissed her,' he said. 'And she kissed him back. I saw it. She probably put her tongue in his mouth, Bertie. You know that?'

Bertie did not think that his grandmother could ever have done such a thing. Besides, he was doubtful if Ranald knew anything about these matters. And the same went for his grandmother, who should be protected, he thought, from such crude speculation.

'She's only kissing him to be polite,' he said. 'If she didn't kiss him, then he'd think she thought he had germs. People in Glasgow are quite sensitive about that sort of thing, Ranald. They know that there are some people in Edinburgh who think there are more germs in Glasgow.'

'Are there?' asked Ranald, looking about himself with a certain nervousness.

Bertie shook his head. 'There are hardly any germs in Glasgow, Ranald. There's nothing to worry about.'

With that, they entered the factory, led by Hen McQuoist, who was pointing out to Nicola a machine that they had bought cheaply for the bulk mixing of Scotch pie ingredients. To Bertie's eye, it looked remarkably like a concrete mixer, and this conclusion was confirmed by the inscription he saw painted on its side – *Property of Aberdeenshire Council Roads Department.*

'We're very pleased with our new pastry mixer,' Hen said to Nicola. 'It was a real bargain. I got it cheap.'

'Where did you buy it?' asked Nicola.

'The Sarry Heid,' replied Hen.

58. Ranald's Crisis

While Hen McQuoist and Nicola went into the office to look over quarterly sales figures for the Scotch pies produced by Inclusive Pies, Bertie and Ranald Braveheart were taken on a tour of the factory by the production supervisor, Maggie. Maggie, a woman in her mid-fifties from Greenock, had joined the firm thirty years ago, during its early years of expansion from a two-person cottage industry run from the home of its founders, Nicola's uncle and aunt. She was the daughter of a butcher and it had been anticipated that she would have taken over the family butchery on the retirement of her father, Winston Churchill Wilson, generally known as Church Wilson. Church had been a senior member of a local Orange Lodge and chairman of a lawn bowling club. He had lost his wife, Maggie's mother, to sudden septicaemia, but had been a conscientious and devoted single father to the daughter, on whom he doted. Maggie would have liked to take over the butchery when Church retired, but she was then seeing a young man, Eddie Hislop, who had his own hairdressing business in the West End, and wanted to join him in that rather than work in the butchery. Her marriage to Eddie had not worked out; she had discovered that he was having an affair with one of his regular clients, and on being challenged he had confessed to several other infidelities. 'I can't resist these ladies,' he said. 'I know it sounds weak, but I just can't.'

Once divorced, Maggie met Nicola's aunt at a Jimmy Shand tribute concert and was offered a job at the pie factory. She was soon an indispensable part of the operation, and in due course recruited Hen McQuoist, with whom she had been at primary school. She remembered him from those days, but he did not, although they both appeared in school photographs, seated a few places away from one another, polished and smiling through missing milk teeth.

They became lovers, and eventually spouses. Hen had proposed to Maggie twice before she eventually accepted him: once at a dog race, on another occasion in a café at Central Station, and finally in an Italian restaurant on Byres Road. On the first two occasions, she had turned him down as tactfully as she could; certainly, she loved him – and told him so – but her experience of marriage to Eddie had put her off the institution of marriage. 'We can be just as happy as we are,' she said to Hen. 'We don't need to bring the Church of Scotland into this.'

Hen had accepted the situation, although he secretly nursed an intention to propose to her again. They were happy living together – they had a small house in Shawfield – and working as colleagues in the pie factory. People sought greater things, of course; the ambitious would regard their situation as being modest to the point of dullness, but they were wrong. A small, ordered life, lived quietly and without fuss, causing no harm to anybody (if one discounted the widespread arterial damage caused by their Scotch pies) was preferable, surely, to one of excitement and risk.

Maggie smiled broadly when Hen introduced the boys. 'Ever been in a pie factory before?' she asked.

Bertie shook his head. 'We're from Edinburgh.'

Maggie laughed. 'Frae Edinburgh then? And there are no pie factories in Edinburgh?'

Ranald Braveheart Macpherson answered for the two of them. 'None,' he said.

Maggie rolled her eyes. 'So what do you folk eat over there?'

'Healthy food,' said Bertie, adding, 'most of the time.'

'Nothing unhealthy about oor pies,' said Maggie, winking at Hen as she spoke. 'Come with me and I'll show you how we do it.'

Hen went to join Nicola in the office and left Maggie to take the boys to the large mixing machine – ex-Aberdeenshire Roads Department.

'This is a highly sophisticated piece of catering equipment,' said Maggie. 'State of the art, I believe. You put the flour, water and lard in the top there, you see, and then you switch it on and it mixes it.'

Bertie stared up at the towering cement mixer. 'That must make a lot of pies,' he said.

'Oh yes,' said Maggie. 'Each load makes seven hundred. Would you like to see it working?'

The boys nodded eagerly.

'Yous can shovel some of the lard in, if you like,' said Maggie. 'We've already put in the flour and hot water.'

The boys helped transfer the contents of several barrels of lard into the maw of the mixer. Then Maggie instructed them to stand back while she turned on a switch. With a grumble and a shaking, the great machine began to turn its barrel round and round, mixing the ingredients. Maggie increased the speed and after a few minutes flicked another switch. The barrel tilted and the mixture began to pour out into moulds sunk in large trays. These trays had been slipped into position by a young man with ginger hair, who waved to the boys as he expertly manoeuvred the recipient trays into position.

'See him?' said Maggie. 'That's Billy. Big Rangers supporter. Maybe he'll take you to a game one of these days.'

It was a promise beyond the wildest dreams of both Bertie and Ranald Braveheart Macpherson and words might have been expected to fail them. But they both knew that they were representing Edinburgh here, and must be polite.

'That would be very nice,' said Bertie.

And Ranald Braveheart Macpherson said, 'Thank you, I would like that very much indeed. Thank you.'

The boys watched in fascination as the rest of the pie-making process was revealed. Then, moving to the baking side of the factory, they were rewarded with the sight of trays of pies being taken out of the oven and left to cool on racks.

'Fancy a pie?' asked Maggie, handing each boy a still-hot and deliciously aromatic Scotch pie.

They each ate three pies. Then, replete almost to the point of discomfort, they were taken by Maggie back to the office, where Nicola and Hen had just completed their discussion of the accounts.

'Smart wee fellows,' said Maggie, smiling at Nicola.

'Perhaps we could fix them up with apprenticeships,' said Hen. 'A wee bit later on, of course.'

'Yes, please,' said Bertie eagerly. He could think of nothing more exciting than being an apprentice pie-maker in Glasgow. He might be too young at present, but he had heard that at sixteen you could leave school and start an apprentice-ship. That is what he would do. He would not tell anybody in Edinburgh where he was going, as he would not want them to try to stop him. In particular, he was unwilling for Olive to know where he was. She could be told that he was dead: that was by far the best solution, Bertie thought. Olive could be told that he had been swept out to sea or struck by lightning – anything that was swift and final. She would have to find somebody else to torment then.

Nicola said goodbye to Hen and to Maggie and took the boys back to the car. 'Well, then,' she said. 'Now we can get over to Bearsden and the place where you two will be staying for the next month.'

Bertie glanced wide-eyed at Ranald: one month, he

thought, one whole month – in Glasgow – by ourselves. The sheer enormity of what they were about to do came upon him suddenly – and it came upon Ranald Braveheart Macpherson too, who began to cry, the tears welling in his eyes – and spotted by Bertie as they ran their course down his cheeks, although Ranald had turned his head away so that his friend might not see them and think him weak, in spite of the heroic name he bore. He had eaten too many Scotch pies, and he wanted to be sick.

'I want to go back to Edinburgh,' said Ranald. 'I've had enough of Glasgow.'

59. Bacon Recipes

James settled quickly into the new routine that Elspeth and Matthew had planned for him. Each week, two mornings and one evening would be spent helping to look after the boys. To this would be added one Saturday a month and the occasional Sunday, if circumstances required it. For these duties he would receive three hundred pounds a week, along with his accommodation – he would remain in the attic bedroom that he so liked – and his board. This was considerably more than the going rate for the hours involved, but Matthew and Elspeth were generous employers. Matthew had always taken the view that there was something fundamentally wrong in the way in which society increased its rewards as people became older. That, he thought was precisely the wrong way round: people should start off being paid more when they were young and their salaries should gradually tail off with the years. That was only right, he thought, because young people could do more with money than older people: they had fewer of the things that we need in this life, whereas older people had acquired far more. They had mortgages to pay and children to feed and clothe, while such claims on a person's pocket diminished as the years went by.

James said, 'You're paying me too much, Matthew.'

That was a protest that is rarely heard – anywhere and in any circumstances, but James was unusual, as were Matthew and Elspeth. The protest was met with surprised silence, and then laughter. Nothing more was said.

The rest of James's working time was allocated to Big Lou's coffee bar, where James had quickly made himself indispensable. Big Lou had been sceptical at first – 'Do I *need* anybody?' she asked Matthew. 'I can do all the things that need doing myself. I can make the bacon rolls ...'

Matthew had been tactful. The bacon rolls were the problem – not in their *essence*, as they were as delicious as bacon rolls can be expected to be, but in their *singularity*, as they were the only thing on the menu. He wanted to say to her, *We live in an age of choice, Lou*, but he held back. Big Lou was sensitive to criticism, and he sensed that consumer choice was not a priority for her. Nor was any attempt to broaden the customer base: 'We get the people who want to come here, Matthew,' she had said to him. 'We don't get the people who don't want to come. They go elsewhere, you see – to the places they want to go to.'

Bacon proved to be the route by which culinary transformation could be achieved.

'I see you have lots of bacon, Lou,' James observed, as he surveyed the contents of the fridge in the coffee bar's small kitchen.

'Aye,' said Lou. 'We serve bacon rolls, you see, James. That's why we have bacon.'

'I like a bacon roll,' said James, planning to continue with, 'But there are other ... '

Big Lou cut him short. 'So do the customers. That's why we serve them.'

The following morning, James was prepared.

'You know that bacon,' he began.

'Aye, bacon,' said Lou. 'What of it?'

'A very versatile ingredient,' James said.

Big Lou thought for moment. Then she observed, 'Versatile? I suppose it is. You can have it crisp or not-so-crisp. I suppose that's versatile.'

James laughed. 'You could say that,' he said. 'But there's more to bacon than meets the eye, Lou.'

James had brought a book with him, and he now showed it to Big Lou. 'See this, Lou?' he began. *The Little Bacon Cookbook.*

Big Lou glanced at the book, the cover of which showed bacon rashers sizzling in a saucepan. 'You don't need a book to teach you how to cook bacon,' she said.

James smiled. 'But you do need a book to teach you how to cook *Bacon-Wrapped Sweet Potato with Avocado Wedges.* Or

Creamy Bacon Scalloped Potatoes. Or even *Cinnamon-Spiced Bacon Monkey Bread.*'

As he uttered the names of these exotic baconian constructions, James turned the pages to reveal pictures of the dishes in question. Big Lou glanced at the monkey bread, and hesitated. The sweet tooth, so firmly planted in the Scottish mouth, made its presence felt, and she took the book from James and studied the recipe for the sticky confection.

James pressed ahead. 'We could start with one or two bacon-related things, Lou. Not too much. Just enough to give the menu some variety.'

Big Lou handed the book back. 'You'll cook?'

'With pleasure.'

'I suppose it can't do any harm.'

The case was made, and accepted, although James was careful not to make this seem a victory. 'You won't regret having had the idea, Lou,' he said.

But Big Lou was not so easily flattered. 'It was your idea, not mine,' she said.

'Of course,' said James hurriedly.

It was at this point that Matthew came in for his regular morning coffee. After Big Lou had prepared this for him, he beckoned James over to his table.

'Everything going all right?' he asked.

James nodded. 'Fine. And I'm enjoying it. But there's something worrying me, Matthew.'

Matthew waited.

'My uncle,' said James. 'We have to do something, Matthew. I had an email from him yesterday. Would you like to read it?'

He handed Matthew his phone, and Matthew read the message displayed. *Seamus, I just thought I'd let you know I'm all right. Uncle.'*

Matthew frowned. 'Odd,' he said. 'You told me he never called you Seamus. And then ... '

'And then why would he send a message to say that he was all right? Who sends that sort of thing – unless they're *not* all right? We must do something,' said James. 'We have to. We can't let things go on like this.'

They had been absorbed in the message and had not noticed a figure approaching their table. Now the figure was upon them. It was Sister Maria-Fiore dei Fiori di Montagna, and she was carrying a small tray with a cup of coffee and a bacon roll on it.

'Don't let me interrupt,' she said, and then sat down. 'Can't let *what* go on like this?' she asked. 'Not that I'd wish to pry.'

There was silence, and then Matthew introduced James to the nun. She looked at the young man inquisitively.

'I'm worried about my uncle,' said James.

Sister Maria-Fiore dei Fiori di Montagna reached for her cup of coffee. 'Worry is like a monster,' she said, 'that devours its children. We worry about that which we worry about, and then we worry about the fact that we worry. So does our poor world heave and buckle under an ever-increasing burden of worry.'

Matthew scratched his head. 'Or whatever,' he muttered.

'We must do something,' said James.

'Doing something is often just the right thing to do,' said Sister Maria-Fiore dei Fiori di Montagna. 'Do nothing, and you'll find that the nothing you do becomes the background for the things that you should do – were you to do something rather than nothing. Nothing becomes something – and something becomes nothing. I have seen that happen so many times before.'

She sighed, and Matthew sighed too. James pursed his lips.

'I want to go round there tonight,' he said. 'I want to go round and help get him out.'

'We must indeed help one another,' said Sister Maria-Fiore dei Fiori di Montagna. 'None of us is a peninsula.'

Matthew grinned. 'Island,' he said.

'That too,' said Sister Maria-Fiore dei Fiori di Montagna.

'When all is said and *Donne*,' said Matthew, who wondered whether to explain the allusion, but decided not to. James belonged to a generation for whom such things must seem remote echoes of an ancient culture, and Sister Maria-Fiore dei Fiori di Montagna had Petrarch and Dante to contend with.

But James surprised him. 'That's *Clare* enough,' he said, and fixed Matthew with a look that said, *Don't condescend, Matthew.*

'Very amusing,' said Sister Maria-Fiore dei Fiori di Montagna.

60. A Fine Tenor Voice

As an adult, Matthew rarely admitted that he was slightly afraid of the dark. This was precisely the opposite of what people advised: 'Talking about a problem,' he had read, 'deprives it of its power.' He understood why this should be the case, but he could still not bring himself to confess that if alone in the dark, he felt, at best, uncomfortable and, at worst, close to panic.

It was a fear that had been with him from early childhood, when he had been unable to sleep without a light's being left on in the room. His parents had tried to wean him off this dependence, but the results had been too traumatic for them to persist with their programme of gradually lowering the brightness of his bedroom light. Although he might drop off to sleep with his bedside lamp dimmed, if he woke up in the middle of the night to a room in subdued lighting, his terrified sobbing would awaken the whole household. A clinical psychologist had diagnosed his nyctophobia when he was eight, and had embarked on treatment, but it was not until he was almost fourteen that he could face going to bed in anything approaching real darkness. He was ashamed of this, of course, and felt miserable too, just as a child will be made miserable by nocturnal enuresis, and his shame compounded the problem. By the age of sixteen, though, patient and gradual desensitisation had enabled him to turn out his light at night without the immediate onset of panic. That made life easier, but every so often the residue of the old phobia would manifest itself, and he would struggle to keep calm if he found himself in darkness, natural or otherwise.

Now, as he stood with James outside the house at Nine Mile Burn, underneath the high and empty night sky, Matthew shivered, and felt the touch of that old fear. They were about to get into the car and drive down to Single Malt House, six miles away, where James was convinced his uncle, the Duke of Johannesburg, was being held against his will by his Gaelic-speaking driver, Pàdruig. In daytime, under the rational light of a Lothian sun, Matthew had readily agreed to accompany James on his planned rescue mission; now, under this velvet emptiness, with the land spreading out around them, dark and mysterious, the hills' black shapes crouching like malevolent shadows, Matthew was not so sure that this was what he wanted to be doing. But it was too late to withdraw and he would have to see the whole escapade through, no matter what misgivings he had about it.

James patted the pockets of his Barbour jacket. 'I've got a torch,' he said. 'And I have a sterile dressing. And a hip flask with some brandy. Brandy revives people, I believe.'

Matthew expressed surprise. 'Nobody's going to get hurt, I hope. Or need revival.'

'I hope so too,' said James. 'But what if we find my uncle in need of first aid? What if Pàdruig has tied him up?'

Matthew laughed, although his laughter was hesitant and nervous. 'I very much doubt if we'll find that,' he said. 'In fact, I suspect we'll not discover anything untoward. We'll probably find your uncle sitting in his chair, reading, and looking rather surprised to see us coming in the window.'

'I wouldn't be so sure,' said James. 'I think he's been kidnapped.'

Matthew shook his head in disbelief. 'You've been watching too much Scandinavian noir. Those things make out that kidnapping happens every day – it doesn't. Nobody I know has ever been kidnapped – not a single person.'

And yet, even as he spoke, Matthew gave an inward shiver at the thought. There *was* something amiss at Single Malt House, even if it was not a kidnapping. There was something about Pàdruig that made him feel uneasy – a hint of menace that Matthew could not quite put his finger on, but which he sensed just below the surface.

'We need to get going,' he said, looking at his watch, but unable to read the dial in the darkness. When he was a boy, he had found an old luminous watch in a charity shop and had bought it. He was proud of its glowing dial, which cast a tiny green light over the skin if one held it to one's palm, and had protested vigorously when his mother had taken the watch from him and disposed of it. He had been too young to understand her warning him of the dangers of radiation and was only silenced when she told him that the people who painted such watches in the factory eventually lost their fingers. 'They also licked their paint brushes to make a suitably delicate point,' she said. 'They lost their lips from that. The radium ate their lips away.'

James checked his pockets and then slipped a dark balaclava over his head. He had one for Matthew, and handed it to him now.

'I'm not putting that thing on,' said Matthew. 'Or at least, not yet. What if people saw us driving along like that?'

James sheepishly took off the balaclava. 'Later,' he said. 'We can use them later.'

They got into the car and drove off in the night. In the middle distance, a slight glow in the sky told them where Penicuik was, Edinburgh's orange light being hidden by the rising bulk of the Pentland Hills. They travelled in silence. Matthew was thinking of a film he had seen of resistance fighters in the mountains of Greece, and of how they lay in wait in the darkness to capture a German general. This was a bit like that, he thought, or the closest he was likely to come to that sort of thing. How would I have been if I had been there, he asked himself, in *real* danger, rather than merely taking part in this ludicrous schoolboy escapade? I would have been too cowardly, he told himself. I would never have done anything remotely brave.

As they approached the driveway of Single Malt House, Matthew switched off the headlights and drew the car to a halt. James now donned his balaclava, and Matthew followed suit. Then, together they crept through the shrubs that lay between them and the lumpy shape of the farmhouse. Light escaped from a window on the upper floor, and some, too, came from the kitchen. Otherwise the house was in darkness.

'We'll go in the same way as last time,' whispered James. 'I'll go first.'

A few minutes later, they were in the scullery, having climbed through the window, and were listening for any sounds of occupation. There was music playing some-where, the notes finding their way down the long corridor and through doors. Matthew cocked his head. 'Kenneth McKellar,' he said.

'Who?' asked James.

'He had a wonderful tenor voice,' said Matthew.

He strained to make out the tune. *I Love a Lassie*.

'Yes, that's him,' he said.

James signalled it was time to go. 'We'll try my uncle's bedroom first,' he said.

I love a lassie, sang Kenneth McKellar. *A bonnie Hielan' lassie . . .*

61. Brochan Lom

They made their way along the narrow, unlit corridor leading to the stairs at the back of Single Malt House. As the light of their torch fell upon walls lined with faded wallpaper and dusty picture frames, Matthew's practised eye could not resist appraising the pictures within the frames – after all, he was, first and foremost, an art dealer, and only secondly a reluctant housebreaker. Even in these tense circumstances he found himself glancing at the pictures, trying to make out what was what in the dim and moving torchlight.

He reached out to touch James's arm. 'Look,' he whispered. 'Look at this painting.'

James shone the beam of the torch onto a small oil

painting in an elaborate gilt frame. 'We need to get on,' he said. 'We can't stand here and . . . '

Matthew cut him short. 'Have you seen this one before?' he asked.

James bent forward to peer at the painting. He seemed uncertain. 'Maybe. Maybe not.' And then, after a short pause, 'Yes, I think so. I think my uncle showed it to me. I can't remember what he said about it.'

Matthew took the torch from him and held it closer to the painting. There was something about the painting that made him feel uneasy. Was this a clue, in a sense, to the mystery that hung over the life of the man who lived in this house?

Matthew glanced at the picture next to the one he had just examined. It was a McIan print of a Highlander bedecked in tartan, standing beside an illicit still. Printed below was the title, *Beyond the Reach of the Excise Man*. That was more the sort of thing one would expect to see in a farmhouse of this sort, he thought – particularly one called Single Malt House.

They reached the backstairs and began to make their way up to the bedroom floor. The music became louder now, as it was emanating from a room on this floor. Kenneth McKellar had finished his paean to his Scots bluebell and had moved on to a rendition of *Brochan Lom*, a familiar nonsense song about thin porridge. Matthew smiled to hear it – he had learned the song as a child – but then he remembered where they were, and why, and his smile quickly faded.

Now, at the top of the stairs, James pointed at a door on the other side of the landing. 'That's his room,' he whispered.

Matthew moved past James. Reaching out, he put a hand on the door handle and twisted it slowly. As he did so, the memory came back to him of something he had just read. Elspeth had given him a copy of Somerset Maugham's *The Painted Veil*, and he remembered Maugham's chilling description of the woman watching the twisting of the handle of her locked bedroom door while she lay inside with her lover. It was something capable of generating a very particular dread: seeing the handle of a door turning while not knowing who is on the other side, and now here he was performing that very action. *How did I let myself in for this?* he asked himself. *I should have said no. This is the second time I have come into this house uninvited. The second time ...*

'It's locked,' said Matthew, his voice just above a whisper. Even so, he wondered whether whoever was inside would hear him, or whether, further away, Pàdruig, whom he supposed to be listening to Kenneth McKellar, might hear their whispers above the jaunty Scottish music.

James tried the door handle himself, more forcefully than had Matthew, who winced at the noise that this more energetic turning made. Again, the door did not move.

'I'm going to break it down,' said James, hardly bothering to lower his voice.

Matthew made a cancelling gesture. 'No,' he hissed. 'We can't ...'

But his objection was ignored and, taking a few steps back, James hurled himself at the locked door, his shoulder meeting the central panel with a heavy thud.

The door withstood the onslaught. James stepped back, again ignoring Matthew's protests, and charged. This time the collision produced results, and with a sharp, cracking sound the lock gave way and the door swung open. For a moment it seemed as if James might lose his footing and fall into the room, but he recovered his balance and was still standing when the door swung back in rebound and hit him painfully on his right arm. Involuntarily, he let out a yelp of pain.

Matthew expected Kenneth McKellar to come to an abrupt stop, but no, the mellifluous crooning continued, moderately seamlessly, into *Mairi's Wedding* to the accompaniment of an accordion quartet. Now James was flashing the torch into the room, the beam revealing a large four-poster bed in which the Duke of Johannesburg, wearing a pair of striped flannel pyjamas, was sitting bolt upright, wide-eyed with shock at the sudden intrusion. Matthew's eyes fell on the Duke, took in his entirely understandable astonishment, but then moved to the lock of the door they had just broken down. *There was no key on the inside.* And at that moment, Matthew knew that breaking in, risky though it had been, was the right thing to have done. The Duke had been locked into his room. He had not locked himself in; he had been detained by somebody else. And that person, of course, was Pàdruig.

Things now moved very quickly. James ran to his uncle's side. 'Are you all right?' he asked. 'Are you hurt, Uncle?'

The Duke looked puzzled. 'Hurt?' he asked.

James took his uncle's hand and began to haul him out of bed. 'Quick,' he said. 'Get your dressing gown on.'

The Duke tried to resist, but his nephew was insistent, bundling him off the side of the bed and into the dressing gown that Matthew had taken off the back of a nearby chair.

'And your slippers,' said James. 'Quickly.'

'Why …' the Duke began to ask, but Matthew was already pushing him across the room.

'Later,' said James. 'We can talk later.'

A light was switched on outside the room. There, fully dressed, stood Pàdruig, his eyes narrowed, holding a golf club – a driver – in his right hand.

The Duke looked at one driver, and then at the other. 'Go away, MacCrimmon, or whatever your name is,' he shouted. 'You can go back to Stornoway tomorrow.'

Pàdruig glared at his employer. 'But …' he lamented.

Matthew shook a finger. 'You heard him,' he said, and then added, 'You're a …' Matthew was not a vindictive man; he was moderate in his views and his language. And the vocabulary of the moderate may often fail to rise to an occasion of real challenge. And so he said, simply, 'You're a really …' Silence fell over the other three as they waited for his condemnation. And then it came: 'Bad influence. You're a really bad influence.'

There might have been laughter, but instead there was a sharp intake of breath from Pàdruig.

'Influence?' the driver growled. 'Who are you calling an influence? Influence yourself!'

The Duke tried to defuse the situation. 'Now, that's a bit steep, Matthew. He's an enthusiast – that's all.'

The Duke looked almost apologetic as he continued: 'And we must remember, Pàdruig comes from Stornoway and may look at things differently.'

Matthew stared at the Duke. The realisation came to him suddenly, but with great clarity. *Stockholm Syndrome*, he thought.

62. Stockholm Syndrome

They took the Duke back to the house at Nine Mile Burn where Elspeth had remained up, anxiously awaiting their return. Matthew had promised to telephone her once the mission was accomplished, but in the excitement of the rescue he had forgotten to do so. He might have thought of Theseus, who famously returned from Crete without replacing his black sail with a white one – a mistake that led King Aegeus to believe his son was dead, and to kill himself in his misery. But he did not, and he only remembered the promised call when he was minutes away from home, and it was too late. Elspeth half expected him to forget – men were like that, she thought – but she certainly felt growing concern until the lights of the car appeared through the rhododendrons to tell her that Matthew was safe.

'We're back,' announced Matthew, peeling off the balaclava that, in his excitement, he had failed to remove.

Elspeth fussed about the Duke. She had prepared hot chocolate and cheese sandwiches, which she now offered to him.

'The Duke is very tired,' said Matthew. 'He needs to get to bed. He can take his hot chocolate and sandwiches with him.'

James took his uncle to the spare bedroom where a bed for visitors was already made up.

'We can talk tomorrow, Uncle,' James said. 'You should get some sleep now.'

The Duke nodded. He had said very little in the car on the way back, and James sensed that he was in no mood for conversation. James seemed tired, too, and so they decided that discussion of the night's events could wait until tomorrow, when the light of day, and a chance to hear the Duke's side of the story, might make everything clearer.

Matthew and Elspeth slept in. It was Josefine's turn to deal with the triplets, and they were already dressed and had left for their play group in West Linton. Elspeth had been relieved to discover that Josefine drove, as this meant she could do her share of taxi-ing the boys to and from the village hall where their play group met.

James was also up and about, as was the Duke. James had made him breakfast, and the Duke was now finishing a slice of toast spread with Dundee thick-cut marmalade. He rose to his feet as Elspeth and Matthew came into the kitchen.

'We jumped the gun for breakfast,' the Duke said. 'James said you wouldn't mind ... '

'Of course not,' Matthew reassured him. He noticed that the Duke was wearing clothes that he had seen on James, and he remembered that they had brought him to the house the previous evening clad in pyjamas and dressing gown.

The Duke smiled. 'My garb is unusually fashionable,' he said. 'Cool, even. Thanks to James.'

'Not everyone's uncle could carry that sort of thing off,' said James.

Elspeth busied herself with preparing boiled eggs while

Matthew sat down at the table with James and the Duke. 'Well,' Matthew began. 'Here we are.'

The Duke nodded. 'Indeed.' He looked at James. 'James, you might . . .'

'We've had a chat,' said James. 'Uncle has explained everything.'

Matthew waited. Elspeth half turned, an egg in her hand, poised above the pot.

'It was Gaelic immersion,' James went on. 'Pàdruig was determined that Uncle should learn Gaelic.'

'I wanted to,' said the Duke. 'I've always liked the Gaelic language.'

'Yes,' said James. 'I know that. But he took it too far. He started to force you. And he had no right to lock you up.'

'It was perhaps a bit extreme,' mused the Duke. 'But language immersion is, by its very nature . . .'

Elspeth interrupted him. 'It was an outrage.'

The Duke stared at the floor. He looked embarrassed, thought Matthew – rather like a person who has done something foolish and finds it hard to explain his actions. 'I found it hard to resist,' he said. 'Pàdruig is very persuasive.'

'Stockholm Syndrome,' muttered Matthew.

They all looked at him. 'What?' asked James. 'Stockholm?'

Matthew hesitated. 'It's a condition,' he explained. 'Not Stendhal Syndrome, of course. Different.'

Elspeth remembered Matthew talking about Stendhal Syndrome after Angus had described to him Antonia Collie's unfortunate episode in the Uffizi Gallery in Florence. Surrounded by great art, she had begun to breathe heavily, feel flushed, and had eventually succumbed to artistic overload.

'When I first heard about it, I found it hard to believe,' Elspeth said, 'that Stendhal Syndrome actually existed. But it does, apparently. And this ... this Stockholm Syndrome – what does it entail?'

The Duke looked up, with the interested expression of a patient about to hear his diagnosis.

'It's identification with a captor,' said Matthew. He had not intended to air his suspicions in the Duke's presence – his muttering had been unintentional. But now he could hardly refuse, and the Duke himself appeared to be interested.

'I'm no expert,' he said.

'Do go on,' the Duke encouraged. 'I don't mind in the slightest.'

'Well,' Matthew continued, 'I've read a little bit about it. I can't remember where, but it piqued my interest, I suppose. It's called Stockholm Syndrome because of an early case of it in Sweden. A bank robber took hostages, and the hostages eventually seemed to side with him. They declined to give evidence against him when he was eventually arrested.'

The Duke's eyes widened.

'And then,' Matthew said, 'there was Patty Hearst and the Symbionese Liberation Army. She was kidnapped and then joined her captors, doing their bidding, signing up, effectively. That was Stockholm Syndrome, or so it seems.'

The Duke continued to look thoughtful.

'She was eventually pardoned by President Clinton,' said Matthew.

The Duke looked up. 'I didn't do anything wrong,' he said.

Elspeth looked at him with sympathy. 'Of course you didn't.'

James agreed. 'You were the victim, Uncle. You weren't immersing anybody in Gaelic – you were immersed.'

'I still want to learn the language,' said the Duke, looking miserable.

'Quite right,' said Matthew. 'It's very important that Gaelic is kept alive. It's just that Pàdruig was trying to force you. He had no right to lock you up.'

'He meant well,' said the Duke.

'You're free now,' said James. 'You're free to speak English or Gaelic – as you wish.'

'I didn't really make much progress,' said the Duke.

Matthew smiled. 'No harm done then.' But even as he reached this cheerful conclusion, he was wondering about the psychological implications. Discreetly, he switched on his phone and navigated to his music streaming programme. *Kenneth McKellar* – there he was. And there, too, was *Jimmy Shand and His Band*. He touched the screen and Jimmy Shand's band sounded through the phone's speakers – distant, tinny, but immediately recognisable.

The Duke looked up. His lower lip quivered. He began to breathe deeply.

Matthew glanced at Elspeth. 'We need to get him to a doctor,' he whispered.

63. Widdershins or Deasil

Angus was telephoned by Domenica while he was walking Cyril in Drummond Place Garden. It was Cyril's second walk of the day, the first having taken place, as it always did, at eight-thirty in the morning and having led them up Dublin Street, along Abercromby Place, and then down Dundas Street to Big Lou's café. It was, in a sense, a *paysage moralisé*, as charged with moral meaning as Piero di Cosimo's *The Discovery of Honey by Bacchus*: Dublin Street, which rose sharply up towards Queen Street, represented an early challenge: reaching a summit requires effort whatever the nature of the elevation – Angus understood that, and he thought that Cyril grasped it too through the fog of limitation that swirled around the mind of a dog. Cyril knew that certain rewards had to be earned – that dog biscuits, enticing in their musty meatiness, the canine equivalent of Belgian chocolate truffles, were only obtained after you had done something: fetched a stick or a ball, pointlessly thrown, in the way in which humans, for unfathomable reasons, threw sticks and balls for dogs to retrieve; extended a paw for an unhygienic handshake (the *namaste* gesture was so difficult if you were a quadruped); or otherwise performed in a way that met with favour from your *comptroller*. (Edinburgh dogs do not have owners – too prosaic a term – they have *comptrollers*.)

Turning right into Abercromby Place, the effort of ascending Dublin Street was rewarded with a pleasant meander, on the level, with more gardens opening up to the south. These gardens had their role in the *paysage moralisé* in that they revealed a terrain of trees and squirrels, a city as celestial as that glimpsed by Christian beyond Bunyan's wicket gate. But, like Christian, Cyril was held back from entry at this stage; further temptations had to be overcome once they reached Big Lou's. There, under the table, with its distinctive sub-tabular smells, Cyril's self-restraint was frequently tested almost to breaking point as he contemplated the ankles that he might so easily and deliciously nip. He did not bite; lesser dogs did that; dogs brought up in ill-disciplined homes; dogs with *comptrollers* who did not care what their dogs should do, or who excused it on the grounds that dogs will be dogs. Such dogs might bite, rather than nip, and were responsible for much bad feeling in the functioning of the otherwise seamless social contract between dogs and man.

That was the first walk of the day; the second walk had less variety, and was confined to the path that led round the internal perimeter of Drummond Place Garden. This walk took place widdershins or deasil, depending on the mood in which Angus found himself. There was no underlying reason for choosing between these two directions, although going widdershins – anti-clockwise – meant that the garden would always be kept on their left, the iron railings on the right. Around widdershins movement there hung a vague feeling of ill luck, and Angus knew that some users of the garden preferred to walk deasil because of intuitive preferences to having the open possibility – in this case the garden, rather than the railings – on one's right. Such things can be mere superstitions, or can be based on some ancient memory of being able to deal with threats more easily if they emerged from the right side. For Angus, though, it was a question of mood: a positive mood naturally proposed the deasil alternative, while doubt or a plain lack of *oomph* predisposed one to the widdershins option. For Cyril, it made no difference: smells were what counted for him; they came at him in delicious, jostling profusion, from every direction, and the angle of shadows was a matter of complete indifference.

On that particular morning they were halfway through a deasil walk when Angus's mobile phone rang. Cyril's ears perked up at the disturbance, but he was quickly distracted by a distant scent of squirrel – a cold trail, he knew, but one to which attention would have to be paid.

It was Domenica.

'I know you'll be back soon,' she began, 'but I just had to speak to you. There's been a bit of drama.'

The expression, *a bit of drama*, was used by Domenica to describe anything from Chernobyl to running out of Earl Grey tea, and so Angus was not alarmed by this portentous opening.

'Government fallen?' he asked. 'Market crashed? Electric toothbrush fused?'

'Very droll,' said Domenica. 'No, it's news from Dr Colquohoun.'

'Ah,' said Angus. 'And what's the verdict from Chambers Street? A genuine Neanderthal skull?'

'No,' said Domenica. 'Or, put it this way – that's still a possibility.'

Angus waited.

'It's rather unfortunate,' Domenica continued. 'You may recall him saying that he was going to catch the 23 bus back up to George IV Bridge.'

'Vaguely,' said Angus.

'Well, he did. And he's just phoned to confess that he left the skull on the bus.'

Angus was silent. This was almost unbelievable. Then, after a few moments, he said, 'You mean to say that he left our Neanderthal skull on the 23 bus? That he got off without it?'

'That's exactly what happened.'

Angus groaned. 'And?'

'And he reported it to the lost property office of Lothian Buses. At first, they thought he was joking. They asked him if his father knew he was playing with the phone. But then they realised it was all deadly serious. They went off to check up whether any skulls had been handed in – they get all sorts of things. apparently, including, last week, a set of false teeth and a first edition of MacDiarmid's *A Drunk Man Looks at the Thistle*. But no skull had been handed in. They asked him how to spell Neanderthal and then they suggested listing it as an item of household furniture, possibly an ashtray. He didn't bother to disabuse them of the notion and let them put it down as *ornamental skull (poor condition)*.'

'Perhaps it'll turn up,' said Angus.

'The museum people very much hope so. I've been on to them since the call, and they are very apologetic. They said they had not lost anything for seventeen years, the last object to go missing being Prince Charles Edward Stuart's toothbrush, which was of dubious authenticity anyway. That was eventually found in the staff washroom, where, judging from the traces of toothpaste on its bristles, it had been well used by a member of the museum's curatorial staff.'

They concluded the conversation, and Angus agreed to return home immediately in order to discuss this distressing development. As he left the garden, closing the gate behind him, he became aware of a figure approaching him. It was Sister Maria-Fiore dei Fiori di Montagna, and he was not at all sure that he had the energy to talk to the aphorism-coining Italian nun. But she clearly intended to speak to him, and so, with an inward sigh, Angus prepared himself for the encounter.

64. In Deepest Morningside

Sister Maria-Fiore dei Fiori di Montagna had been shopping in George Street and had bought herself a new pair of sunglasses. She had dropped her last pair into the Water of Leith when on a walk with her friend and flatmate, Antonia Collie. Antonia had valiantly tried to retrieve them, but had failed, and had to be dissuaded from wading further into the water on her mission of recovery.

'A pair of sunglasses is nothing,' protested Sister Maria-Fiore. 'A human life is of far greater value. There can be few who doubt that, I think.'

Antonia had retorted that the Water of Leith, which was at its lowest level that year because of a prolonged dry period, was hardly a raging torrent, and could be crossed, bank to bank, without any risk of wetting anything above one's ankles.

Sister Maria-Fiore shook a risk-averse finger. 'Most drownings occur in very shallow water,' she warned. 'A puddle is enough in some cases. The Blessed Alberto degli Olivi Santi, rest his soul – a kinsman of mine, as it happens, on my late, sainted mother's side – was drowned in a small basin of water when he fell forward into it in a transport of ecstasy. You cannot be too careful.' She paused. 'He, of course, was reanimated through the direct intervention of the Holy Ghost, and was thereby granted a further fourteen years in which to do acts of exceptional goodness through-out Puglia.'

Now, through the newly acquired glasses, her gaze fell on Angus and Cyril emerging from Drummond Place Garden, and she strode to meet them. She enjoyed Angus's company, and never lost an opportunity to regale him with her views on a wide variety of subjects, theological, deontological and artistic. And now that she was on the Board of Trustees of the Scottish National Gallery there was so much more to opine upon. Angus was in no mood for this now: he wanted to get home to discuss with Domenica the dramatic news that the Neanderthal skull he – or rather Cyril – had found in the lower Moray Place Gardens had been lost by Dr Colquohoun.

Poor man, he thought. He could just imagine the sense of horror he experienced when he arrived back at the museum and realised that the priceless relic he had been carrying was well on its way to the furthest point of the 23 bus route – deepest Morningside. Morningside would not be a place that one would expect to be in sympathy with Neanderthal items, and a local resident travelling on the bus might well consider the skull to be rather distasteful, unhygienic rubbish and dispose of it accordingly. One might remind such people of the fact that two per cent of our human genome was made up of Neanderthal genes, but Angus did not think that Morningside was the sort of place where such information would necessarily be welcomed. He imagined the reaction: 'Neanderthal, you say? Ai'm not at all sure theat theat applies to all of us, if Ai may say so.'

He reflected on the vagaries of fate. It would be a great loss to palaeontology if *Homo watsoniensis*, as he now thought of the skull, were to be altogether lost. If only we had taken a photograph, he said to himself; if only we had insisted on delivering the skull in one of those security vans used for carrying money to and from the bank. If only . . . There was no point in berating himself, or Dr Colquohoun for that matter, thought Angus. What is lost on the 23 bus stays on the 23 bus . . . so to speak. And there he stopped himself. The skull might stay under a seat for some time – at least until the bus received a thorough cleaning and it was discovered. If that were to be the case, then there might be plenty of time still to retrieve it. This led him to speculate as to whether Dr Colquohoun had been rigorous enough in his enquiries of the transport office. It would not be enough, Angus thought, simply to ask if a Neanderthal skull had been handed in: one would surely have to be more proactive, getting on as many

23 buses as possible and conducting a thorough search of the spaces under the seats. It might be difficult to explain to people what one was doing in conducting such a search, and there would be plenty of room for misunderstanding, but one could brazen it out. Should he do it? he wondered. Perhaps he could take Cyril, who would move from row of seats to row of seats, sniffing like one of those sniffer dogs the customs authorities employed at airports. Such dogs were looking for drugs, of course, but could presumably be trained to sniff out other things. Hypocrisy, for example. Angus imagined a very specialised dog at Edinburgh Airport, moving amongst the passengers, sniffing out hypocrites, or subversives of one stripe or another, doubters of our current orthodoxies perhaps ... There were so many possibilities. Involuntarily – for he did not feel like smiling – he smiled.

Sister Maria-Fiore dei Fiori di Montagna mistook the smile for encouragement. 'My feelings too,' she said. 'Pleasure on seeing an old friend is all the greater when it is unexpected. Saint Augustine of Hippo tells us that friendship ... '

Angus did not allow her to finish. 'Ah,' he said. 'Saint Augustine of Hippo. Of course, of course.'

And with that, he tried to sidestep Sister Maria-Fiore dei Fiori di Montagna.

But he did not succeed. 'You may be interested to hear,' she said, her voice rising to forfend any evasive tactic on Angus's part, 'that we are to have a most interesting meeting at the *Galleria Nazionale Scozzese di Arte.*'

'I'm sorry,' said Angus. 'I'm in a bit of a rush.'

'Aren't we all?' said Sister Maria-Fiore dei Fiori di Montagna. 'We rush through life, our busyness rendering us unaware of the beauty of the world about us. We never pause, nor stop to take stock of who we are and where we are going.'

'I was actually going back to our flat,' said Angus.

Sister Maria-Fiore dei Fiore di Montagna smiled sweetly. 'We are all on a journey home,' she said, adding, 'one way or another.'

65. Man Bitten by a Snake

There was no escape for Angus Lordie as Sister Maria-Fiore dei Fiori di Montagna began to explain to him about the agenda she had received for the meeting she would be attending later that day. The trustees of the Scottish National Gallery, amongst whose number she now counted herself, were concerned with the larger issues affecting Scotland's national collection. These included requests for the loan of paintings to other galleries, issues of conservation, outreach initiatives, and so on: on all of these the trustees might be called to guide the curatorial staff in their task of bringing art to the public. Sister Maria-Fiore's qualifications for this role were not immediately apparent, but the success that she had enjoyed since she first burst on Scotland's social scene had carried her to this, and other heights, unchallenged. There were few photographs in the social columns of *Scottish Field* or *Edinburgh Life* that did not feature the seemingly ubiquitous Italian nun: there she was at the release of a new single malt from Ardnamurchan Distillery, her nose buried appreciatively in a whisky glass; there she was at the Annual Dance of the Scottish Motor Trade Association, dancing the Gay Gordons with prominent motor trade figures; there she was at Publishing Scotland's Annual Reception, engaged in earnest conversation with Val McDermid and Ian Rankin. She was everywhere! It was no surprise, then, to anybody that a small announcement should appear in the *Scotsman* to the effect that Sister Maria-Fiore dei Fiori di Montagna, an acknowledged authority on the Sienese School, should have been appointed a trustee of the Scottish National Gallery. To call her an authority was generous – in the extreme – as her only publication had been a minor note, written in the brief period she spent as a postgraduate student and published in the *Rivista d'Arte*, on the influence of Ambrogio Lorenzetti on the later work of Domenico Beccafumi, a subject on which nobody else had written anything before and indeed nothing had been written subsequently. But publication is not everything, and those who have never expressed a view on a subject may sometimes enjoy a reputation based on what it is thought they *might* know, and in the case of Sister Maria-Fiore dei Fiori di Montagna, what she might lack in knowledge she certainly made up for in enthusiasm. And of course her facility with aphorisms, unrivalled in all Scotland, gave her remarks an additional *gravitas* that all agreed added to the weight – and the sonority – of the Board of Trustees' published minutes.

Now she said to Angus, 'The trustees will be called in to pronounce on warnings this afternoon. Should our paintings – or some of them – be accompanied by a public warning?'

Angus frowned. 'A warning? About what?'

'A warning that the more emotionally sensitive members of the public might be distressed by what they see.'

Angus, in spite of himself and his desire to get back to his flat, was intrigued. 'Do you mean that there'll be notices?' he asked. 'Like those Government health warnings? That sort of thing?'

Sister Maria-Fiore dei Fiori di Montagna, pleased to have engaged his attention, nodded gravely. 'That is what some people are proposing. We have had several concerned members of the public making the same point. There have been letters in the *Scotsman* too. That is why we are to discuss the matter at the trustees' meeting.'

Angus rolled his eyes. 'I can hardly believe this. I really can't.' He had heard about the ban on boiled sweets being thrown to children from the pantomime stage – on the grounds that somebody might be hurt – but this was a new and shocking instance of that overly cautious mindset.

Sister Maria-Fiore dei Fiori di Montagna gave more details. 'It has all arisen over a painting we borrowed from the National Gallery in London,' she said. 'We lent them one of our Poussin *Sacraments* and they lent us their *Landscape with a Man killed by a Snake*. I suspect you know the painting.'

Angus did. He liked Poussin, in spite of the neoclassical coldness, and had spent two full hours some years ago while on a visit to London, standing in front of that particular painting, reflecting on the vague sense of menace it conveyed.

'It's a very powerful painting,' said Sister Maria-Fiore.

'There is a whole book devoted to it, you know – Professor Clark's *Sight of Death*.'

Angus nodded. 'I don't know that book.' He paused before continuing. 'But there are so many books I don't know, I suppose.'

The comment had come out unplanned, and he had not thought much about it before he spoke. But it seemed that a conversation with the aphoristically inclined Italian nun produced just such reflections. There were so many books; there was so little time.

Sister Maria-Fiore absorbed this, and Angus thought that he had probably prompted another aphorism. But she returned to her theme. 'It has been suggested that we identify our most disturbing paintings and put a warning sign in front of them. A red triangle, I believe. Or we could simply have a large notice outside the gallery warning people that some of our paintings might upset them.' She paused. 'I believe universities have to do this now. They have to warn their students if they are going to be asked to read anything upsetting.'

Angus sighed. What could one do, he thought, but sigh? He looked at his watch. They could talk for hours, he imagined, about intellectual freedom, and maturity, and tolerance, and related topics, while all the time the darkness closed in, but he had to get back to Domenica.

'I'm sorry,' he said to Sister Maria-Fiore dei Fiori di Montagna, 'but I must get back to my flat. Nothing to do with Poussin, but we have had our own disturbing news.'

Sister Maria-Fiore looked anxious. 'I'm very sorry to hear that. We like to hear things that are unexpected; we do not like things that are not expected, and ...'

Angus cut short the aphorism. 'Yes, yes. My dog, Cyril, found an old skull, you see – a potentially interesting one – and now it has, alas, been lost.'

Sister Maria-Fiore frowned. 'How funny,' she said. 'Because I was on the 23 bus yesterday, I think it was, and I found something that looked a bit like a skull. It couldn't have been, though. Not on a bus.'

Angus froze. 'And?'

'Oh, I threw it in our kitchen bin,' said Sister Maria-Fiore. 'It was muddy and messy. It was the best place for it, in my view, Mr Lordie.' She paused and then continued: 'It's probably still there, come to think of it.' There was a further pause. 'What we dispose of we do not always dispose of, Mr Lordie.'

66. *Doon the Watter*

Nicola liked the look of Mrs Campbell. And it seemed to her that Bertie and Ranald Braveheart Macpherson thought the same as they were ushered into the sitting room of the house in Bearsden.

'They're very excited,' Nicola told the teacher as Mrs Campbell's husband showed the boys round the house. 'Ranald was a bit too excited, in fact. He was sick in the car, I'm afraid. He talked about wanting to go back to Edinburgh, but Bertie seems to have settled him and he's perked up a bit.'

Mrs Campbell looked sympathetic. 'They're very young to be away from home,' she said. 'But the fact that there are two of them should make all the difference.'

Nicola agreed. 'Yes, and Bertie is terribly happy to be in Glasgow. He's talked about nothing else over the last few weeks.'

'Dear wee soul,' mused Mrs Campbell.

'Glasgow is a sort of promised land for him,' Nicola continued. 'The background is a bit complex, I'm afraid. I'm his grandmother on his father's side. The mother ...' She paused. How could one describe Irene in her full enormity?

'Pushy?' prompted Mrs Campbell.

Nicola nodded. 'I'm afraid so. Although *pushy* doesn't quite do it justice. She's pushy on an ocean-going scale.'

Mrs Campbell laughed. 'Edinburgh is full of pushy mothers. It's very strange – travel a few miles west, and the pushiness disappears. We don't have that sort of thing in Glasgow at all.'

'You're very fortunate,' said Nicola.

'We can be a bit boisterous,' went on Mrs Campbell, 'but we're not pretentious. Unlike Edinburgh.'

Nicola's smile faded. 'Not everyone in Edinburgh ...' she began.

Mrs Campbell flushed. 'Oh, I'm sorry, that was a bit tactless of me. I don't really know Edinburgh. I went there once, but didn't stay long, I'm afraid.'

'Well, there you are,' said Nicola. 'I've brought you some pies, by the way. We visited a pie factory on our way here.'

She handed Mrs Campbell the packet of Scotch pies that she had been given in the factory. The teacher looked at the label. 'Inclusive Pies? Oh, I love their pies. My absolute favourite. And Will's too. He likes nothing more than a Scotch pie and these people make the very best in Glasgow.'

This pleased Nicola greatly, and she was still smiling when Will Campbell brought the boys back from their conducted tour of their new temporary home. He had shown them, too, the workshop at the back of the house, where he made and restored cellos. He offered to start them off on a woodwork project while they were staying – and Bertie and Ranald had eagerly accepted. If he could not be an apprentice pie-maker in Glasgow when he turned sixteen, Bertie thought, then he might become a woodworker instead. For his part, Ranald's life ambition was rarely disclosed, although he did occasionally mention it to Bertie. He hoped to be a soldier in a Highland regiment and to lead his men against the English at some point.

After that, Nicola thought it best to go, as a prolonged leave-taking might bring on a recurrence, she feared, of Ranald's incipient homesickness. Her departure, though, was a cheerful one, with the two boys standing at the window and waving to her as she got into her beige estate car and began the journey back to Edinburgh.

Mrs Campbell helped the boys unpack their clothes and place them in the drawers that she had cleared for them in the guest room. Then she revealed what was planned for the following day, a Sunday.

'Have you heard about the *Waverley*?' she asked. 'It's a paddle steamer. A very famous one.'

Bertie had. Ranald Braveheart Macpherson had not – which did not surprise Bertie, as he had found that Ranald knew very little about anything. 'Do you mind not knowing anything?' he had once asked his friend, and Ranald had replied, 'Not really, Bertie. I might know a bit more when I'm a bit older. Who knows?'

They went to bed early, as excitement had taken its toll and they were both exhausted. With the light in their room turned out, they went over the events of the day, reliving every detail of the visit to the pie factory and the drive to Bearsden. Ranald Braveheart Macpherson was still slightly nervous, but Bertie reassured him that it was highly unlikely that Mr and Mrs Campbell, in spite of their name, were directly descended from the Campbells at Glencoe whose standards of hospitality fell so short of what was expected.

They made an early start the following morning, and by ten o'clock they had embarked with the Campbells on the *Waverley*. The ancient paddle steamer drew away from the quay at Greenock, bound for the Isle of Arran; on deck, Bertie and Ranald watched as they slipped out into the Clyde Estuary, the giant paddle wheels drawing them smoothly across the glassy surface of the water. Bertie's heart was full. He was in Glasgow – or close enough – doing something that he knew was an old Glasgow tradition – going *doon the watter*. He had dreamed of this moment and now, so improbably, it had come true.

Will Campbell bought them fish and chips from the café, and they ate these on deck. There was a large party of young Glaswegians, a boys' club, it seemed, and Bertie and Ranald stood shyly by as these boys started to sing *Ye cannae shove your granny aff a bus*: Bertie had heard of the song before, but had never had the chance to sing it in its correct cultural context. One of the boys in the group smiled at him and introduced himself. 'They call me Wee Lard,' the boy said, grinning in a friendly fashion.

Unknown to Bertie, this was the son of Lard O'Connor (RIP), whom Bertie and his father had met before.

'You're no' frae Glasgow, are you?' said Wee Lard.

Bertie shook his head. 'No, Edinburgh.'

Wee Lard shrugged. 'There's some things you cannae help,' he said, and offered Bertie a swig from his can of Irn-Bru, which Bertie accepted.

It was perfect. The sun was out; the river was sparkling; the air was warm. Arran was soon before them, a green hill in a blue sea. Bertie had waited for this for so long. For years he had endured a regime from which freedom and light had been excluded. Now that was over, and in his heart was a chorus of delight, like a swelling of exalting birdsong. No boy was ever happier.

67. Recovery

Matthew and Elspeth had made it clear that they would be perfectly happy to look after the Duke of Johannesburg during the weeks that followed his release from enforced Gaelic immersion.

'There's no hurry for your uncle to go back to Single Malt

House,' Matthew reassured James. 'We like having him here – we really do.'

James looked at Matthew with the look of one who wants to know whether the person to whom he is speaking means what he says. 'You're not just saying that, are you?' he asked.

Matthew laughed. 'I promise you, James – I am not just saying that. Well, I am saying it, I suppose, but I am not saying it just because he's your uncle and just because he happens to be a duke.'

'But he isn't a real duke,' said James. 'The Government promised his grandfather, I think it was, that he could be a duke in return for twenty-five thousand pounds.'

'That was a lot of money in those days,' said Matthew.

'And then the Government took the twenty-five thousand pounds – or the political party behind the Government did – and they never actually made him a duke.'

Matthew looked grave. 'I call that fraud,' he said. 'And yet it happens. Or happened. I don't think it could happen today.' He stopped. He was not quite sure of his ground there.

'And so he thinks he's entitled – or almost entitled – to call himself the Duke of Johannesburg,' James continued. 'Secretly, though, he's worried that the Lord Lyon and his people will catch him. He saw the Lord Lyon the other day in the supermarket in Morningside and he almost fainted. I was with him at the time. It was in the frozen products section and he had to stick his head into one of those big refrigerated displays so as not to be recognised.'

Matthew tried not to laugh. 'Uncomfortable,' he said.

'Yes,' James went on. 'And then he spotted Adam Bruce – he's Marchmont Herald – in the street and he had to run round a corner in order to get away. He's really worried that they'll get him.'

'Oh well,' said Matthew.

'Mind you,' said James, 'he's very happy apart from that. That psychologist who's been seeing him has been very helpful. I spoke to her, too, and she told me that he's been making good progress. She played Jimmy Shand and His Band to him the other day and he was quite calm. She said that he even started to tap the ground with his feet in time with the music. She says that's a very positive sign.'

'I'm so glad,' said Matthew. 'And what about Pàdruig? Has he tried to get in touch?'

'He went back to Stornoway,' said James. 'He wrote to my uncle and apologised for being a bit too keen to teach him Gaelic. He says that maybe some time in the future he can take it up again.'

'At least he realises that it was wrong,' said Matthew. 'Gaelic is a beautiful language and it deserves better.' And he thought: the world would be so much poorer without its endangered languages. As words died, the thoughts behind them died too. And the colours and feelings and the words that went with those colours and feelings.

'It'll be very dull when we live in a monoglot sea of English,' mused Matthew.

James looked up at the sky. 'I agree,' he said. 'I don't want the world to be dull.'

For the Duke's part, he was grateful to have been released from captivity, however well intentioned that captivity might have been. He liked Matthew and Elspeth, and doted on James. He also got on well with the triplets, Tobermory,

Fergus and Rognvald, although, like most people, including – sometimes – Matthew, he could not tell which one was which. He spent hours helping Josefine, the Danish au pair engaged to assist James. Together they would invent new and unusual games for the boys, or bring out old favourites that would be played robustly and noisily on the lawn. There was Chase the Dentist, a version of Tig that involved everybody chasing one player and shouting *Dentist!* on catching him or her. It was not a sophisticated game, but it was one that appealed greatly to the small boys, as did West Highland Steamers, which involved two teams chasing one another in circles shouting, 'Look out, MacBrayne!'

'These Scottish games are very strange,' said Josefine. 'We do not have their exact equivalent in Denmark, although we have one or two games that share certain features. There's Bad Swedes, for instance, in which the children who are the Swedes have to go and hide from the children who are the Danes. When they find them, they have to shout *Bad Swede!* and then it's the Danes' turn to hide.'

The Duke liked Josefine and Josefine liked the Duke. 'We do not have people like him in Denmark,' she said to Elspeth. 'They have all been abolished or have died.'

James liked Josefine, but not quite as much as Josefine liked James. He found it a bit disconcerting that she should stand so close to him when she addressed any remark to him, and he also wished that she would spend less time gazing at him.

'I think that young woman likes you,' whispered the Duke.

'Oh well,' said James, blushing.

Gradually, the Duke grew stronger. His sleep improved,

and he no longer awoke five or six times a night muttering unintelligibly. A spell of unusually fine weather had settled over Scotland, and this meant that the Duke could sit out on the terrace in front of Elspeth's garden room on an ancient cane sun lounger. Elspeth would sometimes read to him and Josefine would ferry cups of tea through from the kitchen. He and Elspeth would talk for hours, about all sorts of subjects, and Elspeth found this helpful and therapeutic, as did the Duke. She told him about her girlhood in Perthshire, and the Duke listened with real interest and pleasure to the stories she related.

'It must have been very sunny then,' he said.

'It was,' said Elspeth.

'Is it easier to be a girl than a boy?' mused the Duke.

'Both can be quite hard,' answered Elspeth. 'I used to think that it would be much easier being a boy, but then I suppose I changed my mind. Now I realise that being a boy – and being a man too – can be very difficult.'

'Especially today, don't you think?' asked the Duke.

Elspeth thought about this. 'It's become harder because men used to skew everything in their favour. They held on to the best jobs. They had all the fun while women had to toil away in the kitchen or look after the children. It was much easier for men in those days.'

The Duke inclined his head. 'I'm sorry,' he said. 'You're right, and I'm sorry.'

'But it's different now,' said Elspeth. 'At least to some extent.'

'I wish people would treat one another better,' said the Duke, looking out over the lawn towards the hills to the south. Blue hills. Gentle hills. Hills that made one realise how lovely a country is Scotland. He looked at his hands, and then at his feet, in his brown brogue shoes. He looked up at the sky.

68. *You've Been a Good Friend*

Leaning against the counter in Big Lou's coffee bar, Matthew said to James, 'And I'll have a slice of that stuff over there, whatever it is.' And then added, 'Actually, James, I'll have two slices – if you think Stuart would like one.' He nodded in the direction of Stuart, who was waiting for him at one of the tables.

'Cinnamon-spiced bacon monkey bread,' said James. 'Stuart likes that. He had it the other day.'

From behind the bar, Big Lou caught Matthew's eye. 'One of James's creations,' she said. 'It's going down very well with the more progressive customers.'

Matthew laughed. 'You flatter me, Lou. Progressive. Very nice.'

Big Lou had not intended it as a compliment. 'Progressive actually means conformist, Matthew. A follower of intellectual fashion.'

James served Matthew with the monkey bread and returned to his task of preparing more bacon rolls. At the table, Matthew said to Stuart, 'That young man is changing everything. Look at the people in here today. Twice as many as usual.'

Stuart gazed about him. 'And a slightly different crowd, as well. A bit trendier, if I may say so. Apart from us, of course.'

Matthew grinned. 'I don't mind if people consider me fuddy-duddy.'

Stuart assured him that he would not think of Matthew in those terms. 'Having been married to Irene for some time, I've had enough of being on the cutting edge.' He paused. 'Not that I want anything to actually go backwards – I don't want that. But I don't see the merit in challenging *everything*. Would you describe your views as conservative, Matthew? In a general sense, that is?'

'Not particularly,' replied Matthew. 'I believe in reforming things that need to be reformed. I believe in social goods. I believe that the most stable and probably the most reasonable position on anything is probably to be found in the centre. I believe in compromise and sharing and making sure that everybody has a chance. I believe that we should listen to one another and accept that those with whom we may disagree have their own view of the good and should be respected. I believe in not insulting those from whom we differ.'

Stuart listened in silence. When Matthew finished, he nodded slowly. 'That doesn't sound like conservatism to me. It sounds more like moderation, perhaps, which is not the same thing, and which is, I suspect, what the vast majority of people want.' He paused. 'And yet that's not what the world is like at the moment, is it? There's all this chest-beating.

On all sides. Bluster. Dislike. Scorn. Blaming others for everything. Posturing.'

'Yes, yes,' said Matthew, ruefully. 'I sometimes wonder why we can't be nice to one another – naïve though that sounds.' Nice, he thought, was a tired little word, even prissy; but everybody knew what it meant.

'It's not naïve to be courteous and respectful of others,' said Stuart. 'It's ... it's the opposite of naïve, in fact, which is ... What is the opposite of naïvety, Matthew?'

'Wisdom?' suggested Matthew. 'Understanding? Perspicacity?'

Matthew studied Stuart as he spoke. There was an elephant in the room.

'And you?' he asked directly. 'How are you doing, Stuart? After ... ' He trailed off. 'After Katie?'

He mentioned her name tentatively, almost apologetically. Sometimes it was better for people not to be spoken of, or at least not named: one never knew what the jettisoned felt about those who cast them off.

'You know she's seeing Bruce?'

Matthew winced. 'I'd heard that. Big Lou told me.' He hesitated before continuing. 'I must confess I was surprised. I mean, Bruce, of all people ... '

'Women like him,' said Stuart flatly. 'They like him a lot. He exercises some sort of power over then. They fall for him. I've seen it so often.'

Matthew sighed. 'It's because of his looks, I imagine. He's very good-looking, isn't he?'

Stuart agreed. But he found it hard to bring himself to say it: many men did not comment appreciatively on the looks of other men because that was an area of taboo: you didn't say it. But Matthew had always thought it odd that men had to say things like 'Women consider him good-looking', the implication being that the female gaze could reach that conclusion, but the heterosexual male gaze should not. Men should be more honest, he thought. We could see male beauty every bit as well as women could.

Now Stuart said, 'Sex, Matthew.'

Matthew said nothing.

'He's better at such things than I am.'

Matthew took a bite of his cinnamon-spiced bacon monkey bread. 'Oh, I don't know about that ...' He realised, though, that he *did* know about it, and Stuart was undoubtedly right. So he said, 'That's not everything, you know.'

'Of course, it isn't. I know that. But ...'

'But,' said Matthew, 'if that's the way she looks at it, you're better off without her. Because one thing's certain, Stuart – the physical side of things is not enough to keep a relationship going in the long term. There's far more to it than that.'

Stuart fished in his pocket. 'She wrote to me,' he said. 'She wrote and told me how sorry she was. She said she couldn't help herself.'

Matthew was dismissive. 'She could, of course. She didn't have to ...'

'She sent me a poem.'

Matthew expressed surprise.

'Would you like to hear it?' asked Stuart. 'It's very short.'

He unfolded the piece of paper and began to read aloud:

You may not believe I loved you once, my dear:
I did.
You may not think I had hoped to be better than I was:
I had.
You may not have thought I'd be unworthy of you:
I was.

Matthew was silent. Then he said, 'What a strange little poem.'

'Yes,' said Stuart. 'I don't know how to take it. I don't know whether it's meant to be an apology or a justification. Or a shaft of self-reproach.'

Matthew decided to change the subject. 'And how's Bertie?' he asked.

Stuart's mood lifted visibly. 'He's having a whale of a time in Glasgow. He's over there with his friend, Ranald Braveheart Macpherson. They've had almost three weeks now and they'll be back next week.'

'You'll be looking forward to seeing him.'

'I certainly am,' said Stuart. And he thought: all right, I haven't got a girlfriend after all and I suspect that it's going to be hard to get one. But at least I've got the children, and my job, and friends, and the flat in Scotland Street.

He looked at Matthew with warmth. 'You've been a good friend to me, Matthew.'

'And you to me, Stuart. You've been a good friend too.'

They finished their cinnamon-spiced bacon monkey bread and drank their coffee. Neither spoke; neither felt the need.

69. Temptation, Its Various Forms

Ten days later, as autumn began to stamp its authority on the last days of summer, Angus and Domenica held a large dinner party in Scotland Street. It was, as they described it, the 'usual affair' – a gathering of like-minded old friends and some new ones, too, for conversation and an eccentric and unpredictable buffet dinner. The conversation was wide-ranging, and often light-hearted, suffused, for reasons that nobody could quite fathom, with a particular sort of celebratory kindness. Things said in the past were encouraged to be said again, in the knowledge that repeated stories are appreciated all the more for their having been aired before. So it was that Angus's story of the unsophisticated local politician who, having heard that certain people had made allegations against him, expressed a wish 'to meet those alligators' could be repeated, savoured, and thoroughly laughed at, even on its sixth iteration.

The guests were invited for six-thirty, but by five o'clock three of them were already there, helping Domenica with preparations in the kitchen while Angus tidied the two rooms in which everybody would be congregating. This advance party, happy to roll up their sleeves and work, consisted of Domenica's old friend, Dilly Emslie, her husband, Derek, and Angus's friend, James Holloway, with whom he and Cyril had found the Neanderthal skull in the gardens below Moray Place.

Dilly had not heard of the find, and was entertained by Domenica to the full story, or debacle, as she called it.

'It was most unfortunate,' said Domenica. 'Poor Dr Colquohoun was very upset. We told him that these things happen, but he seemed to take the whole thing very personally.'

'And you almost recovered it, I gather,' prompted James, as he skilfully jointed a brace of roast guinea fowl.

'Yes,' said Domenica. 'Sister Maria-Fiore dei Fiori di Montagna found it, as it happens, on the 23 bus and took it home. But then she threw it in the kitchen bin and by the time Angus heard about it, Antonia Collie had put the contents out and the men had carted it away. It was too late to do anything about it. We could hardly sift through tons of Edinburgh refuse to find a Neanderthal skull.'

'Such a pity,' said Dilly. 'Mind you, I'm not sure that we want an Edinburgh Neanderthal. We have the Festival, after all – and the Fringe. I'd be inclined to say that's enough. There has to be a limit.'

'My thoughts exactly,' said James.

Dilly remembered something. 'Somebody in Ann Street found a mammoth tusk a couple of years ago,' she said. 'It was excavated from their back garden when they were putting in an ornamental fountain. Everybody was very excited, but the Ann Street Committee decided it would be best not to publicise the discovery. So they took it over to the council refuse place and recycled it.'

'Probably the wisest thing to do,' said James.

They continued to work on the food until the main body of guests arrived. Stuart and Nicola came up from downstairs, and Sister Maria-Fiore dei Fiori di Montagna and Antonia Collie came from around the corner in Drummond Place. Then there were Matthew and Elspeth, the triplets being looked after by Josefine and James. Judith McClure was there, and Roger Collins, too, who was in a mood to celebrate, having just completed the first two chapters of his history of Eurasia – a work of staggering scope.

Angus had invited Glenbucket, whose portrait he had recently completed to the sitter's complete satisfaction. Glenbucket was overdressed for the occasion – wearing full Highland regalia – but seemed indifferent to this fact and enjoyed the vocal admiration of the other guests.

'How adventurous to wear three different tartans at once,' said James Holloway.

Glenbucket might have detected a certain irony there, but did not. 'I'm entitled to all of them,' he said. 'One way or another.'

The conversation flowed freely, fuelled by the generosity of the hosts' cellar. A Portuguese Vinho Verde was available for those who preferred white wine, while those who favoured red had a choice of a Médoc and a South Australian Cabernet Sauvignon.

'Will Lyons recommended this Médoc in his column,' said Angus, as he poured James a glass, 'and he should know.'

'I feel very reassured,' said James.

With the onset of autumn, the evenings were drawing in, and by eight o'clock, shortly before dinner was due to be served, the sky had darkened. Inside the flat, curtains were drawn and lamps switched on, as the hubbub of conversation rose and fell. But then, quite unexpectedly, the light flickered and went out.

'Power cut,' called out one of the guests.

The flat was plunged into complete darkness.

'I'll find some candles,' called out Angus.

'Oh dear,' said Domenica. 'I know it'll be very atmospheric, but there are still things in the warming oven.'

The darkness, although clearly it would be temporary, brought silence. Conversations that had started froze halfway; somebody cleared his throat; another bumped against a small table and sent a glass tumbling to the floor. And then there was a sudden shout – a cry of pain.

'What's happening?' Matthew called out. 'Angus, is somebody hurt?'

The light flickered and returned as suddenly as it had disappeared. Angus, halfway to the cupboard where the candles were stored, turned around sharply.

'Is everybody all right?' he asked.

From a corner of the room, Glenbucket called out in response. 'Something bit my leg.'

Matthew was standing next to the bekilted figure and bent down to examine the place on Glenbucket's leg where the bite was said to have occurred. 'It's your ankle,' he said.

Glenbucket, bent over double, massaged the affected limb. He looked more puzzled than uncomfortable. 'Yes,' he said. 'My ankle. It was a sudden, sharp pain. A nip, I think.'

Angus looked about him. He knew immediately what had happened and he would now find the culprit. He muttered an apology to Glenbucket and left the room. A bedroom door, half open, confirmed his suspicions. Here, underneath the bed, shivering with guilt, lay Cyril, feigning sleep but unable to control his quivering.

Angus, on his knees, stared at the dog for a few moments, and then straightened up.

'I am very disappointed in you, Cyril,' he said, but then smiled. We are all weak, he thought, all of us, and temptation, to which so many of us yield, has so many different – and unlikely – forms.

Cyril crept out, head hung in continued shame. But Angus smiled again, and the smile was understood. Together they returned to the party, where interrupted conversations had now resumed. Glenbucket appeared to have made a full recovery.

'Perhaps I imagined it,' he said. 'Perhaps it's a neurological issue. I occasionally get an odd pain in my calf. Some nerve somewhere, I suppose, waking up.'

'Perhaps,' said Angus.

70. *What Was Always There*

A power cut may dampen spirits, but the restoration of power soon dispels the gloom. Gratitude is the prevailing emotion when the lights flicker back into life, and that was what happened at Angus and Domenica's party. Conversations took up where they had left off and the noise level rose steadily as the exchanges between the guests became more animated. It was past the time at which dinner should have been served, but it seemed to Domenica that people were enjoying themselves so much that it would be a pity to interrupt proceedings with food.

Edinburgh New Town flats are solidly built, and the stone that envelops them is an effective deadener of sound. But twenty or so people engaged in voluble discourse may test even those levels of insulation, and it was this that explained the ringing of the doorbell that now attracted Domenica's attention. Answering the door, she found Torquil, her new student neighbour, standing outside, looking slightly embarrassed.

'Look,' he said, 'this is a bit awkward. We're trying to study downstairs and we wondered whether you might just turn the volume down a little bit – just a little bit.'

Domenica was completely taken aback. Never in the history of Edinburgh had a group of students ever complained about noise generated by non-student neighbours: it was simply unheard of. Complaints the other way – directed against noisy student households – were two a penny, but for students to complain seemed almost inconceivable.

'I'm so sorry,' Domenica stuttered. 'I should have told you we were going to have a party. It's most remiss of me.' She paused. 'In fact, I had intended to invite you and your flatmates to join us, but I completely forgot to do so.'

Torquil smiled. 'Well, in that case ...'

Domenica was quick to continue. 'You wouldn't care to come up?' she asked.

Torquil's reply came quickly. 'Yes, why not? There's plenty of time to study tomorrow. Or the day after.'

'I'm so pleased,' said Domenica.

'There are only two of us,' said Torquil. 'The others are away. So it'll only be me and Dave.'

Domenica returned to the party, leaving the door open for Torquil and Dave to join them. When they arrived several minutes later, she introduced them to Matthew and Elspeth, who were sitting at the kitchen table, engaged in conversation with James Holloway.

'I'm sorry to have interrupted your studying,' Domenica said to Dave.

Dave looked puzzled. 'Studying?' He shrugged.

'We were talking about happiness,' said Elspeth. 'I asked James if he could remember when he was happiest.'

'In India,' said James. 'I was touring with friends. We rented Indian bikes – Royal Enfield 650 Bullets – and went up into the hills. I remember going into a village and the children ran out and threw flowers in front of us. There was a wedding going on – you know those marvellous Indian village weddings – and there were flowers everywhere. And people were dancing in the street and invited us to join them. We stopped, got off the bikes and danced with the wedding guests in all their finery. Those lovely reds. Oranges. We were complete strangers but they invited us to dance.'

Dave said, 'I'm really happy now. Right now. Living here – downstairs – with my friends.'

'I am too,' said Torquil. 'I agree with Dave.'

'We get on very well,' said Dave, and smiled at Torquil, who smiled back.

'And the others?' asked Domenica. 'Rose, Phoebe, Alistair?' Rose, in particular, she thought: how did Rose feel? Torquil had said she wanted Dave back, but had said that this was not going to happen.

'Rose is happy,' said Dave quickly, glancing again at Torquil.

Domenica saw her chance. 'I suppose she's happy sharing with Phoebe.'

'Phoebe's really weird,' said Torquil. And then he asked, 'What about you, Domenica? When was the happiest period of your life?'

Domenica hesitated, but she knew exactly when that was. 'When I was doing my early fieldwork,' she said. 'I was in my mid-twenties. Papua New Guinea. It was so exciting. I had very little responsibility in life – just to get up in the morning and do my fieldwork. And the mornings were so beautiful. I remember birdsong. I remember the air being filled with birdsong.'

Somebody was tapping a glass with a spoon. It was Matthew. Voices died down for his announcement.

'Angus has a poem for us,' he said. 'As he does every year.'

He looked at Angus expectantly.

Angus stood up.

'Do you really . . . ?' he began.

'You must,' called out James.

Angus took a deep breath. He closed his eyes. He had written the lines down, but he did not need to consult the piece of paper he had extracted from his pocket. 'This is about looking for things that are there all the time,' he said. 'We do that, you know.' And then he continued:

Dear friends, of all the irritations of this life,
Looking for things misplaced is perhaps
The most common, the most wasteful
Of time that might be better spent elsewhere,
Doing other things that we would like to do;
I have lost my keys and then recovered them
Three times in one day, have searched
Long and hard for the handkerchief
That was always in my pocket,
Have wasted hours trying to remember
Where I read this or that, a memorable line
Of poetry that isn't where I thought it was.
The hidden things we do not see
Because they are plainly unconcealed,
Not hidden at all, but as obvious
As a really simple crossword clue,
These things we need to learn
Are always there, ready to be seen
If only our eyes were open;
Friendship, love, brotherhood:
The things we want for Scotland
So very much it hurts; these things
Are there, and always have been;
We have not misplaced them,
But not looked hard enough,
Have not looked hard enough.

He sat down. Nobody spoke. Elspeth looked at Matthew, who reached out to touch her arm gently. Sister Maria-Fiore dei Fiori di Montagna looked at Antonia, who nodded in agreement with what Angus had said – if she understood him correctly. Dave looked at Torquil, who returned his gaze with a smile. Nicola gave Stuart a look of sympathy: the look of a mother who knows that her son has suffered. He bit his lip. He might have cried, but would not. He would eventually find whatever it was that he was looking for. Love, he supposed – like everybody else.

The end (Pro tem)

Don't let the story stop here

Visit www.alexandermccallsmith.co.uk

Discover new stories

Find out about events

Sign up to Alexander's newsletter

Help us make the next generation of readers

We – both author and publisher – hope you enjoyed this book. We believe that you can become a reader at any time in your life, but we'd love your help to give the next generation a head start.

Did you know that 9% of children don't have a book of their own in their home, rising to 12% in disadvantaged families*? We'd like to try to change that by asking you to consider the role you could play in helping to build readers of the future.

We'd love you to think of sharing, borrowing, reading, buying or talking about a book with a child in your life and spreading the love of reading. We want to make sure the next generation continue to have access to books, wherever they come from.

And if you would like to consider donating to charities that help fund literacy projects, find out more at www.literacytrust.org.uk and www.booktrust.org.uk.

Thank you.

littile, brown
BOOK GROUP

*As reported by the National Literacy Trust